Luke's jaw twitched furiously.

"Next time you're hot for a man, maybe you should check out his bank statement first and save yourself some grief."

Kelsey stumbled backward, fighting to catch her breath. Blinking away the hot moisture gathering in her eyes, she rearranged her expression into a blank stare and spoke with concealing coldness. "I'd like you to leave, Luke. Now."

"Yeah, I'll bet you would." With that, he lazily sauntered to the sofa and flopped onto the cushions.

"You heard me, Luke. Get out."

"I like it here." He stretched fully. "Besides, this is a community property state, so technically half of this snazzy place belongs to me."

The rationale took Kelsey's breath away. When she recovered, she drew upon hidden strength to maintain a deceptively calm tone. "We're divorced, Luke."

"Correction." He sat up. "We are almost divorced. *Almost* doesn't count...."

Dear Reader,

Spring is on its way in at last, but we've got some hot books to keep you warm during the last few chilly days. There's our American Hero title, for example: Ann Williams's *Cold, Cold Heart.* Here's a man who has buried all his feelings, all his hopes and dreams, a man whose job it is to rescue missing children—and who can't get over the tragedy of failure. Into his life comes a woman he can't resist, a woman whose child has been stolen from her, and suddenly he's putting it all on the line all over again. He's back to saving children—and back to dreaming of love. Will his cold heart melt? You take a guess!

Mary Anne Wilson completes her ''Sister, Sister'' duet with *Two Against the World.* For all of you who loved *Two for the Road,* here's the sequel you've been waiting for. And if you missed the first book, don't worry. You can still order a copy—just don't let Ali's story slip through your hands in the meantime!

The rest of the month is filled with both familiar names—like Maura Seger and Amanda Stevens—and new ones—like Diana Whitney, who makes her Intimate Moments debut, and Dani Criss, who's publishing her very first book. I think you'll enjoy everything we have to offer, as well as everything that will be heading your way in months to come. And speaking of the future, look for some real excitement next month, when Intimate Moments celebrates its tenth anniversary with a can't-miss lineup of books, including Patricia Gardner Evans's long-awaited American Hero title, *Quinn Eisley's War.* Come May, Intimate Moments is definitely *the* place to be.

Yours,
Leslie J. Wainger
Senior Editor and Editorial Coordinator

STILL
MARRIED

Diana
Whitney

Published by Silhouette Books New York

America's Publisher of Contemporary Romance

SILHOUETTE BOOKS
300 East 42nd St., New York, N.Y. 10017

STILL MARRIED

Copyright © 1993 by Diana Hinz

All rights reserved. Except for use in any review, the reproduction or utilization of this work in whole or in part in any form by any electronic, mechanical or other means, now known or hereafter invented, including xerography, photocopying and recording, or in any information storage or retrieval system, is forbidden without the permission of the publisher, Silhouette Books, 300 E. 42nd St., New York, N.Y. 10017

ISBN: 0-373-07491-3

First Silhouette Books printing April 1993

All the characters in this book have no existence outside the imagination of the author and have no relation whatsoever to anyone bearing the same name or names. They are not even distantly inspired by any individual known or unknown to the author, and all incidents are pure invention.

®: Trademark used under license and registered in the United States Patent and Trademark Office and in other countries.

Printed in the U.S.A.

Books by Diana Whitney

Silhouette Intimate Moments

Still Married #491

Silhouette Special Edition

Cast a Tall Shadow #508
Yesterday's Child #559
One Lost Winter #644
Child of the Storm #702

Silhouette Romance

O'Brian's Daughter #673
A Liberated Man #703
Scout's Honor #745
The Last Bachelor #874

DIANA WHITNEY

says she loves "fat babies and warm puppies, mountain streams and Southern California sunshine, camping, hiking and gold prospecting. Not to mention strong, romantic heroes!" She married her own real-life hero fifteen years ago. With his encouragement, she left her longtime career as a municipal finance director and pursued the dream that had haunted her since childhood—writing. To Diana, writing is a joy, the ultimate satisfaction. Reading, too, is her passion, from spine-chilling thrillers to sweeping sagas, but nothing can compare to the magic and wonder of romance.

To Melissa Senate:
Your confidence has urged me to expand self-imposed boundaries, and your unwavering support has given me the courage to try. Thank you.

Chapter 1

A shadow moved, and she saw the glint of a blade.

Kelsey froze against the open car door, her hair crackling with electric terror. This couldn't be happening.

Numbed by shock, she rationalized that the dark figure must be an optical illusion of the moonless night, or head-lights diffused by the translucent fog shrouding the deserted inner-city.

A moment earlier, she had driven into the darkened parking area behind Sontag's Auto Garage and stepped out onto the crumbling asphalt. Illuminated by her vehicle's headlights, an eerie landscape of shapes had emerged like skeletal remains in a steel graveyard. Clammy dampness misted her skin and she'd noted a faint odor of petroleum and burnt rubber. The smell was familiar, and not altogether unpleasant.

Traffic noises emanated from atop the concrete freeway embankment at the rear of the lot behind a chain-link and barbed-wire barrier. Beyond the collage of broken steel was a small travel trailer, its glowing windows piercing the foggy night and beckoning with deceptive warmth.

The subject of Kelsey's quest was fifty feet away, inside that dented tin shell, yet she hesitated, unsure and oddly unsettled.

Someone was watching. The hairs on her nape prickled when she saw the sinister shadow. The silhouette glided smoothly across the graffitied garage wall. There was a chilling hiss, followed by a guttural whisper. "Gimme the car."

Kelsey's breath caught as though smothered by a gloved hand. She was vaguely aware of a tingling sensation where her fingertips touched slick steel and realized that the car's engine was still idling. If she could slide back into the driver's seat and lock the door—

The shadowed figure instantly emerged and grabbed her wrist. "I'll stick you." A gleaming, six-inch blade was pressed against the vulnerable flesh of her throat.

Pale eyes regarded her coldly. Greasy tufts of hair jutted from beneath a knitted cap and as the assailant moved into the refracted light, Kelsey saw that he was a wiry man of slight stature. Hollow cheeks and a thin, twisted mouth gave him a lean, hungry appearance. He smelled bad.

He leaned forward until his face was mere inches from hers, his upper lip curled to reveal a golden glint, and Kelsey heard that same sick hissing as he sucked air between his crooked teeth. "You got money?"

Steeling herself against the nauseating stench of stale sweat and rancid alcohol, Kelsey gestured weakly toward the passenger seat. "In my purse."

The mugger roughly yanked her aside and peered into the vehicle's plush interior without relinquishing his punishing grip. He folded the blade against his thigh, poked the knife into the pocket of his torn trousers, then scooped up Kelsey's white leather handbag and dumped the contents onto the driver's seat.

Ignoring her small cosmetic bag and checkbook, the thief opened her wallet with an expert, one-handed flip, then parted the currency flap with his thumb and forefinger. "Fourteen lousy dollars?" With an explicit curse, he jammed the bills into the pocket of his worn flannel shirt, then twisted Kelsey's wrist until her knees buckled. "Where's the rest?"

"There . . . isn't any more." Automatically clawing at the bruising fingers, Kelsey swallowed a bitter rush of bile and struggled against panic. "I have a credit card."

"Where?" he demanded roughly, so close that Kelsey nearly gagged from the fumes.

"In my checkbook. Please, take it and go."

When the man turned his attention back to her scattered belongings, Kelsey took a frantic gulp of clean air and fought the encroaching nausea. Closing her eyes, she told herself that this nightmare would soon be over. All this creep wanted was money. Once he had that, he'd slink back into the shadows to stalk a more satisfying victim.

Automatically squaring her shoulders, she forced her eyes open, determined to conceal any hint of fear. Then she saw the silver flash in the man's hand and realized that he'd found not only her credit card but the automated bank card that had also been tucked into her checkbook.

He grinned. "Well, lookee what we got here. Guess we're just gonna have to find us one of them all-night money machines." Sharply yanking at her wrist, he slid backward into Kelsey's car. "Get in."

In that terrifying moment, Kelsey realized that he wasn't going to let her go. Her blood iced. A distant siren wailed. She frantically grabbed the car door with her free hand as he tried to haul her inside. "No, please—"

An odd warmth touched Kelsey's back. She sensed movement, then felt a cool breeze brush her ear when a massive hand sliced the gray mist and cracked the thief's forearm with a single, vicious chop. The man howled, released her, then cradled his injured arm and fell against the steering wheel, moaning.

As Kelsey stumbled back, a strong arm encircled her waist and firmly guided her to the rear of the car. She sagged against the trunk and saw a broad-shouldered silhouette reach inside the vehicle, then haul her assailant out by the throat.

Grunting in pain, the pale-eyed man dangled from her benefactor's fist like a flopping fish. The mugger's left arm was hanging at an awkward angle, and Kelsey exhaled slowly, assuming that the incident had ended.

Her relief was premature. The knife suddenly reappeared in the assailant's right hand and as Kelsey screamed a warning, the blade arched toward the big man's belly.

Turning the mugger loose, Kelsey's rescuer leaped backward with surprising agility, then assumed a defensive stance and dodged repeated thrusts of the blade. The pale-eyed man snarled, flexed his arm in a taunting, circular motion, then lunged forward, laughing roughly when his opponent grunted in pain.

Kelsey covered her mouth, muffling a cry of horror. A thin shaft of light from the trailer illuminated the fury glinting in the big man's eyes and the white flash of bared teeth. Assuming a predatory posture, he crouched and slowly circled the perplexed thief. At that moment, Kelsey almost felt sorry for her pale-eyed assailant.

A savage blow snapped the smaller man's jaw and jerked him off his feet. The crack of fractured bone sent a chill down Kelsey's spine, and the knife clattered to the pavement. The mugger crumpled, moaning and spitting blood.

Wincing, her rescuer wrapped one arm around his midsection, then pocketed the knife, wedged a sneakered foot under the prostrate thug's chest and roughly flipped him over.

Sprawled awkwardly on his back, the wiry guy whined, "No more, man," and shielded his swollen face with one trembling hand.

Kelsey's broad-shouldered savior pulled a thin wad of bills from the assailant's pocket, then hauled the shaken fellow to his feet. "You must be new around here," the big man said calmly. "This place is off-limits. Spread the word."

With that, he released the pale-eyed mugger, who quickly limped back into the shadows and disappeared.

The Samaritan bent to retrieve Kelsey's bank card. "Are you okay, lady?"

With a deep breath, Kelsey clasped her trembling hands together and stepped into the light. "Yes, thank you."

The man jerked to a stop.

Pretending that her heart hadn't just climbed up into her rib cage, Kelsey managed a wan smile. "Hello, Luke. It's been a long time."

For a moment, Luke stood rooted to the asphalt, his sharp features frozen into an expression that could have cracked granite. He tossed the currency and bank card into the open door of the vehicle, eyeing Kelsey as though she were now the enemy.

Propping one lean hip against the red fender of her shiny new car, he tucked his thumbs into the pockets of his faded blue jeans. "Yeah, a long time."

Kelsey shifted uncomfortably, then weakly gestured toward the spreading crimson stain on his white T-shirt. "You're hurt."

He dismissed her concern without so much as glancing down at the wound. "It's nothing."

"I could take a look—"

"I said it's nothing," he snapped, then suddenly looked away, as though offended by the sight of her.

Hurt and embarrassed that Luke found her presence so distasteful, Kelsey shrugged off her own distress by reminding herself that he had always been an intractable man. Obviously, that hadn't changed.

But Luke himself was different. Even in the dim light, Kelsey noticed that he appeared gaunt and was thinner than she remembered. He still preferred his T-shirt sleeves rolled up to bare his muscular shoulders, but his trademark tight jeans were slung loosely below his waist, so low that the denim barely covered his slender hips.

That unruly mass of dark hair still curled across his forehead, as wild and untamable as the man himself, and his chiseled features remained raptor-sharp, with probing eyes and a predatory stance that cautioned all to keep their distance or bear the consequences. Luke Sontag had always exuded an aura of danger and pure masculine power that made Kelsey's heart flutter and her pulse race. He still did.

Tension thickened the damp air and Kelsey swallowed hard. "How have you been?"

"Can't complain." Luke folded his arms tightly as his gaze slid over the length of her body, then lingered on the soft folds of her clingy knit skirt. "And you?"

"Good. I've been good." Kelsey licked her dry lips.

"I'll bet." Luke's smile was a little sad, a little bitter. "Nice outfit"

She stiffened, automatically touching the lapel of her soft peach blazer. "Thank you."

He jerked a nod toward her shiny red sedan. "Nice car."

This time she didn't reply.

When their eyes met, she saw a glint of anger and recognized disgust in his voice. "Yeah, looks like you've done real good for yourself. So are you slumming again, or what? That's what bored little rich girls do, isn't it? Check out the real world, have a few cheap thrills, then back to the comfort of Daddy's money."

"Luke, that isn't fair."

"You can drop the hurt look, honey. That doesn't work with me, remember?"

Turning away, Kelsey swallowed the massive lump that had inexplicably formed in her throat and wondered how something so beautiful could have gone so terribly wrong.

Two years wasn't such a long time, yet it might as well have been a lifetime. Kelsey had been a different person back then. Like most college students, she'd been idealistic and wonderfully naive, convinced that the might of righteous morality empowered her to change the world.

And so, two years ago, the invincible Kelsey Manning hadn't the slightest qualm about braving the seedy streets of south-central Los Angeles. She'd been on a mercy mission, determined to save Ruth Sontag, her college roommate and dearest friend, from the tyrannical older brother who seemed hell-bent on controlling his poor sister's life.

At the time, Ruth had been apprehensive about the plan, and Kelsey had sought to reassure her. "Don't worry about a thing, Ruthie. All I'm going to do is drive to your brother's garage and tell him how important this is to you. I'm sure he'll come around. And if he doesn't, I'll chain him to the hydraulic jack and torture him with a torque wrench."

Kelsey smiled at the satisfying image. She'd never met this Sontag character but would relish an opportunity to wreak havoc on a man who could take such cruel advantage of his sister's devotion.

Ruth was still unconvinced, however. Nervously biting her lip, she leaned into the open driver's window of Kelsey's dented compact car. "You don't understand, Kel. Luke means well, he really does. He's just trying to protect me."

Kelsey emitted an impolite noise and inserted the key into the ignition. "Forbidding you from seeing the man you love isn't protective—it's controlling. At twenty-two, you certainly don't need your brother's permission to get married."

"I know, but..." Ruth's words trailed off and she seemed genuinely pained. After a moment, she sighed. "It's just that I couldn't really be happy knowing that Luke disapproved. If he'd only give Joseph a chance, I'm sure he'd change his mind."

"Fat chance of that, since that imperious brother of yours has already declared that any guy named Joseph Ridenour III must be a polo-playing wimp who'd faint dead away if he ever got grease under his nails." Kelsey rolled her eyes. "Honestly, Ruthie, I don't see why you can't just plan the wedding, send your brother an invitation and if he shows, he shows. If not, well, that's his loss."

Ruth couldn't have looked more horrified if Kelsey had suggested that she sacrifice small animals at midnight. "I couldn't do that to Luke. It would hurt him terribly."

Ruth pushed a coffee-brown curl from her face and looked so miserable that Kelsey's heart literally ached. At that moment, she would have fought a tiger with a toothpick to protect her friend from more grief.

Over the past three years, Ruth Sontag had become the sister Kelsey had always wanted. They'd shared everything, and had grown incredibly close despite their vastly disparate personalities. While Kelsey had always been confident and gregarious, Ruth was fragile and quiet, almost introverted, which Kelsey blamed on the demoralizing effect of being raised by a domineering older brother.

Now that same egotistical bully was blocking Ruth's happiness, and Kelsey refused to accept such blatant injustice without one hell of a fight.

Ruth, however, had been consistently reluctant to assert herself, a pathetic situation that both annoyed Kelsey and presented her with an irresistible challenge.

With a glint of determination, Kelsey twisted the ignition key and the worn engine sputtered to life. "Since you won't stand up to your brother, I guess it's up to me to talk some sense into his thick, macho skull." Kelsey smiled brightly and patted Ruth's cold hand. "Don't worry. I can be very persuasive."

With genuine fear in her eyes, Ruth stepped back to the curb and rubbed her arms against the chilly spring air. "Kelsey, wait—"

Waving out the window, Kelsey steered onto the highway and drove off with barely a twinge of doubt.

During the two-hour trip down from the university, Kelsey mentally reinforced the righteousness of her cause, positive affirmations that dissipated as she navigated the final miles into the belly of the barrio.

Derelicts littered every corner, some with signs begging to exchange work for food, others simply crumpled against the faded facade of boarded buildings. This was gang territory, she realized, noting the graffitied walls and clustered homeboys strutting colors. It was difficult to believe that Ruth, who was so beautiful and gentle, could have been raised in such a hostile environment.

By the time Kelsey pulled into the driveway of Sontag's Auto Garage, she was slightly unnerved, but her determination was undampened.

Stepping from the car, she smoothed her crisp cotton shorts and looked around. The entire area was encircled by a chain-link and barbed-wire reminder of the neighborhood's soaring crime rate, and a small travel trailer was positioned in the farthest corner of the asphalt parking lot.

Kelsey recalled Ruth mentioning that her brother lived in a trailer behind the auto shop. After their mother's death, Luke had purportedly sold the family home to finance his sister's college education. Apparently Ruth had viewed that sacrifice with holy reverence. Kelsey was less impressed. After all, one noble gesture wasn't license for the methodical takeover of another person's life, and now that Kelsey was approaching this magnanimous manipulator she actually looked forward to the confrontation.

Since it was midafternoon, the auto shop hummed with activity. Kelsey spoke to a mechanic preoccupied with reattaching a rubber hose to the engine of a battered station wagon.

"Excuse me. I'm looking for the owner."

A greasy face turned in her direction and the man eyed her blankly.

After a silent moment, Kelsey offered her most pleasant smile and tried again. "I have business with Mr. Sontag, so if you'd be so kind—"

"Ah, Señor Sontag." The mechanic's eyes lit up with comprehension. *"Él está en la oficina."* He gestured toward an open doorway inside the cavernous auto bay.

"Oh." Kelsey hesitated, not really wanting to navigate the obstacle course of greasy tools and puddled oil. Still, she hadn't come all this way to wrinkle her nose at a little engine dirt, so she smiled her thanks and carefully picked her way through the busy shop.

Pausing at the doorway, she saw a broad-shouldered man hunched over a dented metal desk. "Mr. Sontag?"

The man straightened and swiveled around.

Nothing in Kelsey's experience could have prepared her for what happened next.

She had planned to hate Luke Sontag; instead, she'd taken one look at those fathomless green eyes and fallen head over heels in love. With a ragged mass of coffee-colored hair and sharply-angled features that crinkled like tanned leather when he smiled, Luke had been strong and arrogant and so damned male that Kelsey had nearly fainted from the scent of testosterone. In less than a heartbeat, Kelsey knew that she simply had to have him, and in those days, Kelsey Manning always got what she wanted.

But that had been a lifetime ago.

Now, as Kelsey stood in the dankness of that same parking lot, in the place where it had all begun, her heart was breaking. Two years ago, she had wanted Luke with a desperation and fire that had permeated every fiber of her body. She still did, but he was gone now, lost to her forever, his bleak eyes still condemning her for tragedies of the past.

When Luke spoke again, his tone was softer but hadn't lost its ragged edge. "What do you want from me, Kelsey? Why the hell are you here?"

The blunt question was deflating. This man had given Kelsey happiness—he'd given her life—then he'd destroyed it; but in spite of the agony and betrayal, she still wanted him. He had invaded her soul; she would never be free of him. That scared the hell out of her.

Suddenly Kelsey was fighting tears, a weakness that she abhorred only in herself. To conceal that frailty, she quickly ducked her head and brushed the strewn contents of her purse from the driver's seat. "I'm sorry. I shouldn't have come."

A strong hand closed over her arm, restraining her, and she was shocked by the faint odor of alcohol wafting from Luke's clothing. He'd been drinking.

That wasn't like him. During the time they'd been together, Kelsey had never known Luke to consume more than an occasional beer, yet judging by aroma and the subtle glaze of his eyes, he had apparently developed a taste for something stronger.

Luke held Kelsey's hand under the dim illumination of the car's interior lights and carefully examined her bruised wrist. A muscle in his jaw twitched. "That bastard hurt you. I should have killed him."

Her skin tingled beneath his touch. "I'm fine, really."

She noted an odd sadness in his eyes, a reflection of regret, and possibly something more. Her breath caught as a glimmer of hope flared, then died when he abruptly released her.

"Go home, Kelsey. There's nothing here for you."

Anger flared as a defense. "There's nothing here that I want." She nearly choked on the lie, then blurted, "Ruth is missing."

Luke stiffened but made no response. Kelsey was bitterly disappointed. Although the Sontag siblings had been estranged for the past two years, they had once been inseparably close, and Kelsey had hoped that Luke still cared for his sister. His immutable expression again dashed her hopes.

Lifting her chin, she faced him defiantly. "I came here hoping that somewhere in that steel-clad heart you could find a pulse of concern for your sister."

Luke's rigid stance warned Kelsey that she was treading on thin ice, but pain dulled rational perception, and she was aware only of the gnawing ache deep in her chest. "You are a hard man, Luke Sontag. If anything happens to Ruth, I hope God will forgive you, because you'll never forgive yourself."

Luke's eyes narrowed dangerously. "I thought you two would have outgrown this kind of college prank."

"This is no joke. Ruth has disappeared." The reflection of genuine fear marring his veiled expression offered small encouragement, so Kelsey spoke more gently. "I was hoping you might have heard from her."

Turning away, Luke rubbed the back of his neck. "I haven't heard from my sister since she married that jerk Ridenour."

Kelsey sighed and pinched the bridge of her nose. The information was disappointing, though not unexpected. In her own quiet way, Ruth was just as stubborn as her brother, so the rift between siblings had widened into a canyon of hurt and mistrust.

Seeming oblivious to Kelsey's presence, Luke gazed up at the line of glittering headlights on the freeway overpass. After a long moment, he spoke. "What happened?"

Leaning against the car door, Kelsey took a deep breath and chose her words carefully. "A few days ago, Ruth showed up at my apartment, suitcase in hand, saying that she'd left Joseph and asking if she could stay with me."

A sad smile tilted one corner of Luke's mouth. "So she finally wised up. Good for her."

Kelsey ignored the remark. "Anyway, for the first day or so, everything seemed fine. Ruth seemed sad, of course, but I assumed that she needed some quiet time to decide what to do with the rest of her life. Then yesterday afternoon, I came home from work and she was gone.''

Luke didn't bother to disguise his skepticism. "She probably went back home."

"I don't think so. All of her clothes are still in my guest room and her cosmetics were left on the bathroom counter. The only thing missing was her purse."

After considering that for a moment, Luke frowned. "Could she have been in a car wreck, or had some kind of accident?"

"Ruth didn't have a car, Luke. She'd taken a train down from Santa Barbara, then caught a cab to my apartment." Kelsey decided not to mention that Joseph had refused his wife access to a vehicle and hadn't even allowed her to renew her driver's license.

At this point, Kelsey also decided to withhold several other facts, including Ruth's shocking bruises. Although the nervous young woman had insisted that the injuries were caused by her own clumsiness, Kelsey had been suspicious.

Besides, Ruth had been uncharacteristically jittery during her stay and, concealed behind partially closed blinds, had frequently watched the street with apparent trepidation. When questioned, she would offer a strained smile and mumble a murky explanation. Kelsey didn't need a psychology degree to understand that her traumatized friend was deeply frightened of something, or someone.

In fact, Kelsey was absolutely convinced that Ruth had been battered, yet hesitated to share her conviction with Luke because she feared his explosive reaction. He'd always been fiercely protective of his sister, and in spite of their past alienation, Kelsey truly believed that Luke was capable of retaliating violently toward anyone who harmed her.

So Kelsey continued cautiously, wanting to convince him that Ruth needed help without disclosing how desperate her situation might really be.

"I called all the hospitals, and then I called the police. They wouldn't do anything, of course, because... how did they put it? There was no evidence of foul play." Kelsey couldn't keep the bitter edge from her voice. "If I'd been able to show them a few blood-spattered walls, that might have piqued their interest.''

Luke stared bleakly up at the caravan of light rimming the concrete embankment beyond the barrier of woven steel. "Why are you telling me this?''

The blunt question took her aback. "Your sister is in trouble. She needs help.''

After a moment's silence, Luke jammed his hands in his pockets. "Ruth made her choice two years ago. If she regrets that decision, it's not my problem.''

Stunned by his callousness, Kelsey touched her throat and stared in disbelief. "You can't mean that.''

Luke's mouth thinned into a hard line as he met Kelsey's shocked expression with one of cold indifference. Then without another word, he turned and strode away.

He'd nearly reached the trailer door when Kelsey finally found her voice. "Damn you, Luke Sontag.'' The tinny door slammed open and he disappeared inside. Furious, Kelsey followed, catching the door before it had closed completely and pushing her way into the stuffy interior.

Without sparing her a glance, Luke lifted a whiskey bottle from the tiny sink counter. "Go home, Kelsey.''

Grabbing a shot glass, he tipped the bottle just as Kelsey angrily snatched it from his hand. Amber liquid splashed over the discolored laminate and dribbled onto the cracked linoleum.

"So that's it?'' she demanded. "You're going to turn your back on the only family you have left just because your precious ego has been dented? What kind of a man are you?''

With green fire in is eyes, Luke yanked the whiskey from Kelsey's grasp and smashed the bottle in the sink. "*I'm a tired man,* tired of being used, then thrown out like yesterday's garbage as soon as something better comes along. I gave my sister a chance to make something out of herself, but all the work and the sacrifice meant nothing. When she met Ridenour, she gave it all up and when she did that, *she* turned her back on *me.*''

"That's what it comes down to, isn't it? You ignore anything or anyone that you can't control. Ruth insisted on living her own life, and that's what really galls you."

"What galls me, honey, is how women judge a man's worth by the size of his checkbook."

Kelsey paled. "Ruth isn't like that."

"No? Is it just a coincidence that she married a man whose daddy is worth millions?"

"She loved him."

Luke laughed unpleasantly. "She wanted him. You, of all people, should understand the difference."

The argument had taken a decidedly uncomfortable turn. Delicately dabbing her moist forehead, Kelsey ignored the innuendo and appealed to his protective nature again. "Ruth needs you."

"Does she?" Luke's eyes glittered strangely. "What's my payback?"

"I don't understand."

"The last time you wanted a favor for Ruth, you offered something in return. That's only fair, right?" Flexing his index finger, Luke caressed Kelsey's cheek with his knuckle.

Her breath caught, and she was affected more deeply by his sensuous touch than by the vulgar suggestion. Before she could gather her thoughts to respond, Luke's voice took on a seductive tone, and he lowered his face until his lips were mere inches from her ear. "Remember, honey?" His breath lifted the fine hairs at her temple. "You give what I want, then I give what you want. It's just business, right?"

Kelsey's stomach turned. How dare he cheapen what they'd shared by insinuating that she'd used her body as a bribe? Did he hate her enough to destroy even the memories? The answer seemed painfully clear.

Pulling away, she inhaled deeply and fought to compose herself so he wouldn't see her pain. Luke Sontag had always been a pitiless and unyielding man. It had been foolish to believe he'd have changed.

Straightening, she wiped a strand of cinnamon-colored hair from her moist brow, stared through the open doorway and spoke in a voice that hardly shook at all. "Coming here was obviously a mistake. I won't bother you again."

With that, she stepped from the trailer and crossed the dismal parking lot. When she reached her car, she saw that Luke was watching from the trailer porch. Without analyzing her motives, Kelsey blurted, "By the way, you're going to be an uncle."

Luke jerked as though he'd been kicked. "What did you say?"

"Ruth is eight months pregnant," Kelsey replied cooly, and with that final, shocking revelation she drove into the night.

Chapter 2

Luke stood in the doorway as rolling fog swallowed the taillights of Kelsey's fancy red car. Beyond the refracted glow from the trailer's bare light bulb, the swirling mist calmed into a drab gray blanket, erasing all visible trace of human presence. For a moment, Luke wondered if her appearance had been an illusion, a specter created by the eerie pall and his own lonely isolation.

For the past year, that evocative woman had haunted Luke's dreams, taunting his restless nights with memories of soft skin and whispered passion. The visions had been so real that he'd frequently awakened, clutching his pillow with humiliating fervor. That's when he'd discovered that a little whiskey numbed his heart and a lot of whiskey deadened his mind. A morning headache was nothing compared to the bleak agony of sleepless, unanesthetized nights.

But this evening had been different. Luke had been sober—well, nearly sober. Besides, the red smear on his shirt was no damned illusion and there was even more evidence to validate her flesh-and-blood presence.

Breathing deeply, Luke inhaled the sweet fragrance still clinging to the humid air. His head spun and his heart pounded with familiar urgency. No apparition could create such a heady scent.

Stepping back into the trailer, Luke closed the door, then reached into a tiny plywood cupboard and extracted another bottle. He poured himself a stiff jolt and leaned against the counter, struggling to get a grip on his raging emotions.

Kelsey hadn't changed much, although her reddish-brown hair had been layered into a shorter, more sophisticated style and she'd been wearing expensive designer fashions. Of course, she'd always liked nice clothes. She'd once told Luke that one well-made dress was better than a closet full of cheap rags. That elitist philosophy had irritated him. To Luke, clothes were a functional body covering, not a shallow display of social status. He was contemptuous of those who defined a person's worth so frivolously, since no garment ever designed could effectively disguise the value of a human soul.

So he and Kelsey had disagreed on fashion, as they had disagreed on almost every philosophical and political issue. Odd, Luke mused, that he'd been viscerally attracted to a woman whose views so represented that which he found callow and materialistic. But tonight, when Luke had seen her standing like a vision in the mist, he hadn't been recalling their philosophical differences. He'd been struggling simply to breathe.

Kelsey still affected Luke, exposing a weakness that angered him to the core. Lifting the shot glass to his lips, he downed its vile contents in a single gulp, then poured himself another drink. He leaned against the small stainless steel sink, lifted his shirt and inspected the shallow cut below his left rib cage. It was just a scratch, really, still oozing a bit but hardly worth a Band-Aid. He splashed a small amount of liquor on the wound, then ignored the fiery sting as his mind recounted the events of the evening.

Luke's first thought was that Kelsey had returned to gloat about having achieved the privileged life-style she'd always craved. Then he'd seen it, the quiet sorrow deep in her eyes. God, how he remembered that desolate expression, the anguished despair. If he lived a thousand years, he'd still go to his grave with the image of Kelsey's grief engraved in his heart.

With some effort, Luke remembered beyond the misery, back to a time when Kelsey's amber-brown eyes had sparkled with mischief and smoldered with promise. That had only been two years ago. It seemed like a century.

Then, Luke's life had been humming along pretty much as he'd planned. Business hadn't exactly been good, but had been steady enough to show a small yet consistent profit. He'd always managed to scrape by, and had invested the proceeds from his mother's home to keep up with Ruth's rising tuition and dormitory expenses.

All in all, he had been feeling fairly confident about his ability to provide for his sister, until she'd brought home an arrogant playboy with a limp handshake and a haughty attitude.

Joseph Ridenour III—*the third*, for crissake. What in hell kind of name was that for a man? The jerk had carried himself like royalty, then taken one look at the greasy auto shop and lifted his blue-blooded nose so damned high it's a wonder he didn't snag a jetliner in his nostril.

Luke had disliked the guy on sight, but had made an effort to be civil for his sister's sake. That's when he'd learned that Ridenour expected Ruth to drop out of college. After all the years of suffering and sacrifice, Luke couldn't believe that his sister would even consider relinquishing her dream of becoming a teacher, but that's exactly what had happened. Ruth had meekly acquiesced, wringing her hands and stammering some ludicrous excuse about the social obligations required of Ridenour women and how being Joseph's wife was all the career that she needed.

Luke had exploded, forbidding his sister to see Ridenour again. To his chagrin, Ruth had defied him.

"You're my brother and I love you," she'd told him, with a calm determination Luke had never seen her display. "I've always respected your wishes, but this time I can't. I love Joseph and I'm going to marry him. Please, be happy for me and give us your blessing."

He had flatly refused.

That's when Kelsey Manning had breezed into Luke's life. He'd been humped over a mound of paperwork, cursing the governmental regulations that seemed hell-bent on driving business owners to the brink of insanity, when a firm, female voice had spoken his name like a challenge.

"Mr. Sontag."

He'd swiveled the chair and looked into the darkest, most provocative eyes he'd ever seen in his life. "Yeah. What can I do for you?"

From the set of her chin, Luke thought the woman must be a dissatisfied customer and wondered if a rebuilt trannie had dropped out on the freeway. Instantly, he discarded the notion. If this beautiful, cinnamon-haired beauty had ever been within ten miles of his shop, Luke would have remembered. She had the tousled look of a woman who'd just rolled out of bed, with a pouty little mouth that begged to be kissed and a body that made his mouth water. No way did a man forget a woman like that.

Then a strange thing happened. Her lips slackened and she suddenly eyed him as though he were the main course at a sumptuous buffet. As her hand touched her throat, her gaze slid down his body and she moistened her lips with her tongue. Luke responded to the sensuous gesture with an instantaneous physical response that took him by surprise. Apparently, it took her by surprise as well, because her eyes widened and she jerked her gaze up, meeting his eyes with an expression of pure shock.

"*Lucas* Sontag?" she repeated. "Ruth's brother?"

Luke's eyes narrowed suspiciously. "Who wants to know?"

She blinked, then instantly composed herself and faced him with the grit and determination that he'd have admired in a man. "My name is Kelsey Manning. I'm your sister's roommate."

Luke frowned. Ruth had mentioned a roommate, of course, and now he regretted not having paid closer attention. "You're the debutante from back east, right? The one with a million-dollar daddy."

"I'm hardly a debutante, Mr. Sontag, although I was born and raised in Connecticut." She seemed amused by the characterization. ''My father makes a good living and although my parents are certainly not paupers, they aren't rich, either.''

She had a nice smile. Luke liked that. He also liked the fact that she hadn't gotten her shorts in a twist when he'd referred to her family's money. He relaxed, just a little. ''So, did you just happen to be in the neighborhood or what?''

One well-curved eyebrow lifted and she cocked her head prettily. ''I came to see you.''

''And do you like what you see?''

The corner of her mouth twitched and her eyes darkened with sensual interest. ''As a matter of fact, I do. But that's not why I'm here.''

Propping his hip against the dented metal desk, Luke rolled up his blue chambray shirt sleeves and met her bold gaze. ''Let me guess. It's about Ruth.''

Kelsey showed no surprise at his bluntness. ''Yes, it is. You're behaving like a pig, you know.''

''What the—'' Startled, Luke's arms sprang apart as though he'd hugged a hot log. ''Who the hell do you think you are, lady?''

''I'm Ruth's best friend,'' Kelsey replied calmly. ''And by the way, macho posturing doesn't work with me, so save the muscle flexing for someone who gives a hoot.''

Before Luke could get his act together, Kelsey had stepped into the small office, brushed off her crisp white knee shorts and delicately seated herself on a vinyl chair that had been shoved beside the metal file cabinet. ''You realize, of course, that you're breaking your sister's heart.''

Luke didn't have a clue what this brash young woman was talking about and since confusion irked the hell out of him, he did what any normal, red-blooded man would do when faced with a spiraling loss of control. He pulled himself up to his full six-foot-two-inch height and gave her the steely look that turned swaggering gang-bangers into quivering sycophants. ''You've got the sexiest legs I've ever seen.''

Her body vibrated in shock. ''Excuse me?''

Luke slid his narrowed gaze from her bare thighs upward, then eyed the rounded contours of her clingy knit top.

"Mmm, curvy but not too big. That's nice. I never liked droopy boobs."

Incensed, Kelsey bolted to her feet, eyes spitting amber sparks. "You are crude and disgusting."

"Yeah. I'm a pig." Grinning triumphantly, Luke sat lazily on the edge of his desk. "If I'm going to wear the name, I'm going to play the game."

Satisfied to have regained the upper hand, he calmly waited for Miss Prissy-britches to stamp her little pink foot and march indignantly out of his life. She didn't. Instead, her anger melted into an unexpected, and quite attractive, sparkle of amusement.

To his surprise, she sat back in the worn chair with an expression of grudging admiration. "Touché, Mr. Sontag. I can see why Ruth is no match for you. I, however, am not so easily manipulated and intimidation tactics just bring out the devil in me. Shall we start this conversation over, or would you prefer to go a couple more rounds?"

Feeling as if he'd just fumbled on the ten-yard line, Luke's smile faded. Behind the facade of fragile beauty lurked a well-honed mind, and enough chutzpah to stare down a snarling grizzly. He'd underestimated her. That had been stupid. It was a mistake he wouldn't make again.

Loosening his stance, he managed an unconcerned shrug. "So, what's my sister's problem?"

"You are her problem," Kelsey replied smoothly. "Ruth is a grown woman, yet you're still trying to control her life."

Luke kept a rein on his indignation and maintained a reasonable tone. "She lives sixty miles away in a university dorm. I'm hardly in a position to control anything she does."

"That's a crock." Kelsey smiled sweetly. "You call her every two days and the poor woman can't even choose her own class schedule without your esteemed approval. The problem is that Ruth believes the world revolves around your admittedly well-formed shoulders, and she'd rather pluck out her fingernails than disappoint you."

"My sister respects me. Is that a crime?"

Kelsey scathed him with a look, then glanced pensively away. "Forcing her to choose between the two people that she loves most is unforgivably cruel."

Luke's neck muscles tightened. "So that's it. Ridenour."

Kelsey leaned forward, her anxiety reflected in her eyes. "Ruth really loves Joseph. What do you have against the poor guy?"

"He's a sniveling drip," Luke growled. "Damned fool whined like a dog because he got an oil spot on his Ivy League pants. Besides, he doesn't love Ruth."

"What makes you think that?"

"I don't know." Luke shrugged. "The way he looked at her, I guess, as though she were a piece of marked-down merchandise."

For a silent moment, Kelsey considered this information, then met Luke's gaze and laid a pleading hand on his forearm. "Ruth wants a real church wedding, Luke, and she wants you to give her away."

"No." The warmth of her soft palm made his skin tingle.

"Please. It would mean so much to her," Kelsey whispered in a sultry tone. "Is there anything I can do that would make you reconsider?"

Luke took one look at her teasing expression and decided that if she didn't stop sending silent messages with those exotic, almond-shaped eyes, he was going to slam the office door shut and shock her preppy socks off. He smiled seductively. "That's a tempting offer."

"It was meant to be." To her credit, she wasn't coy about her interest. "Perhaps we could get together to discuss the options."

They weren't talking about Ruth anymore and both of them knew it. "Yeah. Maybe we can."

As the words left his mouth, Luke knew that there was no "maybe" about it. He would see Kelsey Manning again. Soon.

Before she'd left his office, they'd arranged to meet at a small café halfway between the campus and the auto shop. That evening had been the beginning of a week-long romance that had taken them both by storm.

Kelsey had been different from any woman Luke had ever known. He'd liked her impudence and saucy sense of humor. Although he'd vehemently disagreed with most of her opinions, he'd admired the directness with which she offered them, and had been impressed that she could hold up her end of an argument without becoming defensive or hostile. Most of all, he had liked Kelsey's spontaneity. He'd never known what the nutty woman was going to do next.

One night he'd been working late when Kelsey had appeared at the shop, armed with a picnic basket and a bottle of champagne. They'd spread a calico cloth on the garage floor beside the antique DeSoto that Luke was restoring, but he'd been less interested in potato salad than in the dark-haired beauty who teased him with sly glances.

One look into her flashing, provocative eyes convinced Luke that tonight would be the night. Kelsey wanted him and he instinctively knew that she was going to make a move.

Luke watched hungrily as she arranged their meal on the patterned cloth. Judging by the nervous dart of Kelsey's tempting little pink tongue, she was well aware that his mouth wasn't watering for the rubbery take-out chicken. She fidgeted with a basket of biscuits. Luke found her uncharacteristic shyness appealing.

After offering him a tenuous smile, Kelsey suddenly stood, as though needing a moment to reconsider, then wandered curiously around the shop. She touched various tools—caressed them, really—and Luke envied the cold steel objects that were favored with her delicate touch.

Having completed one circuit of the rambling brick structure, she returned to their improvised dining room. Instead of sitting down, she rubbed the old DeSoto's faded green fender. "This is a lovely car. Have you been working on it long?"

"A couple of years." Luke stood and moved close enough that the sweet fragrance of her hair made him dizzy. "It was my grandfather's first car. Even after the piece of junk blew two engines, he couldn't bear to get rid of it. I can't remember when this pile of bolts wasn't sitting in my mom's backyard."

Kelsey rubbed her finger over the dull finish. "It must mean a lot to you."

"Yeah." Luke hooked his thumbs in his pockets to keep himself from grabbing her. "Sometimes, when I'm working on it, I have this weird feeling that Gramps is handing me a wrench or something."

Frowning, Luke took a step backward. Why had he told her that? He'd never mentioned those feelings to anyone before. Not wanting Kelsey to think that he was into any kind of occult mumbo jumbo, he hastened to mitigate the damage. "When I'm tired, sometimes my mind plays tricks on me, that's all."

"Maybe not. I like to think that in one way or another, the people we love never really leave us."

Their eyes met and Luke held his breath. The air was charged with electric tension, and his groin ached with anticipation.

As he slowly bent to kiss her, she suddenly turned away. She laughed nervously—kind of a squeaky giggle—then knelt on the cloth and encompassed their meal with a jerky sweep of her hand. "I guess we should eat before everything gets cold."

Ignoring the disappointed throb in his loins, Luke painfully lowered himself to the floor. "Yeah. I guess so."

All he really wanted to do was swipe the clutter from the checkered cloth and dine on her luscious body, but good sense and his own warped chivalry insisted that the lady be allowed to set her own pace.

Crossing his legs, Luke placed a soggy hunk of chicken on his plastic plate. "This is swell. Thanks."

"A purely selfish gesture," Kelsey replied, holding a drumstick in one hand as she pushed a mounded bowl of baked beans toward Luke. "You work late every night and by the time I see you, you're too tired to eat. I am not a cheap date, Luke Sontag. I expect to be wined and dined, even if I have to provide my own props. Have an olive." She plucked one from the jar and held it to his mouth.

It was the opening Luke had been waiting for. On the pretext of steadying her hand, he caressed her wrist and gently took the olive in his teeth, touching the shiny black skin with his tongue before cupping it with his lips and sucking it seductively into his mouth. During the sensual procedure, his gaze never left Kelsey's face.

Visibly shaken, Kelsey shivered and slowly retrieved her hand. "Quite a performance," she murmured. "I'll bet your dessert show brings down the house."

"I haven't had any complaints."

Kelsey nervously smoothed her linen slacks, and shifted her weight to one hip, tucking her legs to the side. Luke interpreted her movement as a withdrawal, a signal that he'd been moving too fast and managed to re-leash his rampaging hormones. It wasn't getting any easier. He was so damned hard that it was all he could do to keep from pouncing on her.

Forcing interest in his meal, Luke took a healthy bite of chicken. It tasted like cardboard soaked in diesel oil.

For several minutes, they ate in silence, casting covert glances between bites of bland food that neither of them wanted. A bare bulb dangled from the shop ceiling, casting a golden glow that was strangely erotic. Shadows settled along the curve of Kelsey's shoulders, partially obscuring the drape of her silky blouse. Luke found himself imagining how the delicate fabric might be clinging to the hidden breast, much as it outlined the portion of her bosom that was visible. The image excited him and the air of sexual tension intensified until a fine film of perspiration misted Kelsey's flushed cheeks and Luke was wound tighter than a gear spring.

Finally his taut muscles rebelled, knotting from thigh to shoulder, continuing upward until his throat closed and he was unable to swallow another bite of tasteless food. Placing an untouched chicken thigh on his plate, he glanced around the makeshift table with a pained expression. "Did you bring any napkins?"

Kelsey laid down her fork. "I knew I forgot something."

"No problem." Luke rose up on one knee, preparing to stand. "There's a roll of paper towels around here somewhere."

Kelsey reached out to touch his wrist. He froze, both enticed and perplexed by the conflict he saw in her eyes. Hesitating, she averted her gaze, but her slender fingers still rested against his racing pulse and Luke held his breath, afraid the slightest movement would send her skittering away.

Finally she looked up decisively. "Who needs towels?" she whispered, then slowly brought his hand to her dewy lips. Her tongue touched the tip of his index finer, tickling, teasing, before a gentle sucking motion drew it into her mouth.

Luke's heart rate soared and his gut twisted into a fiery knot. "Don't play games with me," warned a rasping voice that he barely recognized as his own.

Turning his hand, Kelsey rubbed her supple cheek against the roughened skin of his palm. "I want to touch you."

Luke swallowed hard and tested his voice. "I want to touch you, too."

Her lips brushed his thumb, then she looked up, her eyes filled with passion and promise. "Then do it. Touch me, Luke. Please."

Before she'd finished her plea, Luke was on his feet trying to drag her up. She stumbled against him. Olives rolled across the cloth and over the concrete floor.

"Do you know what you're asking for?" Luke demanded.

Kelsey's eyes were half closed and her trembling fingers rested on his collarbone. "Yes." It was more a sigh than a word.

When her lips parted, Luke kissed her with a passion that bordered on roughness, then instantly gentled his mouth. His lips caressed hers, his tongue moving with tender encouragement, until she tentatively followed his lead and explored his mouth with increasing boldness.

Blood rushed to Luke's brain until the vessels in his forehead pounded inside his skull and every inch of his skin was on fire. He wanted her. God help him, Luke wanted this woman more desperately than he wanted his own life.

And he was about to have her.

As he slid one hand under her breast, she arced slightly and he felt her tiny whimper bubble into his mouth. Through the thin fabric of her blouse and soft brassiere, he stroked the erect nipple with his thumb until she gasped. Her head rolled backward, and she closed her eyes, moaning weakly.

More than encouraged, Luke expertly unfastened buttons until her blouse was open from collar to waist, then worked his frantic fingers under her bra by impatiently pushing the flimsy garment away. A pale mound of fragrant flesh appeared, its rose-colored areola gleaming in the golden light. He wanted to take the breast into his mouth, teasing the sensitive nipple with his tongue until she cried out in ecstasy, but forced himself to begin his quest with a series of soft, seductive kisses encircling that most delicate point.

But Kelsey wouldn't be denied. Framing Luke's face with her hands, she pressed his lips against her breast, simultaneously rotating her shoulder to lift the nipple into his mouth. He yielded, giving her what they both wanted. She shuddered and exhaled slowly, emitting a throaty sound of pleasure.

After exposing the other breast, he buried his face between them and tried to control his racing heartbeat. "Slow down," he murmured. "Make it last."

"I...can't." Breathing hard, Kelsey squirmed anxiously against him. "Please, make love to me."

"Oh, I will, honey, but let's take some time. Work with me." Luke was surprised by his own words. Ordinarily, he would have fulfilled Kelsey's desperate request instantly and without a second thought. But for some reason Luke knew that this time, with this incredible woman, the sexual act wouldn't be enough. He wanted their lovemaking to be special, slow and sweet and filled with the promise of a thousand such nights. He wanted to taste every inch of her, from her creamy throat and to the translucent pulse points behind each of her sexy knees.

Suddenly Kelsey took control, startling Luke, but not displeasing him. Still, his noble intention of a slow, sensual seduction evaporated when her seeking hand glided below his waist and held the pulsing core of him. Luke damned near jumped out of his skin. Every nerve in his body screamed for relief.

Then hands were everywhere. Clothes were loosened and discarded without modesty or thought. Skin was exposed and explored with desperate intensity as the sweat slickened their bodies and uncontrollable passion raged.

Luke cupped Kelsey's firm buttocks and lifted her to the rounded fender of the old DeSoto. He barely felt the sting of her frenzied fingernails raking his bare shoulders.

She wrapped her naked legs around his waist and grappled with the button of his fly. "Help me," she whispered hoarsely. "Please..."

Torn between releasing her luscious bottom and accommodating her desperate request, Luke reluctantly turned her loose just long enough to unfasten his jeans and push the obstructing garment away. When his briefs, too, had been dispensed with, he returned his full attention to the gorgeous nude woman reclining on the hood of his grandfather's old car.

Lord, she was a spitfire. Luke had never experienced a woman of such visceral passion and unabashed erotic fervor. Captured in the sweet prison of her encircling legs, Luke tentatively touched the inside of her thigh. Her bottom jerked violently and her heels dug into his spine. Encouraged, he moved his trembling fingers upward, into her warmth.

She sucked in a sharp breath. "Yes...there. Oh, God."

Aroused to the point of pain, Luke reveled in the silkiness surrounding her feminine center and the welcoming moisture within. Then her frantic fingers wrapped around his erect member and Luke thought he would explode. He had to have her. Now.

Grasping her wriggling hips with both hands, he lifted her so quickly that she had to release that personal part of his anatomy and grab hold of his shoulders. Their eyes met. She held her breath, silently pleading for the completion that was moments away.

Luke hesitated—he didn't know why—then pressed into her sweetness, savoring the moment as her heat pulled him deeper, and deeper, and deeper still.

The world went red, then purple, then exploded in shards of white and gold. There was pain, exquisite pain, and pleasure beyond anything Luke had ever experienced.

Now, alone in the silent trailer, Luke reexperienced that exquisite pain, and the kaleidoscope of remembered joy. A shattering sound pricked his brain, and shards of white and gold tinkled into the discolored steel sink. Momentarily disoriented, Luke numbly watched a drop of blood pause on the heel of his hand, then fall onto the sparkling slivers of the crushed shot glass he'd been holding.

Closing his eyes, he drew a deep breath. Even the memories drew blood. It seemed a fitting vengeance from the woman who had destroyed his life.

Absently wiping his hand on his jeans, Luke sat at the compact dinette table and brooded about the past. Once, he had been hopelessly naive, believing that the essence of female love could transform the strong into the invincible. Kelsey Manning had shattered that myth by revealing the true vulnerability of his manhood.

Luke could still taste her honeyed sweetness, still feel how her writhing body had seethed with desire. They'd made wild love that night, achingly sweet yet so explosive that he had damned near blown a blood vessel.

Afterward, Kelsey could have asked him to cut off an arm and he'd have done it. Instead, she'd tricked him, insisting that he bless his sister's marriage. When he'd refused, they had fought bitterly; then Kelsey had marched furiously out of his life.

Two months later she'd returned and coolly informed Luke that she was pregnant. That's when his world had crumbled.

Chapter 3

Kelsey drove down the ramp, stopped at the wrought-iron gate and lowered her window to slide a card into the steel sentry guarding her Santa Monica apartment complex. After approving the silent request, a gate yawned open and she pulled into the dimly-lit underground parking garage. Kelsey despised the cold, concrete structure. It was dank, and perennially dark. She hated that.

After flipping off the ignition, she took a deep breath and rested her head on the steering wheel. It was after midnight, and she was absolutely exhausted, so physically and mentally drained that she actually contemplated spending the night where she sat to avoid the effort of dragging her weary body up to the sixth floor.

Being mugged and nearly kidnapped had been stressful, all right, but that unpleasant incident wasn't the root of her emotional trauma. It was Luke Sontag. The ordeal of seeing him again had been more agonizing than she could ever have imagined. They had shared so much, suffered so much. Now they were little more than bitter strangers. It hurt.

Straightening, Kelsey garnered what strength she had left and opened the car door. When she took her purse from the car, she noticed a shiny object on the floor, nested beside the brake pedal. Her lipstick. She shivered at the unsettling reminder of how the pale-eyed man had emptied her purse, then tried to pull her into the car. If it hadn't been for Luke—

Luke. The memory touched her heart. He had rescued her tonight, but on the universal scale of things, perhaps he'd owed her that much. If it hadn't been for Luke, her life would have proceeded in the structured, orderly manner that she'd always planned for herself. She would have been spared so much pain.

And so much joy.

Shaking off that unbidden afterthought, she scooped up the metallic cylinder and went to the elevator, leaning against the polished brass rail as the lift hummed upward. A soft jolt opened her eyes and the doors slid apart. She stepped onto the soft carpeting, walking a few feet to unlock her apartment door.

Once inside, Kelsey tossed her purse onto the glass-topped entry table and, abhorring even momentary darkness, she quickly flipped on the light. The neat apartment was as she'd left it, a contemporary showplace of white leather, glass and chrome. It was comfortable enough, although not the decor she would have chosen. She enjoyed more traditional things, like the warmth of oiled wood and the homey charm of tapestry. Still, the apartment was adequate, considering how little time she actually spent here. Her promotion to financial analyst earlier in the year had required long hours and extensive personal commitment. Kelsey hadn't minded. After all, the position was a dream job, the one for which she'd groomed herself since junior high school.

She had every reason to be happy. And she was, damn it. She was.

Rubbing her tense shoulders, Kelsey went about the ritual of preparing herself for bed. She showered, soaping herself three times in a vain effort to remove the invisible stain of her attacker's touch, then scoured her hair until her scalp was tender. After slipping on a pair of unattractive but infinitely comfortable flannel pajamas, she slid into bed and stared at the night-light's flickering glow on the ceiling. She wouldn't sleep tonight. It didn't matter. There had been many sleepless nights in the past two years. She'd survived them all. She'd survive this one.

The problem with insomnia was that one's thoughts wandered without permission. Images flashed behind tightly closed eyelids, reminiscences that a busy mind could ignore.

Too exhausted to fight the memories, Kelsey allowed herself to relive them, recalling a special day that she and Luke had spent together.

One beautiful June morning Luke had driven up to the university campus. She'd nervously greeted him and he'd stepped inside, glancing around the dormitory room with detached interest.

His gaze fell on the two neatly made beds. He started to speak, then stubbornly clamped his lips together. Kelsey intuitively recognized the unspoken question and answered it. "I got a letter from Ruth last week," she told him quietly. "She likes Santa Barbara but says that the house Joseph bought is so big that she feels like she's living in a hotel."

Shrugging his eyebrows, Luke conveyed that he couldn't have cared less, but his words betrayed him. "Is she happy?"

"I guess so." Kelsey chewed her lip for a moment, then slid him a wary glance. "She'd be happier if you'd call her. I have a number—"

"Are you ready?" Luke interrupted, shifting impatiently.

Kelsey sighed and nodded. "My suitcase is in the closet. I'll get it."

Before she had finished speaking, Luke strode to the closet and flung open the door. He lifted one large, well-stuffed piece of luggage. "Is this all?"

"Yes." The room seemed extraordinarily hot and Kelsey tugged at the strained waistband of her lovely teal chiffon skirt.

The gesture did not go unnoticed. "It's a long drive," Luke commented. "You should wear something more comfortable."

Kelsey felt the humiliated flush creep up her throat. Having wanted to look especially pretty, she'd chosen the two-piece chiffon because the airy butterfly sleeves were so feminine and the color did wonderful things for her dark auburn hair. The fact that the dress didn't fit properly was beside the point. None of her clothes fit anymore.

"If you want to change—"

"No," Kelsey insisted firmly, willing herself not to cry. "This will be fine."

Luke shrugged. "Okay, then. Let's go."

"Luke..." Kelsey touched his arm as he walked by. He stopped, waiting. The words in her heart evaporated on her lips and she stared at the worn dorm carpet instead. "Are you sure that closing the shop for two days won't be a problem?"

"It won't be closed. The guys can keep things going until I get back tomorrow."

Kelsey knew that "the guys" were the three mechanics who worked for him. Since she also knew that the garage was struggling, she hadn't wanted their time together to cause further financial strain. "That's good," she murmured. "You must feel better about...things."

"Yeah." A muscle twitched in his jaw. "We'd better get going."

Luke's staid demeanor nearly broke Kelsey's heart, and again she struggled against the encroaching tears. Since she'd never been the weepy type, the unaccustomed weakness was immensely annoying, and she steeled herself against the frustrating emotional surge.

Lifting her chin, she offered her brightest, most reassuring smile, sucked in her puffy tummy and jauntily walked out of the building to the curb where Luke had parked his car. "It's going to be a lovely day."

"Yeah." Luke tossed her suitcase into the back seat. "Swell."

Then he'd slid in beside her and they'd embarked on a silent trip to the state line, a salient journey that would herald a turning point in their lives.

Throwing off the stifling covers, Kelsey sat on the edge of the mattress and cooled her face with her hands. She didn't want to think about that day, but couldn't erase the vivid recollections hammering at her fatigued brain, intrusive images of what should have been the happiest moment of her life.

It had been her wedding day. Brides were supposed to be radiant, but Kelsey had felt frumpy, alone and ashamed. Beside her, the man she'd so desperately loved stood stoic and grim, mumbling nondescript vows in a tawdry neon chapel.

It wasn't supposed to have been that way. Kelsey had dreamed of floating in a cloud of white, surrounded by her family and friends. Instead, she'd held a wilted nosegay over her swelling tummy and in a brief, dreary ceremony, Kelsey had become Mrs. Lucas Sontag.

Life could play cruel pranks on the initiated and the naive.

Rubbing her arms, Kelsey stood and walked to her bedroom window, pulling back the sheer curtains so she could watch the activity on the street below. Even in the wee hours, cars drove the boulevard beneath the apartment complex, filling Kelsey's bedroom with welcome illumination. The busy street had been one of the reasons that she'd rented this place. Ever since she'd been a child, Kelsey had never been able to sleep in total darkness. She didn't know why. There was just something unnerving about not knowing for certain if one's eyes were open or closed. Once, when she'd been five or six, she'd awakened from a horrible nightmare, convinced that she'd been struck blind in her sleep.

She had outgrown that irrational fear, of course, yet secretly comforted the memory of that frightened little girl by providing a metaphorical candle in the darkness.

Luke had understood that about her. On their wedding night, Kelsey had nervously waited in the lumpy motel bed. Luke had finally stepped out of the bathroom and hit the light switch, plunging the room into darkness. Kelsey's heart had pounded wildly, yet she'd been too embarrassed to share her secret.

She'd felt the bed move, then the blanket had rustled as he'd moved under the covers. A hand had touched her cold arm, startling her.

"Are you all right?" Luke asked instantly, his voice concerned.

"Yes." She tried to control her frantic struggle for breath. "I'm fine."

The mattress bounced as Luke sat up and turned on the bedside lamp. Blessed light flooded the room, and Kelsey couldn't suppress a grateful sigh as her taut muscles instantly relaxed.

Luke regarded her sharply. "You're not sick, are you? Do you have any pain?"

Feeling guilty, she hastily reassured him. "I'm fine, Luke, really, and the baby is fine, too."

Visibly relieved, he leaned back against the birch headboard and regarded her thoughtfully. "Would you be more comfortable if I slept on the floor?"

She blushed. "Of course not. You're...my husband." The words were music to her ears. Luke, however, winced visibly, and his expression, although fleeting, cut her to the core. Turning away, she aimed a vicious punch in the center of her pillow and concealed hurt feelings with a haughty tone. "If you want to sleep somewhere else, I'm sure we can stretch the budget enough for a second room."

Swallowing a lump of pure misery, Kelsey pulled the bedclothes up to her chin, flounced over onto her side and waited for the mattress to squeak, indicating that Luke had taken her huffy remark to heart.

For several moments, however, nothing happened. Then she felt a tender caress on her shoulder. "I'm right where I want to be." There was no anger in Luke's voice, only kindness and understanding.

Pushing herself up on one elbow, Kelsey shoved her stick-straight bangs from her face and stared into the sexy green eyes that could melt her soul with no more than a glance. "Do you mean that?"

"I never say things I don't mean." He touched her tousled hair with his lips and whispered, "I just don't want to hurt you, that's all. I haven't spent much time around pregnant people."

Kelsey's heart swelled happily. "Neither have I," she admitted. "I guess we'll have to learn about having babies together. Are you up for it?"

He smiled sexily. "At the moment, I'm up for more than that."

She hesitated, then slid her hand under the covers and boldly checked out the facts. "So you are," she murmured. "I guess we'd better do something about that."

"Sounds like a plan," Luke replied smoothly, reaching for the lamp. His hand stopped midair as Kelsey's smile faded, and he regarded her curiously.

She cleared her throat. "Could you please leave the lamp on? I mean, it *is* our wedding night and I wouldn't want to miss a single, delicious moment."

Luke's eyes reflected first bewilderment, then twinkling amusement, although to his credit, he said nothing. Instead, he respected her idiosyncrasy by leaving the lamp on that night and every night thereafter, although they never discussed the matter again.

The honk of a horn startled Kelsey and she stared vapidly at the bustling traffic, realizing with some regret that the vivid image of their wedding night had been nothing more than a memory.

Still, the beautiful vision had been so painfully real that she'd been mentally transported back in time, recalling every detail of how Luke's exquisite tenderness had swept her misgivings away in a wave of fiery passion. In that glorious moment, she'd actually believed that Luke could love her.

Later, she would learn just how cruel that hoax had been.

"Cynthia? Hi. Listen, I'm going to be a bit late this morning. Can you cover for me?" Kelsey took a quick gulp of coffee and listened while her efficient assistant offered to hold the fort. "Thanks. I should be in before noon. 'Bye."

Cradling the receiver, Kelsey held up the torn business card she'd discovered in Ruth's abandoned room—Howard L. Parlow, Attorney at Law. Not much of a lead, but at the moment it was all she had. She draped her purse strap over her shoulder, grabbed her briefcase and headed out to Parlow's Wilshire Boulevard office.

The freeway was clogged, as usual, and when Kelsey became stuck in gridlock, her mind wandered. She fretted about last night, and the apathy Luke had displayed for his sister's plight.

Although painfully aware that Luke and his sister had been estranged since Ruth's marriage, Kelsey had nonetheless been deeply disappointed by his lack of concern. She'd expected better of him. Sadly, last night hadn't been the first time she'd misjudged Luke Sontag, but since he'd always been a distrustful man, he probably wanted proof of Kelsey's dire suspicions.

Proof. That was an infuriating example of the logical masculine mind. If something couldn't be seen, touched and tasted, it simply didn't exist.

Well, Kelsey didn't need proof. She *knew* what kind of person Ruth was, and so did Luke. Ruth was not the type to take off on a lark, ignoring the concern of family and friends. Disappearing without a trace wasn't normal behavior for a woman who had always been the epitome of thoughtfulness and reliability.

Besides, during the short visit Kelsey had become increasingly worried about her friend's health. Ruth's pregnancy had progressed to the point that she was becoming cumbersome and she'd been plagued by heartburn, popping antacid tablets as though they were peanuts.

Then there had been the perplexing, undeniable fear in Ruth's eyes. She'd been so jittery that the slightest sound scared her half to death. Kelsey sobered, remembering how Ruth had quietly related a series of seemingly inconsequential incidents from which had emerged a clear and horrifying picture of the poor woman's life during the past two years.

After her marriage, Ruth had moved to Santa Barbara and within a few months had mysteriously stopped answering Kelsey's letters and the Ridenours' telephone number had been changed to an unlisted one. Kelsey's attempts to contact Ruth had waned during a series of personal disasters of her own that had required all of Kelsey's attention and depleted most of her strength.

Eventually, the two friends had simply drifted apart. That had been a devastating loss, so when Ruth had suddenly reappeared, Kelsey's joy could only be compared to having a severed limb suddenly and inexplicably reattached.

After an hour of hugging and happy tears, Kelsey had ushered the exhausted woman into the guest room, apologetically gesturing toward the cushioned pine frame pushed against one wall. "It's only a futon," Kelsey had murmured, regarding Ruth's grossly swollen belly with concern. "As a matter of fact, I'm sure you'd be more comfortable in the other bedroom."

Shaking her coffee-brown curls, Ruth painfully lowered herself onto the colorful folded pad. "This will be perfect, Kel. You know that a soft mattress kills my back."

"Yes, but—" Kelsey chewed her lip for a moment, then sat down and took Ruth's hand, scrutinizing her friend's unhealthy pallor and the bluish tinge beneath her eyes. "When is the baby due?"

"In a couple of weeks." Ruth offered a tired smile and affectionately rubbed her distended abdomen. "If he doesn't kick his way out first, that is."

"Are you so sure it's a boy?"

"Absolutely. I have the ultrasound pictures to prove it." As Ruth spoke of her child, a maternal light glowed in her soft, blue-gray eyes. Suddenly, the illumination faded and she looked away. "Boys really need their father."

Kelsey squeezed Ruth's fragile hand. "Do you want to talk about it?"

After a silent moment, Ruth shook her head and smiled wanly. "There's not much to say. Things between Joseph and me weren't working out, that's all."

"Why didn't you tell me sooner? Good grief, Ruthie, you never wrote or called—" Cutting off the unintended accusation, Kelsey quickly apologized. "I'm sorry. I didn't mean to rag on you like that. I'm sure you were busy."

"Me? I wrote you every week and Joseph took them directly to the post office. Why didn't you ever write back?" Ruth's eyes widened in disbelief. "Thank God your new address was in the telephone book, or I never would have located this apartment."

That was stunning news. For a moment, Kelsey didn't know how to respond. The pain in Ruth's eyes stung Kelsey to the quick. Finally, she released her friend's hand. "I never received any letters from you, but I *did* write, so many times I lost count."

Suddenly Ruth seemed engrossed in plucking a loose thread from the hem of her oversized maternity blouse.

Kelsey felt sick. "You never received any of my letters, did you?"

Ruth squeezed her eyes shut and shook her head.

"Why not? I don't understand—" The truth struck like an unexpected punch, and Kelsey sucked in a quick breath. "Joseph took them, didn't he?"

Sighing, Ruth delicately massaged her forehead. "I don't know, Kel. Maybe."

"Why would he do such a thing? What have I ever done to offend him?"

"Nothing. It's just that Joseph was . . . well, a bit jealous of my friends. He believed that a wife's place was at her husband's side." She smiled sadly. "At first I was flattered, thinking that he must love me a lot to need all of my time and attention. Then his rules became more restrictive, and I started to feel really confined. I remembered how you and I used to spend Saturdays at the mall, then eat take-out Chinese and watch old Bogart movies on television. I missed that, Kel. I missed a lot of things."

"Is that why you left him?"

Ruth fidgeted with the corded corner of the futon cover, then quickly stood and walked to the window, standing just behind the stacked vertical blinds where she couldn't be seen from outside. "Partly, I suppose."

Kelsey blurted the next words without considering the consequences. "But I still don't understand, Ruth. Why didn't you tell him to shove his damned rules years ago? Why leave now, when you're having a child together? It doesn't make sense."

Ruth's olive complexion paled three shades, but she didn't respond. Instead, she backed away from the window, clasping and unclasping her hands, then crossed the room and made a production of unpacking her suitcase, silently refolding each garment before tucking it neatly in the bureau drawer.

An ominous tingling crawled up Kelsey's spine, but she ignored the implausible notion and switched subjects. "Have you spoken with Luke?"

Ruth shook her head sadly. "Not since before my wedding."

"Why haven't you called him, Ruth? He's your brother. Surely he'd be able to help—"

Cutting Kelsey off with a feeble wave, Ruth sighed, then dabbed at her damp forehead. "I can't, not after what I did to him."

"What did you do, for crying out loud? You got married, that's all. So he didn't like it. So what? Luke has always loved you, Ruth. You're the most important person in his life."

"Once I was. Not anymore." Ruth's tone was more sad than bitter. "You don't understand my brother. He's not a forgiving man."

Kelsey sobered instantly. If Ruth hadn't received Kelsey's letters, she had no way of knowing just how well Kelsey *did* know Luke. Her heart sank like a rock. Ruth didn't know about any of it—not the pregnancy or the hastily arranged marriage or the shattering devastation that had followed.

And Kelsey couldn't tell her. She, like Ruth, couldn't talk about the painful details; not now anyway, and perhaps not ever.

Ruth was right about her brother. Luke Sontag *was* a harsh, unyielding man, yet at this point Kelsey sincerely believed that if Luke realized his sister needed him, he'd have been there in a ring-tailed minute. "Look, why don't you let me call Luke and fill him in? I'm sure he'd be more than happy to—"

"*No.* I mean, no thank you." Without looking up, Ruth spoke in a voice that was unnaturally high-pitched and as tight as a fiddle bow. "The trip made me feel a bit grubby. Would you mind if I took a shower?"

Taken aback, Kelsey stammered, "Of course not."

As Ruth gathered her personal items, Kelsey regarded the taut set of her friend's fragile shoulders and sickly realized something was terribly wrong. Although Ruth had always been quiet, she'd never been fearful or lacking in courage. This mousy, jittery woman bore little resemblance to the sedate, even-tempered roommate with whom Kelsey had shared so many happy moments.

Kelsey tried to convince herself that a certain amount of depression was normal for a person in crisis, and the hormonal chaos of pregnancy would exacerbate that despondency. The strained justification evaporated when Ruth bent over her suitcase and the thick mass of dark curls fell aside, exposing a series of ugly, dime-sized bruises on her neck.

With a loud gasp, Kelsey blurted, "My God, Ruth. What happened?"

Alarmed, Ruth turned and, seeing the direction of Kelsey's horrified gaze, instantly rearranged the curled mass. A portion of her oversized sweater's sleeve slipped to reveal several yellowing blotches on her forearm.

Kelsey was in shock. All she could do was point helplessly and stammer, "Good Lord."

Quickly lowering her arm, Ruth emitted a strained, almost hysterical giggle. "Isn't that something? Honestly, I can't believe how clumsy pregnancy makes a person. It seems like I'm always misjudging doorways or bumping into cabinets. Joseph swears that I should strap pillows to my stomach and wear a crash helmet. Do you have any shampoo, Kel? I forgot to bring mine."

For a tense moment, Kelsey was rooted to the carpet. She wanted desperately to believe Ruth's explanation, but she didn't. Still, having recognized the desperation in Ruth's eyes, Kelsey respected the silent plea and didn't pursue the subject. There would be time for that later, when Ruth was ready.

Or so Kelsey had thought. As it turned out, there hadn't been time at all.

Now, as freeway fumes filtered into the stifling interior of her car, Kelsey wondered if she should have forced the issue. Perhaps if she'd not been so sensitive about upsetting Ruth with obviously unpleasant questions, she might have learned something that could shed light on what had happened since.

Traffic sounds interrupted her troubling thoughts as the line of vehicles moved forward. Pressing the accelerator, Kelsey drove on toward the attorney's downtown office, determined to locate Ruth with or without Luke Sontag's help.

The blasting air compressor vibrated Luke's throbbing head as though a 747 had landed on his skull. He automatically pressed both palms against his temples and swore savagely. Around him, various mechanics continued their cacophonous activities, buzzing, grinding, pounding and riveting, cheerfully oblivious to the fact that the owner's booze-abused brain was preparing to explode.

"Hey, man." A grinning black mechanic leaned on the fender of the dented pickup truck Luke was repairing. "Word on the street is that you had some excitement last night."

Luke scowled at the gritty carburetor. Ordinarily, he would have squelched this unwelcome intrusion with a withering look and stony silence, but Ernie Hawkins was more than Luke's best mechanic. He was a good friend.

Luke and Ernie had grown up on the same block, standing together in the face of intense, sometimes violent, pressure from neighborhood gangs.

Although basically good-natured, Ernie's ebony eyes and sunshine smile obscured a hardened, street-wise soul and if provoked, Ernie could whip any thug in the 'hood without breaking a sweat. So could Luke. Together, they'd won the tenuous and grudging respect of those to whom strength and courage were the only measure of a man's worth.

And so, because it was Ernie who'd asked, Luke managed a sparse reply. "Some punk didn't know the neighborhood rules. I enlightened him."

"Whooooee." Ernie batted at his blue Dodger cap, spinning the visor to one side. "Would've liked to seen that."

"It was no big deal," Luke muttered peevishly.

Ernie emitted a disbelieving snort. "The way I heard it, you busted the dude's arm and smeared his nose all over his face."

Straightening, Luke yanked a stained rag from his rear pocket and wiped his hands. "You heard wrong."

"Yeah?" Ernie cocked his head skeptically. "And I don't suppose there was no woman, either? A so-fine lady, dressed up prissy and driving a set of cherry, uptown wheels?"

Luke's jaw tensed and he jammed the rag back in his pocket. Damn. Street talk didn't miss much. "It was Kelsey."

Ernie sobered instantly. "So that's why you got the red-eyed blues."

Eyes narrowed, Luke issued a silent warning and spoke through tightly clamped teeth. "Have you lubed old man Franklin's Caddy?"

"Nope."

"Then you've got work to do."

"So, what's going on with your wife?"

"Damn it, Ernie—"

"Ain't women the pits? They're devious, that's what. Why, my first old lady was always whining that she couldn't cook, and damn near poisoned me once. So we eat out for six years, you know, then she up and divorces me and guess what happens?"

Luke sighed and rubbed his throbbing head. "Franklin's going to pick up the car at noon."

"The lyin' witch takes a job in a freaking restaurant, as a *cook*. Can you believe it?" Hooking his thumbs in his blue cotton coveralls, Ernie rocked back on his heels and shook his head. "Women. You just can't trust 'em, except for my new lady. She's different. So, what's going on with Kel?"

"Nothing," Luke growled.

"What's it been now, a year? Seems like she must've had a pretty good reason for dropping by."

Gritting his teeth, Luke yanked his head out from under the hood, angrily facing his friend with every intention of pulling rank and ordering the insolent guy back to the lube bay. Instead, he inexplicably blurted, "Kelsey thinks that my sister is in trouble."

"Ruthie?" Ernie's dark eyes mirrored instant concern. "What happened?"

"Probably nothing." Luke's casual tone belied the knot in his belly as he curtly filled Ernie in on the details. He'd expected—hoped—that his friend would validate his own belief that the incident had been blown out of proportion.

That didn't happen. Instead, Ernie's dark brows knitted together and he clucked worriedly. "Kelsey's a passably smart lady. I've never known her to pop a sweat for nothing."

Luke inhaled deeply, then blew air slowly from his lips until his lungs had completely deflated. That wasn't what he'd wanted to hear, although he couldn't dispute the truth of Ernie's statement. Kelsey *wasn't* the hysterical type; never had been.

Damn, his head hurt.

Squeezing his eyes shut, Luke massaged his aching lids. He briefly considered giving up the booze, then discarded the notion. The pain of a hangover was nothing compared to the agony of long, lonely nights with a mind in chaos and a heart cracked into shrapnel.

Ernie's impatient voice interrupted Luke's silent misery. "So whatcha gonna do, man?"

"Nothing."

"Hey, wives are a dime a dozen, but Ruthie's your sister. What with your daddy running out and your momma dyin', she's all you got left. What if she's got big-time trouble?"

The reproachful words struck a chord in Luke's soul, but he stubbornly tightened his jaw. "She got herself into it. She can get herself out."

"Aw, that's no good, man. I know she wronged you, after everything you've done for her and all, but you can't just let her flop."

A sudden flash of anger churned Luke's helplessness into irrational fury. "I don't have to do anything, not one damned thing. The shop phone number has been the same since my sister was ten years old. She knows where I am. Since this is none of your business, get your scrawny butt back to work, or your next employer might be a tougher bastard than I am."

Ernie's black eyes flashed. "Not likely. You're the meanest son of a bitch I know."

"Don't forget that," Luke snapped.

"I won't forget nothing," Ernie replied tightly, balling his big fists. "And don't you forget that if you push me too far, I can whip your pitiful ass."

"In your dreams." Luke straightened, shifting his weight to the balls of his feet and assuming a combative stance without having a clue as to why he was deliberately provoking his best friend. Penance, maybe, the need to have someone punch the guilt out of his gut. Ernie could do that. They'd had a few past confrontations, and although Luke had won his share, none of the victories had been without serious physical consequence on both sides.

An eerie silence shrouded the garage, and Luke was vaguely aware that the other two mechanics had ceased work and were watching the tense standoff with a mixture of apprehension and intense curiosity. Tension mounted and the smell of danger mingled with petroleum fumes until the stifling air was thick enough to slice.

From the corner of his eye, Luke noticed the two other men whispering excitedly; then each fumbled in his pocket before plopping a wad of currency on the fender of a nearby car.

The damned fools were betting on who'd win.

That action provided a mirror to his own stupidity. What was he doing, standing here like a swaggering adolescent, taunting a friend to violence? Had he completely lost his mind?

Apparently Ernie had caught sight of the wager as well, because Luke noted the big man's mouth twitch at the corners, as though he were trying to swallow a smile. When he faced Luke again, there was a hint of amusement twinkling in his dark eyes.

"So, you want me to mess you up or what?" Ernie asked politely.

Luke rubbed the back of his neck. "The problem is that if I break your face now, you'll never get Franklin's damned car lubed."

Stroking his chin, Ernie considered that. "I suppose I could beat you just as bad after hours."

"Yeah." Luke slid a covert glance at the two disappointed mechanics. "Let's get some work done."

Twisting his blue cap until the bill shaded the back of his neck, Ernie started to walk away, then stopped and glanced over back. "Ruthie's your sister, man. She's blood."

With that somber pronouncement, Ernie rotated his big shoulders in a what-can-you-do shrug, then sauntered off to the lube bay.

Frustrated and torn, Luke angrily swiped the neatly arranged tools from the car fender, deriving a perverse satisfaction from their loud clatter as they skidded across the concrete floor. He whirled and glared at the two wide-eyed mechanics. "You guys got a problem?"

"No, sir," stammered the shorter man, a young Hispanic who had worked at the garage for only a few weeks. "We got no problems at all." Instantly the two men grabbed tools and bumped into each other in their haste to return to work.

Folding his arms, Luke braced himself on the fender and tried to focus his aching brain. He usually didn't give a fat flying fig what anyone else thought, but Ernie, of all people, knew the depth of his sister's betrayal.

Luke had always done his best for Ruth, who could barely remember the father who had abandoned them. She'd only been five at the time, but Luke had been eleven, the age when a boy looks to male role models to chart a course for his own life. Luke hadn't been blind, though, and had realized that as fathers went, theirs hadn't been much of a prize.

The grizzled old guy drank too much, whined incessantly, and spent most of his waking hours inventing excuses as to why he couldn't hold down a job. One day, the drunken sod staggered off to the store for a six-pack and never came back.

Luke's mother had been stoic about the abandonment, never complaining or speaking badly about the man who had treated her like a sack of unwanted garbage. Luke had tried to help with after-school jobs and minuscule paychecks to partially alleviate the financial strain, but he could do nothing for his mother's emotional anguish. After four years, the devastated woman finally worked herself to death, leaving the tattered family's survival squarely on Luke's fifteen-year-old shoulders.

At nine, Ruth had been at an age when girls most need maternal guidance. The child had been inconsolable, completely shattered by the loss of their mother. From that day forward, Luke had put aside his own needs and became his sister's parent. He'd acquired a high-school diploma through night courses so he could take on a full-time mechanic job. Over the years, Luke had scrimped and struggled, so that Ruth would never be dependent on capricious masculine whims, as their uneducated mother had been. Forgoing his own dreams, Luke had been determined that his beloved sister wouldn't spend her life scouring some fat matron's toilet.

Then she'd thrown it all away. By marrying Ridenour and dropping out of college, Ruth had devalued Luke's sacrifice. He'd felt betrayed. He'd *been* betrayed.

But blood was thick. Ernie had been right about that, and Luke silently acknowledged that he still cared about his sister's welfare. So why was he being so stubborn?

The answer was shouted by an angry voice in his brain. Because it had been Kelsey who'd asked him, the woman who had shredded his life and shattered his soul. Now she'd returned to tempt and torture him with exquisite memories of all that he'd lost.

Luke swore sharply and snatched a steel rachet from the floor. Women. You just can't trust them.

Ernie had been right about that, too.

Tired and more worried than ever, Kelsey returned to her apartment complex and stepped into the parking structure elevator. Her visit to Ruth's attorney had been a real eye-opener. Although Howard Parlow had been reluctant to discuss confidential client information, Kelsey had learned that Ruth had retained him to handle her divorce, but she hadn't kept her last appointment.

That information, coupled with her own nagging suspicions, had convinced Kelsey that Ruth had definitely not left voluntarily. Something had happened, something terrible, and as certain as Kelsey was of that fact, she was completely bewildered as to what she should do next.

Stepping from the elevator, she wiped a bead of perspiration from her forehead and impatiently tugged at her sticky rayon blouse. It was too hot for March, and too humid for Los Angeles. Even the weather seemed to thwart her every move.

Frustrated, she thrust her key into the lock, stepped into her apartment and absently tossed her purse on the table. With a tired moan, she raked both hands through her feathered hair, then bent into a rag-doll position and tried to shake out the tension. As she rolled her head, her eyes were partially open and she absently scanned the muted off-white carpet, the chrome table legs, the sleek upholstered sofa and a pair of sneakered feet.

Her head froze in mid-roll. For a moment, she forgot to breathe. Her heart hammered wildly. A prowler. There was a man in her apartment. Where did she keep the gun?

She didn't own a gun. Oh, God.

She straightened so quickly that her head spun. Touching her throat, she stumbled back a step and tried to focus on the backlit figure slumped on her couch.

Suddenly the man stood, overwhelming Kelsey with his sheer size, and a gruff but familiar voice demanded, "Where in hell do you keep the damned aspirin?"

Kelsey's jaw slackened in disbelief, then tightened with fury. Of all the arrogant, self-centered, swaggering—

Refilling her lungs, Kelsey struggled to slow her racing heart and regarded the intruder with mounting fury. Since Luke Sontag enjoyed breaking and entering, she hoped he would also enjoy the concrete accommodations that accompanied the activity.

"The aspirin are in the nightstand by my bed," Kelsey replied tightly.

Grumbling and scouring his scalp, Luke ambled toward

the hallway without further comment. When he'd disappeared into her bedroom, Kelsey calmly picked up the telephone and dialed 911.

Chapter 4

"There's an intruder in my apartment," Kelsey announced calmly. "The address is—"

Luke pressed the switch, disconnecting the call. Kelsey's shoulders went rigid and she stared straight ahead, her stubborn little jaw twitching with indignation. It was a good thing Luke had recognized that deviant gleam in her eye and poked his head out the bedroom door, just in case. Lord, she was a pain in the butt.

He pried the handset from her stiff fingers and cradled the receiver. "Now about those aspirin—"

Kelsey whirled and confronted him angrily. "How did you get in here?"

"Through the damned door."

"It was locked."

"So what?" The conversation grated on Luke's nerves. He knew that Kelsey was annoyed by his invasion of her personal space, but that was just tough. His head was about to explode and his tongue felt like a slab of raw liver, so he was in no mood for a freaking third-degree. "You're forgetting where I grew up, honey. On my block, any eight-year-old could jimmy a lock and most could blow a bank vault without dusting up their sneakers."

Folding her arms, Kelsey hiked up her nose with that righteous attitude that had always irked the hell out of him. "Oh, yes. The 'I'm just a poor boy from the wrong side of the tracks' routine. I'd forgotten how effectively you use that worn-out cliché to excuse socially unacceptable behavior."

"And I'd forgotten what a elitist snob you are," Luke growled. "Pull your nose out of the stratosphere, Kel. You may look good and smell good, but inside, you're no better than anyone else."

When her nostrils flared, Luke almost smiled. He could still get to her, still reach the fiery passion boiling beneath that icy crust of control. The achievement was immensely satisfying, a smug reinforcement that he could still expose the emotional core that Kelsey so diligently hid from the world.

With cautious detachment, he noted her silent code of turmoil—the minute twitch of her brow, the awkward angle of her chin—and realized that no matter how intimately he knew this intensely private woman, he didn't understand her at all.

The paradox didn't escape Luke's notice, but never having been a philosopher, he usually ignored anything that required prolonged cerebral activity, preferring the speed and simplicity of physical solutions. That was not the credo of a mentally lazy man; it was simply the logical extension of lifetime of conditioning in an urban war zone.

But Kelsey was fighting her own secret battle, an emotional battle that jeopardized the requisite insouciance that allowed her to function with only half a heart. Luke recognized her carefully constructed pain wall because he, too, had hidden behind a reflexive shield of indifference.

Kelsey suddenly tightened her fists, as though distressed by the mere sight of him and unable to endure the resurgent memories that his presence thrust upon her unwilling mind. Before his startled eyes, her inner resolve crumbled and her wan face was etched by a sorrow so intense that his apathy evaporated, and a burning knot settled in his throat.

When she faced him again, the fire had faded and her eyes were lusterless, two dull brown voids in an otherwise beautiful face. The transformation cut Luke to the quick.

"What do you want?" she asked wearily.

It took a moment for Luke to compose himself, summoning the comfortable dispassion that would conceal his secret heart. "I want to know where my sister is."

"Why? Last night, you were quite clearly disinterested in Ruth's welfare. In fact, I don't believe that you care about anyone who refuses to submit to your paternalistic control, so why are you here, Luke? What's the point?"

The accusation hurt. "You don't have a very high opinion of me, do you?"

Kelsey didn't answer. That hurt, too.

"I tell you what, lady, I don't give a damn what you think of me." The lie nearly choked Luke and he avoided Kelsey's gaze by scrutinizing the elegant surroundings. "Looks like you've come up in the world," he commented, lifting a fancy oriental-type vase.

When she didn't reply, Luke replaced the vase and walked around the well-appointed living room, stung by the tangible reminders of how Kelsey had always loved the pretty things that he'd been unable to provide.

Why are you here, Luke? she'd asked him.

Helluva good question, he decided, for which there was no plausible answer. There were reasons, of course, logical rationales so carefully composed during the long, painful night. Eventually Luke had convinced himself to take a closer look at the situation.

What he had conveniently ignored were his own hidden motives in seeking out the woman who had shattered his soul. He had plenty of excuses, of course, and had even managed to convince himself that he could behave in a calm and rational manner without losing sight of the true purpose of this forced reunion. His relationship with Kelsey was ancient history and he wasn't a man who lived in the past. Or so he'd firmly believed.

That admirable intent had dissipated the moment Luke stepped into Kelsey's ritzy new digs and compared the slick, contemporary furnishings with the shabby one-room flat they'd once shared.

Luke had hated that filthy place, and was still humiliated that he hadn't been able to afford better. Not that Kelsey had complained—not with words—but he could still remember her disillusionment as she'd scrubbed the pitted walls in a pathetic attempt to remove the yellowed city scum.

One night had been particularly traumatic to Luke's ego. He'd come home late, as was his habit in those days, entering quietly because Kelsey was usually asleep on the faded sofa that served dual duty as their bed.

That night, however, she hadn't been sleeping. Luke had found her on her knees beside a soapy bucket, scouring the dingy plaster with a tenacity that would have been admirable, had it not been hopeless.

Luke's stomach knotted. She looked so awkward and vulnerable, with hair sticking to her sweaty cheeks and her distended abdomen covered by an ineffective checkered apron. Guilt sliced into him like a shiv. His wife deserved better than a cheesy apartment with rattling pipes and rotting carpet.

Although she'd never actually said so, he knew that she was disappointed in their life-style. Hell, who wouldn't be? Kelsey loved nice things, Luke knew that. He wished he could give them to her. Someday he would. If he had to work twenty-six hours a day, Luke was determined to provide everything she ever wanted. Someday, she would live like a princess.

But for now, Luke could only watch his wife's silent struggle with helplessness and a gnawing sense of failure. Kelsey continued her task, so intent on her efforts that she was unaware of Luke's presence.

He placed his metal lunch box on the stained melamine dinette he'd bought for five bucks at a local flea market. At the clunking sound, Kelsey gasped and spun so quickly that she hit the bucket with her elbow and foamy water sloshed on to the worn nylon carpet.

The fear in her eyes quickly melted into relief and, as her fingertips brushed her throat, she managed a smile. "Hi."

A lump formed in Luke's throat as she grasped the sofa arm to heave her ponderous body into a standing position. "You shouldn't be working so hard," he admonished. "You'll hurt yourself."

"I'm fine. A little housework is good for the circulation." She absently placed both hands at the small of her back and rolled her torso, as though working out the kinks. "I kept dinner warm for you."

"Thanks." Luke pulled a chair away from the ratty old table, wincing at the cracked plastic seat. Actually, he wasn't the least bit hungry, his appetite having dissipated at the sight of his pregnant wife on her hands and knees like a scullery maid. The image brought back unpleasant memories of his own mother's drudgery, and how she'd spent the final years of her life slaving in other people's homes.

Kelsey set a plate of pasta and creamed peas in front of him, then slid into the other chair. "How was your day?"

"Okay." Luke lifted his fork and poked at the bland meal, recalling with growing aggravation how some pinstriped banker had grilled him for two hours before condescending to consider his loan request.

In truth, Luke couldn't fault the guy's reluctance. After all, the shop had been mortgaged three and a half years earlier to finance Ruth's college expenses, so there was precious little equity left to collateralize further debt. The problem was that without modernizing the garage, Luke couldn't hope to increase profits, and until he increased his profits, he couldn't give his wife and child the kind of home they deserved.

It was a financial Gordian knot, and even if the loan *was* approved, Luke realized that the shop's inner-city location placed severe limitations on the income he could reasonably expect. No magic sword could slice through the societal boundaries of a poverty-stricken neighborhood, but relocating his business was out of the question. Besides the obvious problem of finding someone who wanted to buy the shabby brick structure, there was also the small matter of how to feed his family during the years it would take to establish a new client base.

"Luke?"

"Hmm?" Glancing up from his plate, Luke saw that Kelsey had moved from the minuscule kitchenette into the living/sleeping portion of the room.

She shifted nervously, then reached behind the tattered sofa and rolled out a faded wicker bassinet. "What do you think?"

Pushing away from the table, Luke walked over to inspect the item. It wasn't very big, and a flounce surrounded the oval basket, spilling to the floor in a mass of gauzy ruffles. Inside was a soft little mattress decorated with yellow ducks wearing silly blue and pink bows. A pair of plastic handles allowed the bed to be lifted and carried. To Luke, the dumb thing looked like a tacky shopping basket, but Kelsey's eyes were shining like gemstones and her cheeks were flushed with excitement.

Her fingers floated across the satin ribbon trim. "Mrs. Fletcher in apartment 3B gave it to us. Do you like it?"

He hated it. "Yeah."

A dazzling smile lit her beautiful face. "I'm glad. I was afraid you'd think it was, well, too frilly."

Luke cleared his throat. "It's kind of small, isn't it? I mean, the kid will probably outgrow it in a couple of months."

She frowned prettily. "I know, but cribs are so expensive and since the baby is due next month, I figured..." Her voice dissipated and she stared down into the bassinet, nervously fingering a ruffle.

Humiliation heated the back of Luke's neck and elevated his blood pressure. "You figured that since your husband couldn't afford to buy his own kid a decent crib, that this piece of crap was better than nothing, right?"

Color drained from Kelsey's face. "That's not what I said."

Ignoring her feeble protest, Luke clamped his teeth together and spoke without moving his jaw. "I'm not some dirt-bag wino. I can afford a damned crib, and not some used hunk of junk from the swap meet, either."

"Luke, it's all right—"

"Damned straight it is," Luke snapped. "We're going to the mall on Saturday and you're going to pick out the biggest and best crib in the place, got it? I can afford it."

The words stuck in his throat. Yeah, he could afford it, if they didn't eat for a month.

Kelsey extended her hand and the plea in her eyes struck a mortal blow to Luke's heart. "We don't need—" Suddenly, Kelsey's gaze swung downward and her eyes widened in horror. One hand flew to her mouth and the other wrapped protectively around her belly as she backed away. Emitting a choked gurgling sound, she stared into the bassinet with an expression of pure revulsion.

Taking a quick step closer, Luke looked down and nearly gagged as a huge roach scampered across the duck-print mattress, then tried to burrow into the ruffled folds.

Swearing sharply, he snatched the insect and flung it across the room. With two steps he was in the tiny kitchen, repeatedly stomping the creature until it was nothing more than a greasy smear on the peeling linoleum floor.

Sick and disgusted, he dropped into the rickety kitchen chair and propped his head in his hands. He felt Kelsey close behind him, then her calming fingers began to knead his tight shoulders.

"Everything is going to be fine," she murmured.

Luke didn't respond. Everything wasn't going to be fine and they both knew it.

For several moments she quietly massaged his knotted muscles, then spoke in a soft but decisive voice. "I called Hill and Boucher this afternoon."

Luke frowned, then recalled that the company in question was the investment banking firm where Kelsey had once hoped to work. Of course, that had been months ago. Things had changed since then. She was his wife now, and would soon be the mother of his child.

Before Luke could speculate on why she'd called that particular company, she quietly answered the unspoken question. "There's a temporary job opening in the contracts department. It's basically clerical, of course, but it would give me the inside information I'd need to move into something better after the baby is born."

For a fuzzy moment, Luke actually didn't get it. Then, as comprehension dawned, he stiffened. "No way."

Releasing his shoulders, Kelsey rounded the table and sat facing him. "Luke, we need the money. The doctor says I can work up until the baby is due, then after a couple of months, there's no reason why I couldn't get a permanent job."

Luke stood up so quickly that the chair fell backwards with a startling crash. "I said no."

"That's not fair... Luke? Where are you going?" Alarmed, Kelsey stood. "It's nearly midnight... Luke, please..."

That poignant plea was the last thing he heard before he slammed the door behind him and walked out into the city night.

Now, standing in the plush elegance of Kelsey's uptown apartment, memories of those days raised a bitter bile in his throat. In spite of his objection, Kelsey had taken that damned job because she'd doubted his ability to adequately provide for his family. Part of him couldn't blame her, but that lack of confidence had wounded him deeply.

It still did.

As though from a great distance, Kelsey's voice filtered into his consciousness and Luke was vaguely aware that she'd been speaking to him. He blinked, focusing on this new, but not necessarily improved, version of his wife, with emotions still teetering between passion and resentment.

Balancing on clean, leather high heels that perfectly complemented her tailored wool suit, Kelsey absently brushed a layered strand from her face, folded well-manicured hands on her hips and confronted him with an attitude that he interpreted as utter disdain. "My living accommodations are no concern of yours, Luke. If you're truly interested in helping Ruth, fine. Otherwise, *get out.*"

With those final words, Kelsey's voice rose with frantic intensity. That startled Luke. He'd realized that she was upset, and quite frankly hadn't cared, but now he saw hysteria building in her eyes. With the vague intent of calming her, he took hold of her arm.

Suddenly the front door crashed open, and Luke was staring down the barrel of a gun.

"Oh my God, don't hurt him!" Kelsey frantically clutched at the blue sleeve.

"Stand back, lady." The police officer swept Kelsey aside as his partner slammed Luke's head on the tiled foyer floor.

Luke grunted in pain and Kelsey's heart nearly leapt out of her chest. "Please," she begged. "It was all a mistake. Let go of him. Oh Lord, don't do that!"

The handcuffs snapped with a sickening metallic click and Kelsey stumbled backward, unable to believe what was happening. This was a nightmare.

When the officers had kicked open the door, Luke had been holding Kelsey's arm and she imagined that from their perspective, the situation must have looked dire. Meanwhile Luke, startled to see a weapon aimed at his face, had reacted instinctively. After whipping Kelsey protectively behind his back, he'd grabbed at the gun, a gesture the policemen had naturally assumed to be hostile. Their response had been predictable and instantaneous. Before Kelsey could do more than take a sharp breath, Luke's arms had been twisted behind his back and he'd been wrestled to the floor.

Now the two burly officers dragged Luke to his feet and roughly pressed him against a nearby wall. He didn't resist. Instead, he turned his head just far enough to fix Kelsey with a grim, accusatory stare.

"Please," Kelsey repeated hoarsely. "This has all been a terrible mistake."

One policeman, still breathing heavily, tipped back his hat and eyed Kelsey with obvious suspicion. "Did you call 911 to report an intruder?"

"Yes, but—"

"And when we came to the door, weren't you screaming at this guy to get out?"

Kelsey rubbed her head miserably. "I know this all looks rather awkward, but Mr. Sontag is...an acquaintance." Luke's eyes narrowed and Kelsey quickly averted her gaze.

"I didn't have a chance to give the dispatcher my address, so there didn't seem to be a need to cancel the call."

The second officer folded his arms. "You didn't have to, ma'am. The emergency computer automatically logs the originating address as soon as the call is connected."

"I, uh, didn't know that." She licked her dry lips and rubbed her arms. "I'm sorry."

The first officer, a blue-clad block of a man, was unmoved by her contrition. With one meaty fist still pressed between Luke's shoulder blades, he glared at Kelsey. "Improper use of the emergency line is a crime, you know. You could be arrested."

For the first time since the altercation had begun, Luke spoke. "Leave her alone."

The first policeman twisted his knuckles into Luke's back. "No one's talking to you, bud."

Luke winced, but made no sound. Kelsey stepped forward and laid a restraining hand on the officer's sleeve. "Please don't hurt him any more. None of this is his fault. I just made a mistake."

The officer's harsh expression softened. "We're here to protect you, miss," he said kindly. "In domestic disputes, women often believe that if they don't press charges, they won't be abused again. Trouble is, they're wrong. We get called back again and again, until the poor woman ends up in the hospital . . . or worse."

Kelsey stiffened. "I appreciate your concern, officer, but this is not a 'domestic dispute.' "

The second officer rolled his eyes. "Yeah, right."

Impatient now, the first policeman extracted a black, antennaed radio from the leather pouch on his belt. "Look, are you going to press charges or not?"

"I most certainly am not."

Shrugging, he mumbled something to his partner, who simply shook his head in disgust, then pulled out a key and unlocked the handcuffs.

As the metal restraints were removed, Luke turned slowly away from the wall, absently rubbing his wrists, his gaze locked on Kelsey's face. She cleared her throat nervously. "Again, I apologize for the misunderstanding."

The blocky officer gave her a pitying look as his partner used the radio to clear their position. Before they left, he looked over his shoulder, giving Luke a hard stare while he spoke to Kelsey. "Call if you need us, miss. That's what we're here for."

"Thank you," she mumbled, then closed the door behind them.

Kelsey couldn't move for several seconds, unable to face Luke, yet knowing that eventually she'd have to do just that.

Luke broke the strained silence. "Well, hell, that was sure fun. You really know how to throw a party, Kel."

With a resigned sigh, she turned and leaned against the door. "I'm so sorry. I didn't know about that computer thing. It just didn't occur to me..." The useless apology faded away and Kelsey cringed under the force of his black stare.

"No problem," he growled, dropping onto her sleek leather sofa. "A run-in with the law now and again tends to keep a man humble. You like this, don't you? Seeing me humbled, that is."

"You know better than that."

"Do I?" A dark strand of shaggy hair fell across his forehead and he swiped it away. "It serves me right for buying into the stupid story about Ruth being in trouble. Where is she, really? Next door, with her ear to the wall, laughing her head off because her big brother is such a damned fool?"

Frustrated, Kelsey went into the living room and sat a safe distance away from the man who still affected her so deeply. If he touched her, or if she touched him, she'd yield to the eternal fire surging through her veins and throw herself at him as brazenly as she'd done that first time, when they'd made love in his shop. The memory of that night still embarrassed her. And it still thrilled her.

So she forced herself to focus on the situation at hand, and realized that, somehow, she had to convince Luke that his sister was truly in danger. With a deep breath, Kelsey clasped her hands in her lap and took a calculated gamble. "Ruth isn't here, Luke. I think she has been kidnapped."

Only a faint twinge of fear in Luke's eyes betrayed his feelings. "That's a bit melodramatic, even for you."

"It's true, Luke. I believe—" Kelsey forced herself to meet his skeptical gaze. "Joseph took her."

"Joseph?" His forehead furrowed in confusion. "That mealy-mouthed jackass she married?"

Kelsey nodded.

For a moment, Luke just stared at her as though she'd completely lost her mind, then he blew out a puff of air and shook his head. "They're married, Kelsey. Most married people actually live together." He stood quickly and strode toward the front door. "This is ridiculous. Have a good life, Kel."

"Wait!"

His hand froze on the knob and he turned expectantly.

"You don't understand." Kelsey moaned and ran frustrated fingers through her hair. "I think he beats her."

Luke said nothing, just stood there, staring with that bleak, unreadable expression.

Kelsey licked her lips. "It was so strange when the officers were talking about domestic assault and saying that they could protect me. I could barely stop myself from screaming that it was Ruth who needed protection."

After a tense silence, Luke's hand fell from the doorknob. "Did Ruth tell you that?"

"No. She didn't have to." Kelsey stood shakily. "There were bruises all over her body, Luke, on her throat and her arms, and I saw her wearing a slip one morning and there were more marks on her shoulders."

Luke's tanned complexion faded. "Did she tell you what had happened?"

Waving away the question, Kelsey answered more sharply than she'd intended. "Of course not. She just made up some ridiculous garbage about being clumsy and running into doors. Her husband beats her, Luke. That's why she left him—I'm certain of it."

Luke made an odd movement, almost as though his knees had started to buckle, then he straightened and spoke with surprising certainty. "You're wrong."

The statement took her aback. "How can you say that? Joseph is a brute. He isolated Ruth from everyone, kept her a prisoner in her own home. She wasn't allowed to go anywhere without him . . . she wasn't even allowed to get mail. You didn't see her—you couldn't know what she's been going through."

"I know my sister. She'd never put up with that kind of treatment." Rubbing the back of his neck, Luke began to pace. In spite of his protests, a glimmer of real fear shone in his green eyes. "Ruth was just a kid when our father split, but she remembers how he treated our mother. After Pop left, Mom tried, poor soul, but she didn't have more than a ninth-grade education and she struggled with menial jobs to support us. Ruth was determined never to end up like that."

Kelsey's heart ached for him. "I know how difficult it was for both of you back then, but that has nothing to do with what your sister has endured these past two years."

Whirling, Luke faced Kelsey indignantly. "It has everything to do with it. My sister is strong and self-reliant. I taught her how to think for herself, make her own decisions. Ruth is an intelligent, educated woman. She wouldn't allow those things to happen to her. I raised her better than that."

Luke's anger and his blind ignorance of Ruth's true nature infuriated Kelsey. "Your sister has spent her entire life trying to please men—first her father, then you, and finally, her husband. As to your nobleness in having raised her, what you wanted from Ruth, and from every other woman in your life, was nothing short of abject obedience."

Luke's eyes darkened dangerously and he straightened. "Watch out, Kel. I'm not in the mood for this."

Ignoring the warning, Kelsey simply lifted her chin and defiantly met his black stare. "But you must admit that your assertions are rather ludicrous, in light of the fact that you never permitted your own wife to pursue the pride and independence you purportedly sought for your sister."

"My wife—" Luke bit off the words with a sneer. "Now there's one hell of an example, coming from a woman who'd sell her soul for a taste of the good life."

"Excuse me? By 'the good life' are you referring to an apartment that doesn't house an entire colony of disgusting creatures and a dress that isn't held together by mending thread?" Dramatically placing both hands on her chest, Kelsey concealed hurt feelings with sarcasm. "Guilty as charged, your Honor. Lock me up. I mean, how dare I actually yearn to surround myself with sanitary conditions."

Luke's jaw twitched furiously. "So next time you're hot for the bulge in a man's jeans, maybe you should check out his bank statement first and save yourself grief."

The cruel words hit like body blow, thrown with the pinpoint accuracy borne of his intimate knowledge of her secret vulnerabilities.

Kelsey stumbled backward, fighting to catch her breath. Blinking away the hot moisture gathering in her eyes, she rearranged her expression into a blank stare and spoke with concealing coldness. "I'd like you to leave, Luke. Now."

"Yeah, I'll bet you would." With that, Luke lazily sauntered to the sofa and flopped into a prone position. "Nah, I don't think so."

"You heard me, Luke. Get out."

"I like it here. It's cozy." He stretched, cupping his hands behind his head. "Besides, this is a community property state, so technically, half of this snazzy place belongs to me anyway."

The rationale took Kelsey's breath away. When she recovered, she drew upon hidden strength to maintain a deceptively calm tone. "We are divorced, Luke."

"Correction." He sat up. "We are almost divorced. Almost doesn't count. Say, that's a neat lamp. Is it part of my half?"

Ignoring the taunt, Kelsey stiffened her shaky knees. "You've had the divorce papers for months. All you have to do is sign them, and the final decree will be issued."

He stood, idly glancing around the apartment as he rocked back on his heels. "Yeah, this is a real nice place. A bit pretentious for my taste, but there are a few things around here I could use."

Hurt by the unjustified suggestion that she was materialistic, Kelsey fought back by zeroing in on Luke's private insecurity. "If you're still having cash flow problems, I'd be happy to write you a check."

Luke's eyes darkened with pain and humiliation. Kelsey should have been satisfied that her stinging words had evoked the desired effect, but strangely enough, she wanted nothing more than to retrieve the cruel remark and swallow it whole.

But it was too late. Luke smiled, not pleasantly, and took a step toward her. "Thanks for the offer, but I had something else in mind."

Startled, Kelsey regarded him cautiously. "I don't understand."

"Sure you do. You remember how it goes, don't you? Tit for tat . . . so to speak."

She didn't like the look in his eye. "I don't care for riddles, Luke, and I don't know what you're talking about."

Stroking his chin, he allowed his gaze to slide slowly down her body, lingering insolently on the most intimate feminine curves. "Do you want me to sign those papers, Kelsey?"

Her throat closed up, nearly blocking her voice. "Yes."

"Then help me out here, honey. What are you willing to give?"

"What do you want?" She barely recognized the rasping croak as her own voice.

Luke lightly touched her collarbone, then slid his hand downward until his thumb brushed the side of her breast. "You know what I want," he whispered. "I have something you want, you have something I want. It'll be like old times."

For a moment, Kelsey was unable to move, paralyzed with shock and the unwanted thrill of Luke's strong fingers caressing her breast.

It'll be like old times.

She remembered that night, their first night together. It had been beautiful, an experience that had touched her heart and lightened her soul. Afterward, she'd lain in Luke's arms and they had talked about various things—she couldn't remember exactly what. Then the conversation had turned to

Ruth and Joseph's wedding, and Luke's refusal to attend. Kelsey had innocently asked him to reconsider.

She'd never really understood what had happened next. Luke had stiffened and turned cold, accusing her of trying to bribe him with her body. Mortified by the vulgar suggestion, Kelsey had immediately left.

Now, stung by the same crude reference, indignation rose up inside her. Stepping back, she furiously pushed against his chest. "How *dare* you?"

"What's the matter? Do you insist on cash now?"

With an indignant gasp, Kelsey raised her open palm and swung. Before the blow landed, Luke grabbed her wrist, wrapped his free hand around her waist, and roughly pulled her against him.

Kelsey froze, recognizing the heat and determination in Luke's eyes. He was going to kiss her.

And God help her, that was exactly what she wanted.

Chapter 5

Breathless, Kelsey waited—but not for long.

With only the merest hint of hesitation, Luke's mouth crushed hers in a fiery kiss that was meant to punish, yet instantly gentled into something deeper. Heat spiraled up inside her as the familiar aching desire flared from enforced dormancy with an intensity that demanded response.

Without thought of consequence, Kelsey yielded to the cry of buried passion, winding her arms around Luke's strong neck and pressing herself closer, and closer still, returning his deepening kiss stroke for stroke.

Deep inside her, the icy block of denial melted, spilling liquid desire into her belly and beyond, providing tangible proof of her need.

Frantically framing Luke's face with her hands, she desperately sought his mouth, hungry for the remembered taste of his strength and masculine passion.

Luke groaned, a poignant sound pulled from the very depth of his soul and betraying the turmoil within. He held her in a frenzied grasp that conveyed his desperate need to fuse with her, and become an intrinsic part of her flesh.

Then without warning, Luke tore his lips away. He was breathing heavily, his great chest heaving as though he'd just lost a footrace with the devil.

The unexpected movement shook Kelsey and she clung dizzily to his shoulders. Abruptly releasing her, he roughly pushed her wrists away and spun around, leaving Kelsey to sway in bewilderment and steady herself on a nearby wall.

With some effort, she managed to focus and saw only Luke's muscular back. He was bent slightly forward with his fists on his hips, and his shoulders vibrated convulsively. After a moment, he straightened, roughly raked his thickly tangled hair and swore bitterly.

Kelsey's stomach tightened with a leaden knot of disappointment. When Luke finally looked over his shoulder, she saw the familiar fury that he invoked to conceal emotional frailty.

His eyes were hot; his voice, cold. "So now you've got everything you've ever wanted . . . the fancy car and designer duds. Are you happy now?"

Wounded by the rejection, Kelsey raised her chin and responded with too much emphasis. "Yes, yes I am. I'm doing what I want to do and I'm a success at it."

Luke's expression hardened. "I hope you choke on your damned success."

Kelsey *was* choking—on regret. Suppressed pain burst forth as she lashed back without mercy. "A cheap garage on the south side might be good enough for you, Luke Sontag, but I'm going to do something worthwhile with my life."

The hurt in his eyes would have touched Kelsey had her own suffering not been so intense.

"I guess being married to a grease monkey put a real crimp in your social status, didn't it?" Luke encompassed the sophisticated surroundings with an angry gesture. "You must be in fat city now, with this classy, uptown apartment."

"At least I'm not afraid to walk the street at night, but you never cared about that, did you?" Pent-up fury spewed with uncontrollable force. "You spent sixteen hours a day at that damned shop. Did you ever wonder what my life was like? It was hell, Luke, unadulterated hell. I languished in that dreary room, isolated from the entire world, with the television blaring all day so I wouldn't forget the sounds of human speech. You didn't care that I was lonely, you didn't care that I was frightened, you didn't care that I felt more like a pet hamster than a wife, and that was the crux of the problem, Luke. *You just didn't care.*"

Drained by the outburst, Kelsey propped one hand on her hip and used the other to cover her face. The grief in her heart was unbearable, pounding deep in her chest like a dirge drum. Trembling inside and out, she tried desperately to compose herself. She hated being out of control and despised having allowed Luke to see her like this.

Closing her eyes, she took a shuddering breath, then another, and eventually regained some semblance of composure. When she lowered her hand, Luke was staring pensively across the room with the merest hint of uncertainty in his eyes. Kelsey recognized that expression, and the memory twisted her heart.

It had been eighteen months ago—perhaps longer—on a sultry summer night when the air had smelled of hot asphalt and human sweat. The smothering heat, combined with advanced pregnancy had increased Kelsey's discomfort, so Luke had used a damp cloth to sponge her sticky body.

That particular night stuck out in Kelsey's mind because the soothing sensation of being pampered had been a sweet anomaly in her otherwise stark existence.

But during that humid summer night, Kelsey had been relaxed and deeply contented, stretched luxuriously on the sofa bed and thoroughly enjoying Luke's tender ministrations. Suddenly, he'd stroked her taut belly with that same pensive expression, then softly asked if she was happy. The hushed question had surprised her, but before she could respond, he'd silenced her with a kiss.

So Kelsey hadn't revealed the secret of her heart, that she had been deeply in love with the man who was her husband.

Throughout their tumultuous relationship, the unspoken purpose of their marriage had always been the legitimization of their child. Kelsey had accepted that sad fact, along with the disheartening reality that she held no true place in Luke Sontag's heart.

But on that particular night, it hadn't mattered. That night, they'd come together with the poignant intensity of two people who had been created for the sole purpose of loving each other.

Months later, the horror had come, the unendurable heartbreak that had torn them apart, brutally exposing the tenuous facade of lies on which their relationship had been built. Self-delusion, Kelsey had learned, was the cruelest lie of all.

Brushing away the bittersweet memories, Kelsey gathered her thoughts. Luke was watching her. She licked her lips and managed a calm, if somewhat aloof, tone. "I'm sorry, were you speaking to me?"

"No." He folded his arms like a shield and stared out the window.

She wondered what he was thinking, but dared not ask, so she cleared her throat and turned the topic to a slightly more neutral subject. "Earlier, you said you'd come here to talk about your sister. Do you think we can put aside our personal differences long enough to do that? For Ruth's sake, that is."

Nodding slowly, Luke's distant gaze lingered a moment, then he wearily turned and walked into the short corridor leading to the guest bedroom. Baffled by the odd movement, Kelsey waited for him to return, then heard the muffled sound of activity and went to investigate.

"What in the world are you doing?" she demanded, shock and surprise causing her voice to quiver strangely.

The query was actually quite unnecessary. Having spread a blanket over the reclining futon, Luke scooped two pillows from the floor and tossed them onto the freshly made bed.

"Good Lord, you're not planning to stay here?" She nearly strangled on the question. "Absolutely not. I won't stand for it."

"Your objection is duly noted." Luke sat heavily on the edge of the futon's flat, cotton-stuffed mattress. He rubbed his eyelids. "I'm tired."

"I don't care. You can't sleep here."

He flopped onto his back. "Watch me."

Sharing space with this man for even one night was unreasonably disturbing. Kelsey's hands were clammy and a fine sheen of nervous perspiration beaded her brow. "What about Ruth?"

Luke hiked one brow quizzically. "Ruth isn't here. She doesn't need the bed. I do."

"But we have to find her," Kelsey insisted, wringing her hands. "We can't just stay here and . . . and . . . sleep."

"My sister is probably back home." Luke rolled on one elbow and wadded the pillow into a familiar knot. "Tomorrow I'll drive to Santa Barbara and settle this whole stupid thing. As for tonight, you can either stare at me or join me, I don't really care which, because I'm going to sleep." With that, Luke stretched out, tossed a muscular forearm loosely across his forehead and closed his eyes.

After a stunned moment, Kelsey backed away and retreated to the solace of her own lonely room.

I can handle this, she told herself, wondering if it were true. The man she'd once loved more than her own life was less than thirty feet away. His masculine presence enveloped her. She was overwhelmed by his distinctive, personal scent. It was driving her wild.

I can handle this, she repeated silently, then added, *for Ruth.*

Mentally reinforced, Kelsey turned on the small corner night lamp, then undressed and put on a nightgown. She sat in bed, hugging her knees, regretting the cruel things she'd said earlier. Verbal brutality was unlike her. She'd always believed that calm, rational discussion was more likely to achieve one's goals, or at least an acceptable compromise. Kelsey rarely lost her temper, and couldn't remember ever having exploded with such emotional force.

Tonight, she'd been deliberately hurtful and that was troubling. She'd even allowed Luke to believe that she was wealthy enough to own the expensive furnishings that had been supplied with the apartment.

But he'd deserved that much. His acerbic remarks about materialism had rankled her, partly because it was untrue and partly because it was an accusation he'd used frequently in the past. Luke had a way of making her feel guilty for not having been born into poverty, and because Kelsey's grandfather had left a trust for her education, Luke considered her to be privileged. She was, of course, but was nonetheless tired of doing penance for good fortune.

And Kelsey's life had not been without tragedy. Luke, of all people, knew that.

The memory of past heartbreak now caught in her throat. She couldn't sleep. She could hardly breathe.

Slipping out of bed, Kelsey knelt on the thick white carpet and quietly opened the bottom drawer of her black lacquered dresser. Reaching under a stack of neatly folded garments, she extracted a small, tissue-wrapped parcel. Caressing the package, she hesitated, but was drawn by a poignant, indefinable need. Carefully drawing back the thin paper, Kelsey lifted the soft, pink garment to her cheek. She closed her eyes, inhaling the faint powder scent that clung to the fluffy yarn.

Then she buried her face in the tiny, hand-knit sweater and she wept.

It was nearly two a.m. when Luke looked at his watch again. As exhausted as he was, his brain simply wouldn't shut off. He tossed fitfully, upset by the argument he and Kelsey had earlier, and the hateful words they'd used like lethal weapons.

Kelsey had accused him of not caring. What a hoot. If she only knew how damned much Luke *had* cared—

With a muffled curse, he flopped onto his side and tried again to sleep. He couldn't, because there was also the matter of Kelsey's other disturbing accusation. Overly possessive, she'd called him. That was crap. Protective, yeah, but that was part of his nature.

Still, he wondered if he'd crossed some invisible line, guarding his wife to the point of obsession. If Luke was truly honest with himself, he'd admit that Kelsey might have some small basis for the misguided belief that he'd wanted his wife to be submissive and dependent, while insisting that his sister not fall into the same trap. She was mistaken, of course, but Luke could charitably see her point of view.

At the time, his actions hadn't seemed such a paradox. After all, he was the man, the breadwinner. It had been his responsibility to protect his family and provide for it. A woman alone on L.A.'s mean streets was a target for tragedy. If anything had happened to Kelsey—

Luke couldn't have taken the risk. Surely, Kelsey could understand that. Or at least, he'd thought that she could.

Now he realized that he hadn't had a clue as to what his wife had been thinking or feeling all those months ago. She'd been lonely. She'd been afraid.

God, how he'd failed her.

Music.

Still half asleep, Luke was lulled by the lyrical strains of a melody that was vaguely familiar, yet which his foggy mind couldn't quite identify. The tune's effect was oddly soothing and a serenity swept over him, a relaxing sense that all was well. Eyes closed, he smiled in the darkness around him, allowed himself to float with the sweet sounds.

Then he heard the scream, a keening lament of horror and grief that shattered the lullaby.

Bolting upright, Luke stared into the blackness, heart racing and blood running like liquid ice in his veins. He didn't know where he was. Strange furnishings loomed like sinister shadows, and he vaguely recognized the rectangle of dim light as a window.

Cold sweat beaded his brow as he listened to the silence. Dropping his legs over the edge of the futon, Luke's bare feet touched an unfamiliar plushness and comprehension dawned slowly. He remembered where he was.

And he remembered the scream.

Standing, he listened, his ears attuned to every nuance. He heard the muffled hum of a refrigerator, and the distant drone of vehicles on the street below. Nothing else.

Tensely, Luke wiped his wet face and wondered if he'd been dreaming again. The red glow of a clock radio on the nightstand confirmed that two hours had passed. He'd fallen asleep. The music had been a dream, the melody of an exhausted mind. But the scream—

Luke's stomach twisted. The scream had been part of the nightmare that had tormented him repeatedly over the past year. Usually, he would awaken, terrified and sickened, reaching for the numbing whiskey that would get him through the night. This time, there was no whiskey.

Unless Kelsey happened to have a bottle stashed somewhere. The possibility was tempting.

No. Luke sat on the futon and rubbed his head again. In a couple of hours, he'd be embarking on a long, tedious journey up the coast. He couldn't afford to slow his reflexes and dull his mind. Liquor was definitely not an option. He'd have to make do with a couple of aspirin.

The problem was that Kelsey kept the aspirin in her bedroom, but she'd always slept like a rock. Once she dozed off, nothing short of an explosion could wake her. That had always amazed Luke, since the hum of a mosquito could arouse him instantly, yet his wife would sleep blissfully through the shriek of a clock-radio cranked to full volume.

Deciding that he could easily obtain the pills without disturbing her, Luke stealthily made his way from the guest bedroom to the hallway. To his right, a thin shaft of light peeked from beneath the door to her bedroom and he smiled. Such a tough lady, he mused, but he knew her secret. Inside that cool, controlled exterior lived a frightened little girl, who hated the darkness.

Luke had loved that part of her.

The smile faded and he mentally reworded the thought. Liked. He'd *liked* that part of her. Love had never been a consideration in their relationship. They'd come to a silent, mutual understanding of the reasons for their union, and love had nothing to do with it. Kelsey had never loved him; he knew that. He'd accepted that.

Still he recalled times that had been achingly beautiful, moments when he'd almost believed—

Damn. He shook his head, trying to exorcise the haunting memories. Believing. That had been his mistake, and, eventually, his downfall.

Taking a deep breath, Luke touched the doorknob and quietly peered into Kelsey's room. The bedding was tossed into familiar piles at the foot of the mattress, and she was curled into a ball on the far right side of the bed, the same position she'd occupied during their time together. Luke thought it odd that she hadn't taken advantage of the extra space. It was almost as though she subconsciously continued to share their marital bed. The thought was ludicrous but gave him a peculiar comfort.

He quietly moved toward the nightstand, then paused to watch the sleeping woman. She seemed so fragile, her lips slackened and tousled hair shading her pale cheeks. He suppressed an urge to push the unruly strands away, wondering if her skin was as smooth as he remembered, and as soft.

His gaze slid to her throat, and to the thin cotton gown covering her slender shoulders. Her arms were pressed tightly against her chest, and her hands, tucked beneath her chin, were protectively clutching something. A glimpse of pink yarn protruded from between her knotted fingers and, as Luke looked more closely, he saw the shape of a tiny sleeve.

His stomach turned, then tightened into a painful lump. Covering his mouth with his hand, Luke quietly backed out of the room, closing the door behind him. Then he stumbled into the bathroom and was sick.

Kelsey slipped into a crinkled-cotton duster and nervously went to the kitchen. Luke was sitting at the table, staring into a cup of coffee as though some mystical prophesy were revealed in its inky liquid depths. His hollow cheeks were shadowed by black stubble and his sunken eyes resembled moldy green olives.

In short, he looked like hell.

She tested her voice. "Did you sleep well?"

"Yeah, great." He lifted the cup to his lips and drained it in a single swallow.

"Would you like something to eat? I could fix some eggs, or—"

"No." Standing he rinsed his cup and laid it in the sink. "Thanks, anyway." He reached into his pocket and extracted a key ring. "I'll call you later."

With that curt statement, Luke strode quickly toward the front door. After a stunned moment, Kelsey followed, touching his arm as he reached for the door knob. He paused, glancing down at the slim fingers resting on his skin.

She instantly pulled her hand away. "Where are you going?"

"To Santa Barbara."

"Ruth won't be there."

"How do you know?"

"I just know."

"Do you have a better place to start?"

"No, I guess not." Rubbing her arms, Kelsey sighed. "Give me a couple of minutes."

Luke scowled darkly. "For what?"

"To get dressed. I'm going with you."

"Like hell."

Kelsey shrugged. "If you find sharing a vehicle with me that distasteful, I'll follow in my own car. But I'm going and that's that."

Luke followed her to the bedroom door. "You can't do anything to help."

"I can talk to the neighbors, see if they've noticed anything out of the ordinary."

"I can do that."

Kelsey eyed his torn jeans and shaggy hair. "The Ridenours' highbrow neighbors would probably size you up as a potential cat burglar and call the cops. Besides, I can be very persuasive."

Folding his arms, Luke scowled darkly. "Yeah. I remember."

Slipping off the duster, Kelsey peered into her closet, trying to ignore the fact that Luke had stopped arguing and was staring at her with a familiar intensity. She could hear his sharp intake of breath and knew without looking that a warm light would be illuminating his eyes. There was a deep satisfaction in knowing that she still affected him, at least in one basic way. It was only fair, she figured, since the mere sight of him turned her innards into quivering jelly.

Trying to ignore the sudden pounding of her own racing heart, Kelsey pulled out a pair of cream-colored linen slacks and her favorite apple-green sweater, then forced a casual tone. "Do you think I should take a jacket? It looks pretty cloudy out there." Without waiting for his answer, she tossed a tailored wool jacket onto the bed, then faced Luke and provocatively slid the gown strap over her shoulders. "I'm going to get dressed now. Would you like to watch?"

Startled, Luke blinked, then sulked like a child who'd been caught with the cookie jar. "Don't flatter yourself, honey," he growled, although his voice held a slight tremor that did not escape her notice. "I'm leaving. You can do anything you want, but you're not coming with me." With that, he spun on his heel and stomped down the hall.

Kelsey smiled.

Shading her eyes, Kelsey regarded the isolated Tudor home tucked behind an eight-foot stone wall. "Well, so much for talking to the neighbors."

Luke leaned his elbow on the steering wheel of his old pickup truck and propped his chin on his knuckles. The place was a freaking fortress.

Kelsey was right. There were no neighbors. The last house they'd passed was at least three miles back and the narrow, hillside road ended at the iron gate blocking entrance to the Ridenour driveway. In his wildest imagination, Luke couldn't envision his delicate, demure sister living in such a cold and forbidding place.

"There's some kind of a box with buttons over by the gate. Maybe it's an intercom," Kelsey said, as she exited the truck. She closed the door, then leaned in the open window. "Are you coming?"

"Hmm? Oh. Yeah."

Without waiting for him, Kelsey trudged around the front of the pickup and scrutinized the electronic gate controls. Luke stepped out, his attention focused on the way Kelsey's beige slacks cupped her neat little rear and how feathery strands of gleaming hair brushed her cheekbones when her head tilted a certain way.

Damn. He mentally shook himself, as he'd been doing during the three-hour drive up from L.A. It had been torture. Kelsey had been inches away, yet he couldn't reach out and touch her. She had no business affecting him this way, not after everything that had happened between them. He couldn't even figure out why she was here. He hadn't wanted her to come.

In fact, he'd left her apartment with every intention of jumping into his pickup and driving halfway to the Valley before Kelsey even had her teeth brushed.

Then he'd remembered he had left his wallet on top of the guest-room bureau, so he'd marched upstairs and retrieved it, then decided to straighten the futon so Kelsey wouldn't think him a slob. By the time he'd finished, she'd been at the stove, beating a bowl of eggs, while a pan of simmering sausage filled the room with a mouth-watering aroma.

No way was he going to stay for breakfast, of course, but then the sneaky woman had added chopped mushrooms and onions to the eggs, so Luke sat down at the table.

Next thing he knew, his stomach had been comfortably full and they'd been heading up Highway 101 with Kelsey chatting a blue streak and Luke pondering the uneasy feeling that he'd been bested by a mushroom omelet.

"Luke?" Kelsey's voice interrupted his thought. "Look at this."

He walked over and peered through the twisted black bars of the gate. The large, sculpted lawn was overgrown and the extravagant garden was weedy and untended.

Kelsey's words echoed Luke's thoughts. "That's really odd. I'd think that such an expensive home would be scrupulously maintained. And why on earth would anyone close off the windows with those heavy draperies? It's not like privacy is a problem, with this huge wall around the entire yard."

Luke silently agreed. The whole place was pretty eerie, more like a prison than a home. An uneasy chill skittered down his spine. For the past two days, Luke had repeatedly tried to convince himself that Ruth's sojourn in L.A. had been the result of a temporary spat between spouses. He'd been positive that they'd arrived in Santa Barbara and find Ruth lounging in her comfortable parlor, having forgiven her husband for whatever minor trespass had offended her in the first place.

Now he wasn't so sure. There was something about this bizarre situation that made him queasy.

"I don't think anyone is here," Kelsey announced.

Luke didn't either, but wasn't quite willing to acknowledge that yet. "Someone could be inside. Try the intercom."

Pursing her lips prettily, Kelsey scanned the box, which contained a keypad of numbers arranged like a touch-tone telephone. There was also a red button labeled Announce, and she pressed it. Nothing happened. She pressed it twice more, then tilted her head and shrugged. "Now what?"

Luke sighed. He'd hoped it wouldn't come to this. Resolutely, he took hold of the bars and put his foot on the iron cross rail. "Stay here," he muttered, then hoisted himself up.

She snagged his belt, stopping him on the second rail. "What do you think you're doing?"

Irritated, he stared down. "I'm going inside. Let go of my pants."

"That's breaking and entering. We could be arrested."

"Oh, gosh. I never thought of that." He climbed down and feigned a shocked expression. "Gee, we'd better go back to L.A. right now."

"Stop it." Kelsey rubbed her forehead in concentration, then glanced into the yard with a resigned expression. "I guess we don't have much choice, do we?"

"Not much."

She chewed her lower lip nervously, then tested the gate and stepped up one rail as Luke had done. He took hold of her arm. "No way."

"If you go, I go."

Frustrated, Luke jammed one hand in his pocket and used the other one to prop himself against the wall. Stubborn woman. She was driving him nuts. "Look, you stay here and when I get into the yard, I'll open the gate, okay?"

Clinging to the wrought iron like a frustrated cat on a screen door, she eyed him suspiciously, then tilted her head back and regarded the height of the fence. "Well..."

Sensing victory, Luke lifted her from the gate and placed her firmly on the pavement. "It'll just take a couple of minutes for me to get over," he assured her, then using the chain-link and barbed-wire experience gleaned from his youth, he expertly scaled the gate and perched atop the block wall, preparing to descend into the yard.

A loud rattle startled him, and he looked down to see Kelsey shaking the gate. She gazed up. "I don't think you can open it from inside. It's got some kind of key lock."

Luke shook his head. You'd think she'd have learned by now. "Trust me, that's not a problem."

Kelsey was suddenly focused on something inside the yard. "The lock may not be a problem," she replied, stepping away from the gate and pointing inside. "But that certainly is."

When Luke heard the nasty snarl, his heart sank. A damned dog. Moaning, he glanced down and saw a hundred pounds of churning black fury heading right at him.

The huge Rottweiler hit the fence at full throttle and for the space of a heartbeat, Luke thought the furious beast was going to climb straight up the wall. Pulling his feet up, he swore viciously. Luke hated dogs, particularly the large black kind with chainsaw teeth. One of his childhood friends had sneaked into a wrecking yard and been mauled by such an animal. Afterward, the poor kid's face had looked like a road map.

Luke shuddered at the memory, then stared bleakly down at the frantic animal. God, it even had drool coming out of its mouth.

From the corner of his eye, he saw Kelsey move closer to the gate, and to his horror she actually spoke to the disgusting beast. "Hi, handsome. What's your name?"

Whirling, the dog snarled and lunged against the wrought iron until the entire gate bowed out. Luke nearly fainted. "Kelsey... for God's sake, get into the truck and lock the doors."

"Don't be silly, Luke. He can't get out—can you, big guy?" The animal stood on its hind legs and clawed at the gate with a savage snarl that didn't seem to faze Kelsey at all. "Are you hungry, fellow? Do you want something yummy?"

It was all too much for Luke. Here she was discussing canine cuisine with that demonic animal while Luke's legs dangled over the fence like human drumsticks. The woman was obviously quite mad.

As Luke watched in disbelief, Kelsey ran back to the truck, fumbled in her purse, then, clutching something in her palm, returned to the gate. "Here you go, boy," she said breathlessly, tossing a tiny blue disk into the yard. The dog hesitated, alternately growling at Kelsey and eyeing the strange object.

Luke was completely bewildered. "What in hell is that?"

"A breath mint," Kelsey replied. "I had a cat once who loved them."

If the situation hadn't been so damned miserable, Luke would have laughed out loud. Breath mints. That was the dumbest thing he'd ever heard.

Then the idiotic dog spun backwards and sucked the blue disk into its mouth. Luke's jaw slackened in surprise and he was astonished when the animal returned to the gate, wagging its stubby tail. "I'll be damned."

"Good boy," Kelsey crooned to the dog, tossing another mint, which the dog snagged in its massive jaws. She squinted up at Luke. "You can open the gate now."

He snorted. "When hell freezes."

"Luke, he's just a big pussycat. He's not going to hurt you."

"He's not going to get the chance." Glancing across the yard, Luke noticed a chain-link dog run with the gate slightly open. "Throw me those mints."

She hesitated, then shrugged and tossed the roll into Luke's waiting hands. Luke dropped one to the animal. "Here, you ugly, flea-bitten hunk of crap. I hope you choke on it." The dog scarfed up the mint, then turned his attention expectantly upward.

Over the next few moments, Luke moved along the top of the block wall toward the kennel, tossing mints to encourage the dog to follow. The ploy worked. When Luke threw the final mint into the fenced enclosure, the animal loped inside and Luke dropped quickly to the ground and slammed the kennel gate.

After wiping the sweat out of his eyes, Luke crossed the yard to where Kelsey was waiting, then pulled out a tiny pocket knife and deftly jimmied the lock. The gate swung open.

"Nicely done," she told him, a hint of amusement twinkling in her dark eyes.

Luke used one hand to fold the blade, then pocketed the knife. "Don't celebrate yet. We've still got to get into the house."

"That shouldn't be a problem for a man with your dubious talents."

"That depends on what kind of alarm system Ridenour has."

Kelsey's smile faded. "Alarm?"

Luke was already on the front porch, examining the door jamb. He didn't find anything, but then he hadn't expected to. Usually, wires or magnetic switches were concealed so that the current would be broken when the door opened, thus triggering the alarm. Straightening, he circled the massive house, checking each window for visible wires. When he located the circuit box, he pulled out his trusty knife and dispatched the padlock.

A sweet fragrance enveloped him as Kelsey peered over his shoulder. "Are you going to turn off the electricity?"

"No. Most alarms have a battery backup and as remote as this place is, there's probably a direct telephone hookup to the alarm company's switchboard."

"What does that mean?"

Luke replaced the circuit cover. "That means that if we cut off either power or phone lines, a squad car will meet us in the driveway."

Wringing her hands, Kelsey was obviously distressed by the thought. "So we've come all this way and we can't get inside?"

"I didn't say that." Glancing around the yard, Luke shrugged out of his denim jacket, then picked up a medium-sized rock. He wrapped the rock and twisted a portion of the sleeve as a handle, then took aim at a small, frosted glass window that he assumed would lead to a bathroom. "Stand back."

Kelsey grabbed his shoulder. "You can't just break the glass."

"Why not?"

"Well . . . someone might hear the noise?"

"Who? The neighbors, two miles down the road?"

Kelsey considered that. "You have a point. But can't you just disarm the alarm?"

"I hate to disenchant you, honey, but in spite of my checkered past, I'm not too good with alarm systems. Most of them are designed to keep people from opening windows or doors, so unless there are tiny wires running through the glass, the circuits are probably wired into the jambs."

Oh." Kelsey eyed the window. "No wires in the glass, huh?"

"Nope. I'll check for motion detectors inside. Now move back and turn your face away."

"Luke?"

Irritated, he lowered the rock sling. "What now?"

"We're going to have to pay for the damage, you know."

"Oh for the love of—" Frustrated, he raked his hair and spoke with exaggerated patience. "I'll send them a check, okay?"

"Well . . ."

"Your choice, Kel. We go in or we go home. Which is it?"

After a hesitant minute, she stepped away and shielded her face with her hands. "Go ahead."

He tightened his grip, reared back, then slung the wrapped rock against the frosted glass. The first blow shattered the window, but it took several whacks to clear the sharp shards from the frame. He draped the jacket on a bush, planning to retrieve the garment later, then cautioned Kelsey to wait while he carefully hoisted himself through the broken window and dropped onto the tiled bathroom floor.

Glancing around, Luke noted that the room seemed oddly vacant. There were no personal items on the gray marble vanity, and the slate-blue towels had a fluffy, pristine texture. The door opened into a carpeted hallway and Luke decided that this sterile, unused room was probably a guest bath.

Luke used the towels to pad the glass-encrusted frame and helped Kelsey climb into the room. For a moment, they stood silent and tense, waiting for a police bullhorn to demand their immediate surrender.

Finally, Kelsey swallowed hard and managed a nervous laugh. "Looks like we made it."

"Yeah." Luke chose not to mention the possibility of a silent alarm. Instead, he moved out and followed the hallway toward the front door.

After crossing the polished granite foyer, Luke jerked to a stop at the entrance of the home's expansive living room, sickened by what he saw.

Beside him, Kelsey clutched his arm and gasped in horror.

There was no doubt in his mind now. Ruth was in terrible danger.

Chapter 6

"Dear God." Pressing one fist against her lip, Kelsey stepped into the devastated room. "It looks like a bomb went off in here."

"Yeah," Luke said tightly, stepping over a shattered crystal mess. "A human bomb."

The thought was terrifying. "You don't think Joseph did this?"

Luke's grim expression was answer enough. Turning away, Kelsey's stupefied gaze swept over the shambles. An end table had been overturned and a mauve ceramic lamp, miraculously unbroken, lay sideways on the plush gray carpeting. Broken glass littered the baseboards, as though someone had flung fragile items with great force. The textured walls had been scarred by repeated blows and a jutting fireplace poker impaled the plaster like a war lance.

The room reeked of uncontrollable fury—and of vengeance.

Kelsey's eyes widened and she whirled, recognizing her worst fears reflected in Luke's bleak eyes. "Ruth," she whispered.

Grasping Kelsey's arm, Luke pulled her firmly toward the front door. "Go outside, Kelsey. Now."

"You think Ruth's still inside this horrid place, don't you?" Kelsey shook him off, fighting the terrifying vision of her beloved friend crumpled in a pool of blood. "You think Joseph killed her."

Luke's jaw tightened but he didn't deny it. "Wait in the truck."

"No." Stumbling backward, Kelsey's gaze darted around the shattered space. *"No."* When Luke reached out for her again, she spun away and ran toward an open doorway at the rear of the parlor. *"Ruth!"* Kelsey dashed through the elegantly appointed dining room into the kitchen area. Pausing, she whimpered aloud at the piles of smashed china and dented cookware littering the counters and floors.

"Kelsey...don't." As though from a great distance, his voice barely filtered through her mounting panic.

Ignoring him, Kelsey alternately sobbed and screamed as she kicked her way through the mess, then emerged in a carpeted corridor.

The room to her right was a den or study, complete with desk, bookcases and file cabinets. It was neat and orderly, having escaped whatever alien wrath had been vented on the rest of the house.

Whirling, Kelsey saw a set of double doors at the end of the hallway. One door was partially open and revealed the foot portion of an unmade king-size bed. Kelsey darted toward the room and hit the doors with the heel of her hands. She stopped abruptly, bracing herself on the jamb. "Oh, God. Oh, no."

Kelsey swayed and felt Luke behind her. Strong fingers gripped her shoulders and for several seconds, they silently stared at the carnage.

Shredded clothing was everywhere, strewn across the floor and bed, while dresser drawers had been yanked out and emptied, then heaved across the room. Slashed dresses and torn lingerie littered the bed, and a pair of scissors had been discarded near the doorway. Personal items had also been flung around the room—books and crumpled papers, cosmetics, jewelry, shoes—any item usually found in a closet or dressing area had been reduced to heaps of ragged rubble.

Releasing Kelsey, Luke carefully stepped over the maze of ripped cloth and wire hangers, then went into the adjoining master bath. Kelsey's lungs started to ache and she realized that she'd been holding her breath. Exhaling, she sagged against the door jamb. What kind of monster could have done this?

Joseph had always seemed like nice enough—a little arrogant, perhaps, but basically decent. There had never been a hint of clandestine brutality lurking beneath that facade of smooth charm. How could such a thing have happened?

Luke reappeared, obviously relieved. "Ruth isn't here."

Kelsey's eyes fluttered and closed and she uttered a silent prayer of thanks. But the situation was still grim, she knew that. Fighting to compose herself, she shakily stepped over a pile of slashed clothing and sat wearily on the disheveled bed. "Do you think Ruth is all right?"

Luke touched a piece of tattered silk, draped over the thick, carved foot post, then his eyes hardened ominously. "She'd better be."

The unspoken threat was not an idle one and Kelsey shivered. Luke could be a dangerous man. If Ruth had been hurt, Kelsey fervently hoped that the police would find Joseph before Luke did. Not that she felt any sympathy for Ruth's abusive husband, but she didn't want Luke imprisoned for having dispatched the cowardly worm.

Suddenly Luke swore violently and kicked a pile of ripped fabric. Alternately balling his fists and scouring the back of his neck, he paced the room with an expression of murderous rage mingled with abject terror.

Instantly, Kelsey suppressed her own fear and sought to calm him. "I'm sure Ruth is just fine." She wasn't sure at all, but encompassed the devastation with a sweeping gesture. "In fact, she probably wasn't even here when all this happened."

Luke halted abruptly. "How do you know that?"

Kelsey moistened her lips. "I don't, really, but when Ruth arrived at my place, she had a suitcase packed with perfectly good clothing. She mentioned that Joseph hadn't been home when she left, so my guess is that when he discovered that she was gone, he had a major tantrum, and this was the result.''

Luke quietly considered her theory. "That makes sense, but it doesn't explain why Ruth would have disappeared from your apartment. She was safe there.''

Kelsey remembered how Ruth had constantly peered out the windows, apprehensively scanning the street below. "I don't think she *was* safe, Luke, and what's more, I think she realized that. I believe that she was frightened, afraid that her husband would come looking for her.''

Averting her gaze, Kelsey wiped her damp palms on her slacks, unable to endure the terrible comprehension dawning in Luke's murky gaze. He said nothing; he didn't have to. They were both agonizingly aware that Joseph probably *had* come looking for Ruth, and he'd probably found her. The crucial question now became, where had he taken her? They didn't have a clue, yet with every passing moment, Ruth's situation became increasingly dire.

They had to do something, and soon. Ruth's life depended on it.

Resolutely, Kelsey stood. "I saw some file cabinets in the den. I'll start there.''

Luke frowned. "Start what?''

"If Joseph forced Ruth to go with him, he probably took her to some predetermined spot. If we search this dreary mausoleum, we might find a clue.''

"Yeah,'' Luke replied bitterly. "He might have even jotted down the address and phone number.''

"I know it's a long shot, but what other choice do we have?''

To Luke, Kelsey's idea seemed as useless as spitting at the sky and waiting for rain, but since he couldn't come up with a more productive suggestion, he simply shrugged helplessly. With a brusque nod, Kelsey disappeared into the hallway.

For a moment, Luke stood quietly gazing at the remains of his sister's clothing. Kelsey's rationale, farfetched as it was, had a calming effect. He wasn't foolish enough to believe that they actually had a prayer of discovering a real clue in this godawful mess, but hoping to gain insight into

Ridenour's twisted mind, Luke set to work methodically examining each piece of wadded paper and torn garment.

After a few moments of frustration, Luke noticed that the telephone on the nightstand was undisturbed, its receiver still neatly cradled. Since everything else in the room had been overturned or smashed against a wall, Luke scrutinized the phone more carefully. On a hunch, he depressed the Redial button and waited. When the operator for Los Angeles information answered, a cold chill slid down his spine.

Cradling the receiver, he spotted a scratchpad lying on the floor at the base of the nightstand and inspected the item more closely. The blank top sheet held an imprint of earlier writing. Idly, he recalled the clichéd staple of bad television movies and decided that it couldn't hurt to give it a try. Picking up a shiny gold cylinder, Luke lightly brushed the lipstick color over the impression. From the void slowly emerged legible print.

"Well, whadaya know," Luke mumbled under his breath. "It works."

In fact, it worked too well. A stark white scar in the crimson smear spelled out the address of Kelsey's apartment. Luke crumpled the paper in his fist and flung it into the clutter.

So what if Ridenour knew that Ruth had been staying with Kelsey. They had already figured that much out. What Luke needed was information on what had happened afterward, and unless Ridenour had been thoughtful enough to leave an itinerary, there wasn't much chance that scrounging through the scraps of his sister's life would shed any light on that.

Suppressing a renewed wave of hopelessness, Luke stiffened his spine and continued on what he was certain would be a fruitless search. What else could he do? The police had already refused to get involved and since there was no law against trashing one's own home, Luke doubted that another call would yield any better results.

So, because Luke couldn't give up, he went on, and moved to the master suite's closets. Joseph's closet was still intact and tidy, with expensive suits and designer polo shirts arranged in neat, color-coordinated rows. A metallic gleam on the floor caught Luke's eye. At first, he thought that the cylindrical object to be another lipstick container, but upon closer examination he saw the telltale point on one end.

Tensing, Luke scooped up the item for closer examination. It was a bullet, a .38 caliber jacketed hollow point to be exact, and judging by its size and configuration, not the kind of ammo used for sport. This bullet was meant to kill.

Although Luke immediately searched for a corresponding weapon, he found none and hadn't expected to. He had a fairly good idea where the gun was now, and the realization that Ridenour was armed added to Luke's fear and frustration.

Dropping the cartridge into his pocket, he closed the closet's double bi-fold doors and turned his attention to Ruth's closet. The skinny, eight-foot interior had been completely gutted, but there was a dark shadow in one corner that turned out to be a flat zippered case, which he promptly removed.

The portfolio transport was the type used for large, flat items such as blueprints and drawings. Folded beneath the black plastic handle, a leather flap fastened to the body of the case with a tiny keyed lock.

For a moment, Luke hesitated. Having always respected his sister's personal possessions, he was still loath to invade her privacy. Since the situation was too desperate for such noble restraint, he finally slipped his trusty pocket knife under the lock, popping the flimsy metal with a quick twist.

Unzipping the case, Luke reached inside and pulled out a handful of his sister's personal documents—her high-school diploma and college transcripts, a dog-eared program from her sixth-grade Christmas play, a certificate of honorable mention from a junior high creative-writing contest and, surprisingly enough, copies of engineering schematics for some of Luke's original mechanical designs.

Each item carried its own memory for Luke, and he touched them reverently, as though by caressing the inanimate object he was offering psychic comfort to the sister that he'd always cherished.

Laying the papers aside, Luke reached back into the case and retrieved an envelope of old photographs. He leafed through the pictures quickly at first, then slowed as he recognized and relived images of happier times. There was a photo of Ruth as a gangly eleven-year-old struggling to wash an indignant, wriggling puppy.

Smiling, Luke remembered the day he'd taken Ruth to the mall for a new pair of shoes and instead, she'd fallen in love with a tiny beagle in the pet store window. Luke had taken one look at the price tag and nearly gagged. He'd been seventeen at the time and earning minimum wage working at a nearby gas station. No way could he afford a damned dog that cost more than a month's groceries.

When he'd pointed that out, his sister had been stoic, but her eyes had misted ever so slightly. Her disappointment had nearly broken his heart, so he'd taken her to the animal shelter, hoping one of the cheap mutts would bring that same excited shine to her eyes. None had.

The next day, he'd emptied their small savings account and bought her the damned beagle. She'd cried and named the creature Freddie. Luke hadn't much cared for Freddie—he was a dog, after all—but had decided that any beast that could make his sister happy deserved to be treated with at least a modicum of respect, so Luke and his sister's dog had managed a peaceful co-existence for the duration of Freddie's nine-year life.

Setting the puppy photo aside, Luke picked up another and his smile faded. This picture was of Luke and Ruth in front of Disneyland's fantasy castle. Luke's arm was around his sister's slender shoulders. He was smiling; she wasn't. It had been Ruth's sixteenth birthday.

He stared soberly at the photo, a moment frozen in time. Suddenly, every hour of that day was etched in his mind as though it had happened yesterday instead of seven years ago.

"Smile, folks."

The Iowa tourist had aimed the camera, waiting patiently while Luke had tried to coax his sullen sister into displaying a pleasant expression. "Come on, sis, just one smile, then I'll take you on the teacup ride."

Ruth had folded her arms stubbornly. "Wow. I just might die of excitement."

"Hey, there's a million kids in the world that would kill for a chance to see Disneyland." Luke tossed one arm around the teenager's rigid shoulders. "If you smile for the picture, I'll buy you a Mickey Mouse hat."

With a disgusted snort, Ruth lifted her chin, turning away just as the camera clicked. Sighing, Luke dropped his arm, thanked the flustered tourist for her effort and retrieved his camera. Slipping the small plastic case in his breast pocket, he swallowed his disappointment. "Do you want to go on the Matterhorn? You love roller coasters."

Ruth used the toe of her sneakers to poke at a glob of gum sticking to the warm pavement. "Uh-uh."

Raking his hair, Luke propped one hand on his hips and glanced around the Magic Kingdom with mounting frustration. "Well, hell. It's *your* birthday. What *do* you want to do?"

She sniffed audibly. "You know."

Luke pinched the bridge of his nose and tried to control a temper that was fast spiraling to the point of explosion. After a moment, he decided to give logic one final try. "Look, we've been through all that. You're too young for girl-boy parties."

"All my friends are allowed to date."

"I don't give a damn what your friends do. You're too young."

"I'm sixteen," she pointed out, rather haughtily Luke thought. "Our grandmother was married at sixteen."

The familiar argument held no water with Luke. "Yeah and Gramps was a field hand, but that doesn't mean I expect you to pick lettuce for a living. Quit trying to grow up so damned fast. There will be plenty of time for boys later."

"When?" she demanded. "After I graduate from college?"

Luke considered that. "Yeah, that's about right. Say, do you want a Sno-Kone?"

"Damn it, Luke!"

"Hey!" Luke shook Ruth's arm. "Don't you ever let me hear you use language like that again."

She lifted her chin defiantly. "You do."

"That's different. I'm—" He was going to point out that he was a man, then thought better of it and switched tactics. "I'm older."

"So when I'm twenty-two, I'll be able to swear a blue streak?" Ruth asked sweetly. "How old do I have to be for sex?"

Luke's jaw slackened. "Sex?"

"Uh-huh." She batted her eyes coyly. "You know, what men and women do together when the lights go out?"

It took a moment for Luke to regain his composure. "Sex is for married people."

"Really?" Feigning surprise, Ruth delicately chewed her lower lip, then slid her brother a sly glance. "Then you must still be a virgin. Are you?"

Luke nearly choked. "Where in hell do you learn about this stuff?"

"Everybody at school talks about sex," she cooed, obviously enjoying her ability to shock him. "Most of my friends do it all the time."

Luke glared menacingly. "Then you need new friends."

The veiled threat didn't faze her. "I like the friends I have. That's why I wanted to have a party for them."

"Forget the damned party. I told you, you're—"

"Too young," she finished sharply. "I know. I'm too young for parties and too young for dating and too young for sex. Tell me, big brother, do you plan to keep me in a bottle for the rest of my life?"

"Don't be melodramatic. You've got all the freedom in the world."

She emitted a sarcastic hoot. "Sure. Of course, I can't even spend the night at a friend's house unless you've cased the joint, then you call six times to make sure I'm still there, and as for after-school activities, well, forget that. You wouldn't even let me audition for the senior play."

Luke clenched his jaw. "The rehearsals ran too late. You'd have missed the bus and had to cross the barrio after dark."

Hands on her hips, Ruth confronted him angrily. "Cheerleader practice is during school hours, but you wouldn't let me try out for that, either."

Turning away, Luke felt a humiliating flush rise up his neck. Ruth was right, he *had* refused to sign the try-out permission slip and had been too embarrassed at the time to give her the reason. Logically, he realized that he owed her an explanation, yet the words still stuck on his tongue. Finally, he took a deep breath and spit it out. "I couldn't afford it."

The cryptic statement startled Ruth. "You couldn't afford what?"

"The damned cheerleading uniforms," he replied angrily. "There were 'home' uniforms and 'away' uniforms and liability insurance and transportation expenses—" He muttered a sharp expletive. "The whole ball of wax ran over five hundred bucks, and I flat didn't have it. There. Are you satisfied?"

Ruth's blue eyes softened. "I guess I was too excited to actually read the forms. I'm sorry—"

"Sorry about what?" Luke was unreasonably angry, he knew that, but being unable to provide something that his sister wanted left him feeling powerless and inadequate. "Sorry that your brother is such a damned failure?"

"That's not what I meant." The hurt in Ruth's eyes drove a stake into Luke's heart. "You're not a failure. How many men your age have started their own business?"

Luke snorted disdainfully. The business in question had driven him even further into debt and at the moment, the minuscule profit was barely enough to keep a roof over their heads, let alone set aside money for Ruth's education. "I fix cars for people who don't want to get their hands dirty. Big deal."

"You won't do that forever. You're a smart man, Luke. Look at that self-lubricating piston thingamabob you designed. You even got a patent on it. If you really wanted to, you could get a mechanical engineering degree and maybe even start your automotive-parts design firm. Think about the possibilities."

Luke *had* thought about the possibilities, then he'd considered the realities and relinquished his dream. There simply wasn't enough money. Ruth's education had to come first. Luke could always take care of himself, but his sister needed that degree, or she'd end up with nothing more than a slew of runny-nosed kids and a monthly welfare check.

Still, the unpleasant reminder of personal sacrifice served to fuel his inner turmoil. "Don't start putting on airs, pretending you come from aristocratic stock," he snapped. "Your daddy was a lush, your ma scrubbed toilets and your brother is a grease monkey. That's how it is for us, but things can be different for you. You're going to get the chance to make something of yourself. Don't blow it by letting some swaggering jock turn your head, hear?"

Ruth's complexion paled. "I didn't mean anything. I'm proud of you, Luke, really I am."

At the time, Luke hadn't really digested those final conciliatory words. He'd been hurt by his sister's rejection of the Disneyland visit, which had been his birthday gift to her, and angered by the untimely reminder that in spite of his best efforts, he hadn't been able to supply everything that a young woman apparently needed.

So he had firmly taken Ruth's arm, then hustled her to the parking lot, and a day that should have been so special had ended with sullen silence, a precursor to the estrangement that had eventually destroyed their relationship.

Luke turned the photograph facedown on the floor. All Ruth had wanted for her sixteenth birthday was a party with her friends. Because he'd refused to acknowledge that his baby sister was growing up, he had dragged her off to an amusement park, as though forcing her to cavort in a child's playground would somehow negate her blossoming sexuality.

Luke sat on the floor of Ruth's bedroom and realized just how oppressive his actions had been. It was a real eye-opener, because he now recognized that there had been many such incidents with his sister.

And with his wife.

He'd smothered them both. He'd lost them both.

Regret was the most bitter, and the most useless, of emotions. Regret twisted a man's guts and tore at his soul, but history was immutable. If Luke's deepest wish could be granted, he would atone for the pain that he'd caused. But wishes were capricious flights of fancy, as elusive as the wind and as fragile as life itself.

There was nothing Luke could do about the past except curb the memories and look toward the future, but as he surveyed the surrounding devastation he realized that his sister might not have a future. That was the cruelest blow of all.

When Kelsey returned to the master bedroom, she found Luke sitting cross-legged on the floor amidst a jumble of papers and snapshots. His strong shoulders were slumped forward as though crushed by some enormous, invisible weight. An immense lump wedged in her throat as he carefully set another photograph on top of the stack, then surreptitiously wiped his face.

Knowing that he would be humiliated by her intrusion into his grief, she stepped back into the hallway and loudly called his name. "Luke?"

Kelsey counted to five, then reentered the master suite. Luke was standing in the middle of the room, ramrod stiff, with a hint of dampness still smeared across his left cheek. He cleared his throat and questioned her roughly. "Did you find anything?"

"I think so— Oh, for goodness' sake. Aren't those some of your designs?" Before he could answer, Kelsey knelt and spread out the prints with renewed amazement at the detail and complexity of the neat engineering calculations.

During their time together, Kelsey had admired Luke's fascination with mechanical design. His specialty had been improved engine components and he had spent hours working on the complicated schematics. Although Kelsey had been baffled by the engineering intricacies of the devices, she'd been awed by his brilliance in having designed them.

She inspected the plans that were spread across the bedroom floor. "I recognize your drawing style, Luke, but I don't think I've ever seen these particular designs. Where did they come from?''

Without speaking, Luke gestured toward a flat, leather case yawning open on the floor.

''Ruth had them?'' Kelsey smiled, returning her attention to the drawings. ''In college, Ruth was always bragging about how talented you were and how many patents you owned. She always believed that you had a very special gift.'' After replacing the papers in the case, Kelsey stood. ''Ruth was right, you know. You are very talented.''

Shifting uncomfortably, Luke curtly pointed to the manila folder Kelsey had brought from the den. ''What's in there?''

''Hmm? Oh, Joseph's property-tax records.''

Luke accepted the proffered folder, then leafed through the contents without visible interest. ''So the guy paid his taxes. So what?''

''His family owns a lot of property,'' Kelsey announced. ''Or rather, they used to. Two years ago, the Ridenours were paying taxes on a condo in Aspen, a couple of hundred unimproved acres outside of Portland, two separate homes in upstate New York and a fishing cabin north of Yosemite.''

Luke still didn't get it. ''Am I supposed to be impressed?''

Puffing her cheeks, Kelsey exhaled slowly and retrieved the manila folder. ''These receipts show that right after Joseph and Ruth were married, the senior Ridenours transferred most of these properties into their son's name. Joseph instantly liquidated one of the New York homes and purchased this place.''

Crossing the room, Kelsey perched on the mattress and opened the folder. ''Now, look at these.''

Luke sat beside her and dutifully eyed the two tax receipts. ''Those are for this year's payments.''

''Exactly. And there are bills for only two pieces of property, this house and the fishing cabin. Everything else has been sold.''

''How do you know that?''

''I came across some escrow documents in the file and according to Joseph's bank statements, there were sizeable deposits corresponding with the dates of those documents." Kelsey flipped the file shut and drummed her fingers on the thin cardboard. "There are also a lot of cash withdrawals. Frankly, Joseph now has less in his bank account than I do, and that's a pretty sad state of affairs, considering what he started out with."

"You mean the guy is broke?"

"Not yet, but he's certainly on his way."

Standing, Luke rubbed his chin and Kelsey noted the merest hint of satisfaction in his eyes before he turned away and slowly crossed the room. When he faced Kelsey again, his expression was bleak. "Do you think that Ruth left because her husband was running out of money?"

"Of course not," Kelsey replied indignantly. "Ruth left because Joseph abused her."

"Then what has all this money business got to do with finding my sister?"

Kelsey moaned. "You've missed the whole point here, Luke. Joseph still has *two* properties left, remember?"

"Yeah. So?"

"So we've already searched one."

Luke's eyes widened slightly. "The cabin."

Unscrewing the pickup truck's gas cap, Luke inserted the unleaded nozzle and pressed the trigger. A cold rain drizzled from the turbulent sky and the gas pump clicked rhythmically.

They were just outside of Bakersfield, at one of the service areas scattered along this stretch of interstate highway. The Yosemite cutoff was two hundred miles north, then another fifty or sixty miles to the wilderness lake where this stupid cabin was supposed to be located. At least six more hours behind the wheel; maybe more, depending on just how remote Ridenour's property turned out to be.

Luke hadn't given much thought to how he would find this elusive little cabin. In fact, he hadn't given much thought to anything over the past two hours except pointing the damn truck north and stomping the accelerator to the floorboards. If the horrible scenario of Luke's imagination was accurate, every hour that passed represented another hour of torturous terror for his sister.

Deep inside, his worst fear was that Ruth—and her unborn child—might not even be alive. Since his conscious mind couldn't deal with that possibility, Luke suppressed the macabre speculation and focused on speed without dwelling on details. Even if they found the godforsaken place, the entire trip could be a wild goose chase.

A loud click broke into his thoughts. Pulling down the pump lever, he replaced the gas nozzle, then glanced around the roomy parking area and saw Kelsey talking with one of the mechanics. Absently rescrewing the gas cap, Luke watched as she showed the young man a photograph of Joseph and Ruth. The guy squinted at the picture, then shook his head and turned away.

Kelsey was obviously disappointed, but what did she expect? Luke had told her the stupid photo was a dumb idea. Thousands of people used these service areas every day. The possibility that anyone would remember two particular faces was so small as to be nonexistent.

Still, she'd stubbornly insisted, so Luke had figured that if it made her feel better, what the hell.

An irritated patron diverted Luke's attention, and he realized that there were several vehicles lined up to use the pump. He entered the truck, then pulled across the lot and parked beside the small mini-mart that served as a cashier's booth. At these self-service stations, one had to pay in advance, so Luke had handed the clerk a twenty-dollar bill just to get the pump turned on, and now went to retrieve his change.

When he returned to the truck, Kelsey was inside with a road map spread out on her lap. Luke slid into the driver's seat, slammed the door and fired the ignition. Kelsey didn't look up and he felt a twinge of guilt. During the past two hours, he hadn't spoken a syllable, and Kelsey had respected his silence. Luke had always required time for quiet thought, and she'd never resented that need, as other women had. Instead, she'd always recognized his subtle signals without comment, then had allowed him the space that he'd needed. Strange, he mused, that he'd never noticed how perceptive she'd been about his moods, nor appreciated the solace of her silent support.

There were many things about Kelsey that Luke had never noticed or appreciated in the past, and he decided that he must have been either blind, or completely self-absorbed to have allowed such unique qualities to escape his attention.

As he pulled back onto the highway, he sidled a glance and saw that Kelsey was still studying the map. "We're going to turn off in Modesto, right?"

Seeming startled by the sound of his voice, Kelsey looked up and hesitated briefly before replying. "Yes. Highway 108 veers east into the Sierras and passes within a few miles of the lake."

"Which offramp?"

"I'm not sure." Kelsey stared out at the blurred scenery. "The tax records showed a parcel number, so I called Tuolumne County before we left Santa Barbara. I spoke with a woman in the assessor's office, but all she could tell me is that the parcel in question is fairly remote, on one of the private, unpaved roads along the northeast corner of the lake."

Luke regarded the clever woman with renewed respect. He'd been so consumed with simply getting to Ridenour's cabin that the logistics of how the hell he expected to find the damned place had escaped him. Kelsey was more practical, thank God.

Actually, they wouldn't even have gotten this far if not for her. Luke had always admired his wife's initiative. Once, she'd saved his floundering business by convincing the bank to use future receivables as collateral for a low-interest loan. Luke had been proud of her.

He'd also been a bit intimidated, having asked himself how a woman so highly educated and exceptionally intelligent could be happy with a struggling mechanic. The answer had been clear, at least to Luke. She couldn't, not for the long haul.

God knows, he'd tried. It had damn near killed Luke, watching how hard Kelsey had worked trying to make a home of that ratty roach trap they'd lived in. So he'd worked longer hours in a desperate attempt to pay off his debts and give his family a decent place to live.

It hadn't been enough. Over his furious objections, Kelsey had taken a job and they'd fought bitterly. Deep down, Luke hadn't faulted Kelsey for wanting pretty things, but had been wounded by his own inability to provide them. Seeing his pregnant wife at the corner bus stop had been a daily reminder of his failure. Kelsey had tried to reassure him, Luke would give her that, but all the assurance in the world couldn't heal the massive rift in his ego.

Now, chasing a painted line down a monochrome highway, Luke recalled that he and Kelsey had never resolved that particular problem, but had put it behind them as they'd always done—in the bedroom. Afterward, they'd rarely discussed her job and the cloud of hurt and mistrust had remained.

From the corner of his eye, Luke examined Kelsey's pale complexion and the strain lines bracketing her funny round mouth and realized that she, too, was fighting resurgent memories and reflections of what might have been. During their journey, neither had spoken of the past, although both were shrouded in it. They were helpless, spinning victims of a haunted history and an uncertain future.

Actually, their future wasn't uncertain—it was nonexistent. He and Kelsey *had* no future, at least not with each other. Why couldn't he accept that?

There seemed only one answer to the perplexing question circling his bedeviled brain. It was an answer that Luke refused to acknowledge.

Chapter 7

By the time they reached Modesto, the gray drizzle had evolved into serious rain. Luke cranked the wipers up to full speed, then noticed a quiet rumbling and ducked his head to inspect the clouds that obscured the distant Sierra peaks. "Was that thunder?"

"No." Kelsey smiled wanly and fidgeted with the torn corner of the map. "It was just my stomach. Sorry."

Luke glanced at the dash clock and moaned. It was past dinnertime and they hadn't even stopped for lunch. No wonder she was hungry. His jaw tightened. "We'll get off at the next ramp."

"That's not necessary, really—" Another audible growl cut off her words and she shrugged, seeming embarrassed by the fact that she obviously required sustenance.

Ignoring her feeble protest, Luke veered right and steered onto one of Modesto's busy surface streets. Conveniently enough, a coffee shop blinked a neon welcome and he drove directly into the parking lot.

Kelsey was still staring at her lap.

"The break will do us good," Luke told her. "Besides, I'm hungry, too."

She smiled then, just a little. "Thank you."

Luke enjoyed that smile, and inexplicably sought to encourage another one. "Maybe they have marbled-fudge ice cream."

Instantly her head lifted and she hiked one neatly tweezed brow. "Do you think so?"

"If they don't, I'll personally drive to the nearest supermarket and bring you an entire gallon," Luke promised, meaning every word. At that moment, he'd have climbed Mt. Everest barefoot just to keep that soft glow in her eyes.

Even during the most difficult times of their marriage, a carton of marbled fudge could always defuse the tension by transforming his proud, self-respecting wife into a servile mass of quivering gooseflesh. Luke had loved watching her savor the treat, closing her eyes and emitting delightful humming sounds with each creamy mouthful. Afterward, he'd take her into their bed and she'd recreate those sounds while he made love to her.

The image still burned in Luke's brain as Kelsey stirred restlessly in the passenger seat. Their eyes met and held for a moment before he looked away.

Kelsey noted Luke's wistful expression and wondered what he'd been thinking. Before she could ask, he turned sharply and exited the truck.

Sighing, she let herself out, then allowed him to take her arm and guide her into the restaurant. The little diner was bustling with activity. They slid into a booth just beyond the lunch counter. Several menus had been propped behind the napkin holder, and Luke extracted two, offering one to Kelsey.

"I'll just have a hamburger and coffee."

"Yeah." Luke replaced the menus and turned to the frazzled waitress who had suddenly appeared, pencil poised over a small green pad. "Make that two."

The woman nodded, tucked a wild strand of strawberry hair behind her ear, then hustled away.

"You look tired," Luke said suddenly.

Startled by his unexpected concern, Kelsey responded defensively. "It's been a long day."

Luke started to speak, then hesitated, pursing his lips and absently twirling the plastic salt shaker. "Look, Kelsey—"

A distressed wail from a nearby table interrupted Luke and Kelsey's stomach tightened instantly. She stared down at the laminated tabletop, willing herself not to focus on the source of the cry, yet even as she formed the silent command, her gaze wandered expectantly around the busy restaurant. Then she saw it and the breath caught in her throat.

Less than fifteen feet away, a fussy infant kicked in a small carrier that had been set atop the table. A woman, whom Kelsey assumed to be the mother, placated the child by rubbing its round tummy. Kelsey's heart ached at the sight. The baby was so tiny, perhaps two or three months old, yet it sported an abundance of dark, feathery hair that had been neatly twirled atop its head and fastened with a bright red barrette.

A little girl.

Kelsey closed her eyes, blinking away the sudden sting. She remembered it all. The details of that moment had been seared into her brain, and now flared into vivid images that overwhelmed her senses and transported her instantly into the past.

The lights had been so bright.

Strange faces had surrounded her, kind eyes exposed over sterile blue masks. Air had brushed her face as the gurney was wheeled quickly down the hospital corridor. Someone had patted Kelsey's hand. "Here we go, Mommy. Junior is preparing for his debut."

Since Kelsey had been in labor for nearly nine hours, that was definitely good news. What wasn't so good was the force of those final contractions. All the Lamaze in the world couldn't have prepared her for this—

"Oh!" The force of the pain jolted through her like an electric shock, raising her shoulders off the gurney. "Ahhh—"

"Breathe, Mommy," said a crisp female voice and Kelsey felt a gentle hand on her distended abdomen. "My, this is a lovely contraction."

Gritting her teeth, Kelsey squeezed the handrails as the pressure faded. "Easy...for...you to say," she mumbled, falling back onto the firm, padded surface. Blinking, she glanced around and realized that she was in a small room cluttered with electronic gadgets and frightening medical devices. A gowned figure bent over her. "Hi, Kelsey," crooned a male voice that she recognized as her obstetrician's. "It looks like we're ready to have a baby."

We? Where on earth did he get the "we" business? Kelsey wondered irritably. After all, the doctor-man wasn't strapped to a table, panting like a whipped dog. "Ahhhhh—" Doubling up, she rolled to her side and tried not to scream.

The searing pain was the worst yet, twisting from the small of her back to her navel with such unexpected force that she nearly panicked. Reaching out blindly, she sought to grab something—anything—but instead felt herself being lifted and rolled.

When the contraction eased, she licked her dry lips and squinted up at the halogen lights. She was on a different table now, and someone was hoisting her leaden legs into a pair of humiliating devices that jutted out from each side of the bed.

"Giddyap," said the disgustingly cheerful nurse who was tucking her feet into the icy steel stirrups.

A cold breeze touched Kelsey's bare thighs, then a square of crinkled blue fabric was draped from her suspended knees to her grossly swollen belly. "Where's...my husband?" she whispered, the effort of speaking almost too much for her. Craning her neck, she pushed herself partially upright and tensely scanned the room. "Where's Luke? Please...I want my husband."

"Now, now. He'll be along, don't you worry."

But Kelsey *was* worried. For the past three months, she and Luke had planned for this moment. They'd both read everything they could get their hands on about childbirth and attended birthing classes with religious fervor. During her long, exhausting labor, Luke had been by her side, watching the electronic monitors as though the secret of world peace had been encoded in the blinking red numbers.

Then the contractions had changed, suddenly and irrevocably, and now, when Kelsey was so desperately frightened and needed him most, he had suddenly disappeared.

Dear God, she couldn't go through this without him.

A now-familiar pressure swelled up each side of her abdomen. "Luke!" she cried, her upper body curling forward with the force. *"Luuuke!"*

Then a strong arm encircled her rigid shoulders. "Shh, honey. I'm here."

Although her eyes were squeezed shut, a distinctive male scent confirmed Luke's presence and Kelsey was instantly soothed. When the pressure faded, she looked up and had she not been so exhausted, she would have laughed out loud.

There stood her macho husband decked out in a shapeless blue gown with disheveled strands of dark hair peeking out from beneath what appeared to be a gauzy shower cap.

"You look silly," she whispered.

He squeezed her hand and glanced toward where her bare feet were poking out of the blue drape. "So do you."

Lifting his hand to her lips, she kissed his roughened palm. "Where have you been?"

With a crooked grin, Luke shrugged self-consciously. "Dressing for the party."

The obstetrician peered over Kelsey's curtained thighs. "Speaking of parties, I think the honored guest is about to arrive. Start pushing with the next contraction, Kelsey."

Luke went pale. "So soon? I mean, I thought this stuff took time." Kelsey gave Luke a withering look, but he was preoccupied with the process going on just beyond her view. Still holding her hand, he sidled along the bed until he could peek around the drape. Instantly he straightened and made an odd, gurgling sound. He looked ill.

The contraction hit with jackhammer force and Kelsey bolted upright. She would have cried out, except she couldn't suck in enough air even to breathe, let alone scream. Her entire body shook with the force, and she was numbly aware that there was less pain, but the intense pressure was terrifying. It felt as though a tank had just roared down the inside of her spine and was trying to push her lungs out through her navel.

From a great distance, she was aware of familiar voices issuing sharp commands.

"Push, Kelsey!" Was that her doctor?

"Breathe, honey, breathe."

"Push!"

"Breathe!"

"Push!"

"Arghhh—" Kelsey fell back onto the hard table, desperately sucking air into her deflated lungs. Her muscles uncoiled, just slightly, and she was too weary to do anything more than roll her head.

Luke's cool palm brushed her forehead and she felt his lips touch her damp face. "Are you okay, honey?" Kelsey wanted to open her eyes but was too tired. Then she heard Luke's voice again, and recognized the desperate edge. "Hey, Doc, her face is turning white. Do something, man, this is my wife!"

The doctor murmured a calm reply that Kelsey couldn't quite hear, but the fear in Luke's voice gave her the strength to console him. "I'm . . . swell. The baby?"

A pair of twinkling eyes appeared over the drape. "Everything down here is just fine, Kelsey, and by the way, your baby could use a haircut."

Suddenly buoyed, Kelsey lifted her head far enough to rest her chin on her chest. "You can actually see him?"

Luke tightened his grip on her hand, then sidestepped and ducked under the drape for a quick look. Kelsey heard a muffled thud and Luke instantly reappeared, holding his forehead. "Sorry, Doc," he mumbled, then turned to Kelsey, excitement lighting his eyes. "He's got dark brown hair, honey, a whole head full of it."

Another contraction hit and Kelsey pushed for all she was worth, squeezing Luke's hand and concentrating on the sound of his voice. "It's coming, honey! Oh, God. Oh, God. His head is out. Oh, God. His eyes are open . . . he's looking right at me!"

Panting, Kelsey blinked the stinging sweat from her eyes and managed a weak smile.

Luke was bouncing with excitement. "He's got blue eyes, honey, the biggest, most beautiful blue eyes in the world." Again peering beneath the curtain, Luke continued briefing Kelsey on each tantalizing detail. "He's kind of wrinkly, and there's a knobby red thing in the middle of his face, so he's got your nose. Other than that, he looks just like me.''

"Ah, Mr. Sontag, if you could just step back—"

Kelsey stiffened, then clamped her jaw until her teeth ached and pushed, focusing all her strength on giving birth to her beautiful, blue-eyed child.

"His shoulder is out! Oh, man. This is so great. Push hard, honey! He's almost here."

She fell back. "You push," she mumbled weakly. "I'm tired."

Instantly Luke was beside her, wiping her wet brow and murmuring sweetly. "I wish I could do this for you."

"So do I." Kelsey licked her lips and prepared for the next contraction. She didn't have long to wait. Suddenly, she felt a tearing sensation, as though her liver had been pulled out with a chain.

Luke emitted a strangled sound, then disappeared from her side.

Kelsey's head was spinning. She tried to focus, too dizzy to see more than a blur of activity and hear the garbled hum of distant voices. Something was happening. She tried to prop herself up but was too weak. She tried to speak but managed only a raspy croak. She tried to reach out but her hand seemed to weigh a hundred pounds.

Then Luke suddenly reappeared again, cradling Kelsey's head against his hard chest and brushing the wet hair from her face with a tenderness that made her heart ache. She felt his warm breath brush her cheek. "Our baby is here, honey," he whispered. "We have a daughter."

A magical warmth washed over her then, a peculiar feeling of physical emptiness and spiritual completion. They were whole now. They had a child.

"I...want to see..." Kelsey struggled briefly, then melted against Luke's strong arms as he lifted her upper body. Across the room, two blue-garbed people were preoccupied with something small and limp and oddly colored. Confused, Kelsey blinked and tried to focus. "Where's my baby?"

Against her shoulders, she felt Luke's muscles grow taut and the operating room atmosphere was suddenly humid, thick with tension.

Even her doctor's voice had changed. "Relax, Kelsey," he commanded curtly. "Your work isn't done yet."

"What's wrong with the baby?" Luke blurted. "Why is she all purple?"

"Everything's under control," the doctor replied brusquely. "Lie back, Kelsey, and work with the afterbirth contractions."

Although Kelsey was aware that her abdomen was still knotting with rhythmic cramps, her attention was completely riveted on the somber activity at the far side of the delivery room. Two medical technicians were handling what appeared to be a discolored rag doll, and Kelsey watched the process with dazed detachment, wondering if her baby had already been taken to the nursery.

One technician held a bulb to the tiny doll's mouth while another briskly rubbed its lavender skin, removing the waxy mucus and reddish smears.

It occurred to Kelsey that the room was strangely silent. There should have been noise . . . a cry. That's it. The baby should be crying. Babies always cried in the movies. A doctor would hold the infant up by its little pink feet, then slap its little pink bottom and the baby would start crying. That's what was missing here, Kelsey thought dizzily. Their baby hadn't made a sound.

Suddenly Kelsey felt a cold breeze as Luke released her and quickly crossed the room.

"What are you doing?" he demanded of the two technicians, one of whom was forcing a translucent tube into the rag-doll's tiny throat. "Why isn't she breathing?"

A nurse stepped up and took Luke's arm. "Please, Mr. Sontag, they're taking care of the situation."

"What *situation?*" Luke's eyes were wild with panic. "What's happening?"

"Childbirth is just as difficult for the baby as it is for the mother," the nurse explained patiently. "The infant's nose and mouth must be cleared, and sometimes the baby has to be coaxed into taking that first breath."

For several moments, Kelsey watched the peculiar exchange without fulling grasping the ominous implications. Then it hit her. That pitiful, discolored object wasn't a doll; it was her child.

A low moan filled the room, escalating into an unnatural sound, like an animal in pain.

Instantly, Luke was at Kelsey's side, murmuring words that she couldn't understand. Again, the air was filled with the keening lament, and Kelsey knew that the sound was coming from her but was helpless to stop it.

The doctor issued a brusque command. Luke shouted something. A male technician took hold of Luke's arm, restraining him. The nurse loomed over Kelsey, her veiled face distorted. Kelsey felt a sharp prick in her arm.

Then the room went black.

"Kelsey?" Luke's voice seemed so far away.

Kelsey stirred, wincing at the sharp pain in her hollow belly. She opened her eyes, confused by the strange room with its darkened windows and antiseptic scent.

"Are you awake, honey?"

Blinking because even the dim light stung her eyes, Kelsey winked up at the source of the concerned query. The features were blurred, out of focus, but Kelsey still recognized him and smiled weakly. "Luke?"

"Yeah. It's me."

Stretching, she grimaced at the aching throb deep inside her. "Where are we?"

There was a pause. "In the hospital."

"Hospital?" Kelsey shook her head and the drug-induced cobwebs dissipated. The hospital. The delivery room.

The baby.

She sat up so rapidly her head spun. "My baby," she cried, her glazed eyes darting rapidly.

Then she heard it, a tiny squeak of displeasure followed by a lusty howl. Turning toward the sound, she saw only Luke's back as he bent over what appeared to be an open-topped plastic box set on four chrome legs.

Luke straightened, his elbows poking out at odd angles, then turned and Kelsey saw that he held a small wrapped bundle from which a miniature fist was extended.

Tears sprang to her eyes. "Oh."

Luke carefully laid their precious daughter in the crook of her arm. Overcome, Kelsey could do nothing but touch the healthy pink fingers and caress the infant's incredibly soft cheek. The baby responded by turning her head and making little sucking noises.

Kelsey looked up apprehensively. "Is she all right?"

"She's great," Luke assured her. "Once they got her crying, she wouldn't stop for almost an hour. Doc says she's healthy as a horse."

"She's . . . so beautiful," Kelsey whispered.

"Yeah." Luke's eyes shone with a spiritual reverence as he caressed his daughter's feathery head. "She looks like her momma."

Kelsey laughed. "I thought you said that she looked like you."

Luke grinned. "That's when I thought she was a boy."

"Always the chauvinist," Kelsey chided.

Luke's grin faded. "Not anymore. My kid is going to have nothing but the best."

"She already does." A knot of joy lodged in Kelsey's throat. "She has you for a father."

Settling gently on the edge of the bed, Luke brushed his thumb across Kelsey's lips. He said nothing, but the tenderness in his eyes expressed volumes. Lifting Kelsey's chin, Luke gently brushed his mouth over hers, then cupped one large hand gently around his daughter's tiny head and kissed the infant's cheek. He seemed in awe of the miracle they'd created and too choked up even to speak.

When Luke caressed the baby's diminutive hand, she promptly wrapped her teensy fingers around his thumb. "Happy birthday, princess," he whispered.

Then the valiant man who deterred hardened criminals with no more than an icy stare, lifted his newborn daughter into his arms and cried.

That had happened seventeen months ago. Now, in the noisy coffee shop, Kelsey relived that joyous moment, along with the tragic days that had followed. Across the dining area, the infant's cries had been silenced with a bottle, and the young mother seemed massively relieved.

A feminine arm stretched in front of Kelsey's paralyzed gaze. "Here you go, folks." The weary waitress placed their meal on the table. "Enjoy your dinner."

The steaming food no longer held any interest for Kelsey, yet somehow she managed to utter quiet thanks as she twisted the paper napkin in her lap.

Suddenly, Luke spoke. "Wrap it up," he commanded gruffly. "We'll take it with us."

The confused waitress hesitated only a moment, then smiled stiffly as she lifted the plates. "Certainly, sir," she mumbled, then disappeared into the restaurant's small service area.

Luke stood. "Let's go."

Sliding out of the booth, Kelsey complied without comment. Having recognized the ridges radiating from Luke's eyes and the thin line of his mouth, she'd realized that he, too, had been deeply affected by the fussy child. Since Kelsey's appetite had dissipated with the baby's first wail, she was anxious to leave and allowed Luke to escort her to the exit without comment.

Luke pushed open the double glass doors. "Wait in the truck. I'll be out in a minute."

Kelsey nodded without looking at him, then walked into the night drizzle. A few moments later, Luke entered the truck and set two white bags on the seat. He slammed the door shut, then gripped the steering wheel and, without starting the engine, stared straight ahead. Rain pelted the windshield, its velocity increased by the strengthening force of the storm. His eyes were bleak, his expression grim.

"Your hair is wet," he announced without so much as a glance in her direction. "There's a towel behind the seat."

Absently touching her dripping hair, Kelsey wiped the dampness from her face and dully noted the spreading stain of moisture on the upholstered bench seat. "Sorry," she mumbled, turning awkwardly to retrieve the towel. As she did so, she noted that Luke was staring at her with a pained expression.

"I don't care about the damned seat," he said roughly. "I just don't want you to catch cold."

Kelsey dabbed her hair with the towel and responded blandly. "Thank you."

Luke stared for a moment longer, and Kelsey saw a brief flash of anger before he turned away. Swearing softly, he jammed the key into the ignition with more force than necessary, shoved the truck into gear and burned rubber.

The acceleration caught Kelsey off balance and she fell against Luke's shoulder, then quickly grabbed the door handle and righted herself. He said nothing but slowed slightly as he steered out onto the busy highway.

Trembling, Kelsey laid the damp towel in her lap and reached for one of the take-out bags. "Would you like me to unwrap your hamburger?"

Luke checked the rearview mirror and steered into the left lane. "I'm not hungry."

Kelsey slowly reclosed the bag and replaced it beside the other one.

He slid her a quick glance. "You go ahead."

She shook her head listlessly. "I'm not hungry, either."

Returning his gaze to the road, Luke tightened his jaw. "Eat anyway," he growled. "I don't want to spend the next three hours listening to your grumbling stomach."

Ordinarily Kelsey would have contradicted the stinging order with a sharp retort. At the moment, however, she was mentally drained and didn't want to argue. There was enough pain between them without adding more hurtful words, so she opened a bag and pulled out a limp French fry. Her stomach revolted at the thought of ingesting the greasy thing, so she simply held it in her hand and hoped he wouldn't notice.

He did notice.

In fact, he took his eyes off the road long enough to freeze her with a look that Kelsey interpreted as total disgust.

Tears spilled over her lashes as she huddled miserably against the truck door, staring out the wet window. Obviously, Luke still despised her, and she couldn't blame him.

If not for her own selfish stupidity, their beautiful child would still be with them. There was no way Kelsey expected Luke to forgive her. She hadn't even forgiven herself.

Squinting into the blinding rain, Luke followed a blurred smear of neon color into the motel parking lot. He pulled in front of the office and turned off the ignition. Beside him, Kelsey slept fitfully, curled against the truck door, as far away from him as she could get without hanging off the fender.

Her hair had partially dried, but was still plastered against her skull, and a sharp crease marred her forehead. Occasionally, she had moaned in her sleep and had screwed up her face as though silently sobbing her way through a devastating nightmare.

And she probably had been.

Luke could kick himself for having gone into that coffee shop in the first place. Rationally, he realized that there was no way to avoid babies completely. The tiny reminders were everywhere—in supermarkets and parks, sidewalks and shopping centers—hell, he'd even walked into an auto-parts warehouse once and found a grinning toddler strapped into a stroller by the cash register.

He'd left instantly, then had sent Ernie to make the purchase.

Sighing, Luke rubbed his forehead, then speared his fingers through his tangled mass of damp hair. Seeing that kid tonight had been worse than usual. The infant had actually looked like Pattie Sue—the same head full of dark, feathery hair, the same round blue eyes—but the real killer was that Kelsey had been there.

When Kelsey had looked at that beautiful baby, her shattered expression had broken his heart. He would have severed his own limbs to take back that moment, along with the moment so many months ago that had started the pain, the unendurable anguish that had tormented them ever since.

But he couldn't change the past, and he couldn't stop Kelsey's agony any more than he could ease his own aching soul.

She stirred beside him, whimpering quietly in her sleep and Luke touched her cheek. Strands of hair clung to her face, having been wet by the rain and dried into stiff clumps that would have been unattractive on anyone else. To Luke, the sticky spikes made her more vulnerable and alluring.

He'd always been fascinated by Kelsey's sleeping persona. It had seemed incongruous to him that such a willful woman could be transformed into this fragile, childlike entity when darkness covered her world.

His fingertip traced the sharp line of her jaw, then slid lightly across the warm pulse of her throat. Her eyes opened slowly and a confused frown wrinkled her forehead. Luke quickly pulled his hand away and straightened.

Rubbing her eyes as would an awakening child, she blinked at the glowing Vacancy sign just outside the truck window. "Where are we?"

"At a motel." Luke didn't know why his voice sounded so rough, and tried to gentle his tone. "We'll have to wait for the rain to let up before we can navigate the unpaved roads around the lake."

She moistened her lips with her tongue and the guarded expression returned to her eyes and her shoulders lifted with a subtle tautness.

Hurt by her apparent dismay at spending another night with him, Luke responded harshly. "Your virtue is safe with me, honey. I've already sampled the goods, and I'm not interested in a second helping."

Kelsey didn't blink at the cruel remark. Instead, she folded her hands in her lap and continued to stare blankly out the rain-blurred window. "I know that."

Turning away, Luke swore bitterly, angry with himself and the blatant lie, by emotions too deep to ignore and too intense to acknowledge. The fact was that if Kelsey realized just how desperately he *did* want her, it would flat scare the hell out of her. Besides, the poor woman had enough on her mind without worrying about fighting off the amorous advances of a spurned lover. To Luke, feigning disinterest was a kindness.

"Two rooms with a view coming right up," he muttered, giving the door handle a vicious yank and extending one leg into the frigid rain.

"Luke..."

He hesitated, glancing over to see that Kelsey was still staring blankly out the window. "Yeah?"

She neither blinked nor looked his way. "I don't want to be alone."

The statement surprised him, almost as much as the unspoken request. Hope surged, then retreated. Recognizing her fatigue and pained resignation, he accepted her words as a literal statement of truth. She was exhausted, she was frightened, and Luke surmised that at this moment, Kelsey would probably keep company with the devil himself if isolation was her only alternative.

Not trusting his voice, he nodded, then slammed the door shut and pulled up the collar of his denim jacket as meager protection from the stinging rain.

If his presence offered solace, Luke owed her that much, but he held no illusions. They both knew what had happened to their beloved daughter, and they both knew that Luke was to blame.

Chapter 8

Kelsey stepped out of the cramped bathroom, self-consciously smoothing a wrinkled T-shirt Luke had scrounged from an unfolded stash behind his truck seat. Since she hadn't considered the possibility that their journey would extend overnight, she had brought only the few staple cosmetics that she always carried in her purse. Fortunately, Luke's most recent load of clean laundry remained in the truck, stuffed into the tattered pillowcase that served as a Laundromat duffel.

Other necessities had been purchased from the dingy motel office, which carried a meager stock of personal items, including overpriced toothbrushes arranged like an afterthought beside an impressive condom display. This definitely wasn't the Ritz, but since it reminded Kelsey of their sparse wedding night accommodations she felt a nostalgic affection for the dinky little dive.

Two neatly made beds dominated the cramped space and Luke was hunched over a small table by the front door, scrutinizing the road map. Although Kelsey was fairly certain that he'd heard her open the bathroom door, a subtle tensing in his shoulders was the only clue that he was aware of her presence.

She hesitated, then crossed the room and stood behind him. He remained silent, although his back muscles rippled visibly. Desperate to end the tense silence between them, Kelsey gestured toward the Ridenour wedding portrait laying beside the map. "Did you show the picture to the motel manager?"

"Yeah." Without looking up, Luke shifted in the chair, then folded the map to expose only the section surrounding the lake. "He hadn't seen them but said we should check with the guy who runs the general store by the lake turnoff. The manager said that the old geezer knows every road and cabin around the lake."

Kelsey stepped back and sat on the edge of the nearest bed. "Maybe he can give us directions to Joseph's property."

"Maybe." Luke pushed the map away and rubbed his face wearily. "We should get some sleep."

Plucking a fuzzy thread on the worn chenille spread, Kelsey chewed her lower lip and tried to think of something that would keep the conversation going. The turmoil that had been boiling deep inside was bubbling to the surface, threatening to explode if she didn't release the pressure. She needed to talk about what had happened at the diner, about how she had felt when she'd seen that beautiful baby.

But she couldn't, any more than she'd been able to share her feelings a year ago. Luke wasn't comfortable with emotions, his own or anyone else's, and so throughout their mutual agony, they had shared only a wall of silence.

The silence.

Kelsey had hated the silence. Grief had broken her heart but it had been the silence, the isolation of her hemorrhaging soul, that had crushed her spirit.

The chair rattled as Luke stood up and stretched, still averting his gaze. "Are you through in the bathroom?"

"Yes."

He nodded, then turned without looking and took two steps toward the open bathroom door.

"Luke?" When he paused, his arms held stiffly at his sides, Kelsey swallowed hard. "What if Ruth isn't at the cabin?"

He opened and closed his fists. "Then I'll go to New York."

"New York?" Kelsey repeated, momentarily confused. Then she recalled that the Ridenours still owned a home outside Syracuse. She stood. "Oh. Well, I have some vacation coming—"

"I'll go alone," he interrupted gruffly, then spun and faced her. "In fact..." His voice trailed away when he saw her bare thighs, then his gaze moved slowly, stopping midway up her torso. His eyes darkened sensually.

Kelsey drew a quick breath and absently touched her chest, just above her breasts. A downward glance confirmed that the points of her chilled nipples were clearly visible beneath the thin knit fabric. Her first instinct was to conceal herself by crossing her arms, which she did, but when their eyes met, something snapped deep inside her. Kelsey dropped her arms to her side and lifted her chin. Holding her breath, she prayed that he would accept the unspoken challenge.

Sex was a poor substitute for love, but Kelsey's pride was suppressed by a desperate need for tenderness and intimacy. Luke's touch had always eased her pain and so she enhanced the T-shirt's effect by squaring her shoulders, then waited and prayed.

A tight twitch of Luke's jaw revealed that he was not immune to her physical attributes. A small voice in Kelsey's brain screamed that this was wrong, because she wanted so much more from Luke than a breathless coupling in a dreary motel room. She wanted his heart.

But Kelsey had never touched that part of him, and realized that she never would. All they'd ever shared through the union of their bodies had been the pretense of love. For a time, that had been enough, because the affectation had been so poignantly beautiful, and because Kelsey had been in love.

Now, because of the aching void that only Luke could fill, Kelsey pushed away thoughts of love and hypocrisy. She reclined provocatively on the mattress, allowing the T-shirt hem to ride up her hip. "I guess it's time for bed," she murmured, in a sultry voice so unnatural that she almost winced. "We . . . have a long day tomorrow."

Luke took a shuddering breath, balled his fists and tore his gaze from the curves she'd so shamelessly exposed. "*I* have a long day tomorrow. You're staying here."

After a stunned moment, Kelsey bolted upright. "I most certainly am not staying here."

Spinning on his heel, Luke retreated to the bathroom, pushing the door almost, but not quite, shut. His reply was muffled but audible. "The room is paid through tomorrow night. I'll pick you up on my way back."

Instantly Kelsey leapt off the bed. "You wasted your money, because you are not leaving this room without me." Those final words were drowned out by the blasting water faucet.

Furious, Kelsey shoved the bathroom door and nearly knocked Luke into the sink. He swore and whirled, water dripping off his freshly shaved chin, then stared down at the pink finger Kelsey had pressed into the center of his bare chest. "I said, I am going with you. End of discussion."

He flicked her wrist aside as though it were a pesky insect. "I'll tie you to the damned bedpost if I have to, but I don't want two simpering females to worry about."

"*Simpering females?*" Swelling indignation finally snapped raw nerves that had already been stretched to the breaking point. "How dare you threaten me? I won't be bullied and I won't be ordered about like a dim-witted child. If it weren't for me, you'd still be squatting on Ridenour's wall cussing at a dog."

Snatching a towel, Luke quickly dried his face, then reached for the discarded T-shirt he'd draped over the shower rod. "I bow to the power of your obviously superior intellect, but unless you can pin a two-hundred-pound man with your bare hands, you're no damned use to me."

The bigoted statement left her momentarily speechless. The condition passed quickly. "Of all the pompous, arrogant—"

"Quiet, woman!" Luke's fist hit the porcelain sink with enough force to rattle the plumbing. "Why in hell does every conversation with you turn into a freaking argument?''

"What would you know about conversation?" Kelsey flattened against the wall as Luke elbowed out of the bathroom. She followed close behind. "You don't talk to people, Luke, you talk *at* them. Come to think of it, you don't actually talk at all. You growl. You snap. You bark orders, but you never really converse."

Rolling his eyes, Luke flung his wadded shirt on the floor, then threw his arms up in a gesture of total frustration. "Right. Then consider this as just another barked order. *You're staying.*''

Hands on her hips, Kelsey enunciated each word, so he couldn't miss her message. "Stuff it and twirl, bud. I'm going."

Kelsey didn't even blink at Luke's thunderous expression. Fighting was comfortable, and although she was intellectually aware that a screaming match was an ineffective way to resolve problems she liked it better than the oppressive, gut-wrenching silence.

Suddenly, however, words flew from her mouth as though they had a mind of their own and Kelsey was uncomfortably aware that she was losing control. "You don't own me, Luke, not anymore. You never did, but I pandered to your monumental ego and allowed you to savor the illusion of power. Did you believe all the lies, Luke? Did they make you feel like a real man?"

Only when she recognized the flash of pain in his eyes did Kelsey realize that he'd misinterpreted her taunting remark. She had been referring to his over-protective behavior, not criticizing his sexual performance, but the barb had been poorly worded and brutally delivered. "Luke, I didn't—"

Roughly grasping her wrist, he pulled her against him. "So it was all a lie?"

Miserably, she closed her eyes and shook her head. "That's not what I meant."

Luke ignored her weak denial. "Those sweet little sounds when I touched you, were they fake?"

"Please—"

"Let's test that theory," he whispered harshly, cupping her breast with his rough palm. An electric jolt went through her and she shivered, then tried to twist away. He held her firmly in place as he continued caressing her breast. "Look how your nipples harden and press against my hand. Are they faking it too, honey? Or maybe they'd really like me to do this..." Sliding his fingers upward, he rolled the erect nipple between his thumb and forefinger.

Kelsey moaned and her knees buckled.

Supporting her weight with one arm, Luke rested his lips against her ear. "Good acting, baby," he murmured, then brushed his mouth along the side of her throat and touched his tongue to the frantic pulse point he found there. The effect was instantaneous, and incredibly erotic. Her lips fell apart as her head lolled in surrender. "Are those make-believe goose bumps?" Without waiting for an answer—she couldn't speak anyway—Luke tasted each of the tiny chill bumps, emitting a throaty grunt of satisfaction when she shuddered violently.

It was all too good, too deliciously wonderful. Somewhere, in the deepest recesses of her mind, Kelsey knew that, for Luke, this was an act of anger, but she didn't care. There was an aching hole in the pit of her, a hollowness that this man, and this man only, had the power to fill. In spite of his anger, Luke's touch was gentle and sweet, and Kelsey cherished each fleeting moment.

Luke's breathing shallowed and Kelsey felt the heat of burgeoning desire radiating from every inch of masculine flesh. She was driven by the power of her own exploding need and brushed her fingertips over his muscled chest, reveling anew in the power captured just beneath the sleek skin.

Kelsey had always been repulsed by men with hairy bodies, so the first time she'd seen Luke shirtless, she'd been awed by the slick sculptured contours of his strength, and how sinew and bone tapered gracefully into a waist too slender and hips too slim for a man of such size.

The sight still affected her now as it had that first time. She traced a darkened scar beneath his collarbone, and the thin pink line on his forearm, then noticed the partially healed scratch along his rib cage, a reminder of how he'd defended her from the pale-eyed mugger. These imperfections only added to his appeal. Nothing could mar the magnificence of this powerful man, and Kelsey's lungs still tightened at the mere sight of him.

Beneath her probing fingertips, she felt Luke's telltale quiver and was pleased that her touch could still arouse him. Bending her head, she brushed her lips over each sensitive scar, a tantalizing demonstration of what she wanted in return. He understood the message.

With a low growl, he lifted her off the floor and pressed her against the wall, then allowed her limp body to slide down until she stood on her own and the oversized T-shirt was bunched under her armpits. Slowly, tortuously, Luke took one breast into his mouth, nipping and teasing until the excited nipple hardened into a rosy diamond.

She emitted a throaty sound of pleasure.

"Do you like that?" he whispered against her slick skin.

"Yes."

"And this?"

Kelsey managed a weak nod as Luke's caresses moved downward with a series of feathery strokes, barely touching the soft mound of intimacy, then returning to tantalize every inch of her soft belly with tender promise of the passion to come.

A gentle warmth flooded over her. Needing to share the exquisite sensations, she fumbled with Luke's jeans, unfastening the buttoned fly, then peeled his garments down his lean thighs. Touching her mouth to the center of his chest, she methodically lowered herself, until she had tasted every inch of his strong torso and her kisses became excruciatingly intimate.

Luke stiffened and gently framed her head, allowing his fingers to tangle in her hair as he guided her to the heart of his manhood. Cupping him tenderly, she caressed with her lips, and her cheek, rubbing against his hardness like an affectionate kitten, until he could endure no more.

With a strangled sound, he suddenly pulled her up, roughly sandwiching her between the wall and the entire length of his body. Opening her thighs with his knee, he caressed the moist feminine folds while she cried out, overcome by the burst of frantic heat coursing through her veins.

Arching into him, she heard a raw plea and vaguely recognized the sound of her own voice. "Love me, Luke. I need you to love me . . . please."

Kelsey was sick with desire, her fingers clutching at his broad shoulders like talons. Frantic now, she wrapped one leg around his tempered thigh. She was crazed. If she couldn't meld with him now, couldn't hold his heat within her very core, she would surely go mad.

But Luke made no move toward completion.

Moaning, Kelsey squirmed against him as though the frenzied writhing could quench the fire in her belly. Still, he held her mere inches from that which she so desperately craved. Fearing she might die of frustration, she opened her eyes. What she saw reflected in Luke's bleak expression froze her blood. Even before Luke stepped back and his soothing warmth was replaced by an icy chill, Kelsey recognized his shame and disgust.

Jerking away, Luke yanked the unzipped jeans back up and Kelsey felt as though her heart had been surgically removed. She'd tried to share her soul and he'd been repulsed by it.

Mortified, Kelsey managed to conceal her body with the wadded T-shirt, then covered her face with one hand, too humiliated even to look at him.

Staring blankly across the stark room, Luke closed his eyes and tried to get a grip on his rampaging emotions. He didn't trust himself to face Kelsey, so he spoke to the wall. "This is how it all began, isn't it?"

Except for the soft rasp of her breath behind him, the room was silent.

Luke rubbed his neck and swore. All these months, he had selectively altered his memory of that first night and blamed Kelsey for a seduction that he had subconsciously planned since the moment he'd first laid eyes on her. Now he realized that she'd surrendered to him then, as she had done tonight, but he'd allowed her no other recourse.

Tonight, he'd pitted her body against her mind and taken advantage of her emotional exhaustion. Two years ago, he'd taken advantage of her youth, her idealistic romanticism. The results had been the same—or would have been, except that rational thought had finally slapped his raging hormones into submission.

Luke was disgusted with himself. Their physical attraction was undeniable but beyond the realm of sensual pleasure, he knew that Kelsey despised him. He didn't blame her. If he'd actually made love to her tonight, she would have been horrified in the morning.

Clearing his throat roughly, he folded his arms, he rocked back on his heels and stared up at the ceiling. "That shouldn't have happened."

When she didn't respond, he forced himself to look at her. His heart twisted. She was sagging against the wall holding one hand over her face, looking so fragile and child-like that he ached to hold her. He didn't reach out. He couldn't. If he touched her again, he couldn't trust himself to ever let go.

Turmoil tightened his voice. "It's late. You should get some sleep."

From behind the concealing hand, her head bowed in a feeble nod. She shuddered once, then wrapped both arms around herself, stared at the floor as though expecting it to roll out of the way, then shakily crossed the room. Sliding into the nearest bed, she pulled the covers under her chin and turned away.

Luke sighed wearily, sat on the vacant mattress and absently turned off the lamp. The room plunged into darkness. Stretching out, he stared into the blackness for several minutes before he bolted upright. Damn. He'd almost forgotten.

Moving quietly, he turned on the bathroom light, then cracked the door so that a dim spray of illumination fell warmly onto Kelsey's bed. Only a few fringes of cinnamon-colored hair were visible above the pile of covers. The mounded covers quivered erratically as she sobbed quietly into her pillow.

Luke returned to his own cold mattress. There was nothing else he could do.

* * *

Another pair of headlights appeared in the distance, and Luke watched the bright orbs move closer, then pass the motel with a soft hum. Crossing his ankles, he propped one shoulder against the window frame and stared into the night, idly wondering how many more cars would pass the quiet highway before dawn.

He glanced toward Kelsey's bed, as he had done every few minutes for the past three hours. The mounded covers lifted and fell with her rhythmic breathing. Satisfied, he returned his attention to the window and the darkness beyond.

He had hurt her tonight. Again.

All he had ever wanted to do was protect Kelsey and make her happy, yet he'd caused her nothing but pain. The kindest gift he could offer now would be his permanent absence from her life. He'd tried. Even when Kelsey had appeared at his shop and begged for help, he'd instinctively realized that it would come to this, but he didn't have the guts to stay away.

The angry shield he'd so carefully nurtured all these months had eventually dissipated, leaving Luke vulnerable and exposed.

Frustrated, he turned from the window and moved stealthily to the bathroom, turning the faucet to a quiet trickle. He allowed the cool stream to fill his open palms, then splashed his face, hoping the chill would snap his mind out of this pointless reverie.

As he reached for a towel, a muffled sound caught his attention and he paused, listening. After a silent moment, he heard a soft, drawn-out moan, like an animal in pain.

Opening the bathroom door, he saw Kelsey toss fitfully, then roll her head on the pillow. One hand appeared from beneath the covers and slammed into the mattress, then extended as though fighting off an invisible foe.

"No," she whispered, tossing and feebly slapping thin air. "Pattie? Oh, God. No...please, no— *My baby!*" Then, she gasped and screamed, a shrill cry of absolute anguish that shook Luke to the soles of his feet. Bolting upright, she stared blindly across the room, face distorted with horror and hands pressed against her temples as she shrieked over and over and over again, before her screams faded into the agonized wail that had haunted Luke's nightmares.

Only this time, he was awake. This time, the horror was real.

Managing to break his stunned paralysis, Luke took two giant steps to Kelsey's bedside. Her fingers were still knotted in her matted hair and she blinked in bewilderment, as though jarred awake by her own screams.

"Kelsey...honey?" Luke sat on the mattress and slid one arm around her rigid shoulders. "God, what is it? What happened?"

Disoriented, her chest heaved with the force of another jerky breath, then she slowly turned and her eyes met his. Luke saw lucidity in the dark depths, and he saw something else. It scared him half to death.

Before he could speak again, a forceful knock rattled the motel-room door. A deep voice boomed from outside. "What's going on in there?"

Recognizing the motel manager's voice, Luke answered impatiently. "Everything's fine."

Apparently not satisfied, the manager pounded again. "Is anyone hurt?"

Frustrated, Luke realized the guy wasn't going to leave quietly, so he reluctantly released Kelsey and answered the door.

Although dazed, Kelsey was aware of strained voices across the room, the manager's concerned query and Luke's curt response, but was oblivious to the conversational details. Her heart was pounding, her head was spinning and a taste of raw terror fouled her mouth. She was going to be ill.

Yanking off the covers, she dashed to the bathroom and slammed the door. In the space of a heartbeat, the door flew open and Luke pushed his way in.

"What's wrong?" he demanded, his worried expression contradicting the gruff tone. "Are you in pain? Should I get a doctor?"

Kelsey pressed a damp cloth to her face. "I'm fine. It was just a dream."

Looking away, Luke considered that for a moment. "Tell me about it."

"I can't remember," Kelsey lied, then laid the washcloth on the edge of the sink. "It's over now. Go back to bed."

Luke frowned. "But—"

"Please. I'll be out in a minute."

Luke was obviously not pleased with the idea of leaving her alone, but after a moment he backed out and softly closed the door.

Shaking, Kelsey sat down and tried to compose herself, knowing she could never speak of the recurring nightmare that had tormented her for over a year. In that hideous dream, she'd tiptoed into a colorful nursery, the kind with animal cutouts dancing from a mobile over the crib, and bright walls decorated with circus motifs.

Kelsey didn't know where the image of this picture-perfect nursery had come from; it was a place she'd never actually seen. Still, in the dream, she'd been familiar with the room and, having just returned from work, she'd been joyfully anticipating the moment of lifting her baby from the beautiful white crib.

Setting an oversize briefcase on the plushly carpeted floor, Kelsey had softly hummed a melodic tune from her own childhood, then crossed the room, her eyes fixed on the sweet, darkly-furred little head nestled against the duck-print mattress.

But when Kelsey had reached the crib, it had been empty. Then before her horrified eyes, the crib had metamorphosed into a tiny bassinet with tattered bunting, and the gorgeous nursery melted into a drab, one-room flat. Frantically, Kelsey searched for the infant, screaming out for her husband to help.

Suddenly, the front door had blown open. Luke appeared, eyes burning with hatred and damnation, holding a tiny, limp body in his arms.

Then Kelsey would awaken, drenched with sweat and sick to her stomach. The dream had not been a fictionalized figment of her mind; it had been the hideous recreation of a horror that had been agonizingly real.

Their precious baby was dead.

* * *

"Yep, I seen 'em." The grizzled old storekeeper spit on the splintered porch and hooked his thumbs in the bib of his worn denim overalls. "Three days ago, mebbe four."

Luke tucked the photograph into his shirt pocket. "Were they going up to the lake?"

"Far as I know, they was. Headed up yonder, anyway." Since his hands still jutted from his overalls, the old man gestured north with a sharp nod. "Seen the man before. Comes this way once, mebbe twice a year, when the bass is a-biting. Never buys no worms, though. Likes them fancy, store-bought lures."

"Do you know how to get to his place?" Luke asked.

"Let's see now..." The storekeeper rubbed his stubbly chin, then rambled on for several minutes about each parcel on the lake, including gossipy tidbits about the property owners.

Stifling impatience, Luke tightened his jaw and feigned interest, suspecting that the old codger would take offense at any attempt to hurry the story along.

"...So that leaves the piece up to the north corner, across Martha Creek. Funny thing about that creek, y'know? About fifty years ago, mebbe it was longer, this little gal named Martha—"

"How do I get there?" Luke blurted, unable to stand another moment of rural folklore.

The old man frowned. "Can't, probably."

" 'Can't' what?"

"Can't get there." He spit on the porch, then wiped his mouth with his sleeve. "Rain, don'tcha' know."

Luke rubbed his eyes and willed himself to be calm. "It's barely sprinkling."

"Yep." Scratching his sparsely covered scalp, the old man winked up at the gray sky. "Still raining in the high country. Floods the creeks. Makes 'em real messy for a spell."

The warning wasn't lost on Luke, but at this point he had few options. "Assuming the roads were passable, could you give me directions to this north parcel?"

"They ain't, probably."

" 'Ain't' what?"

"Passable." The guy's lips disappeared into his toothless mouth and his wrinkled chin vibrated. "But if they was— passable, that is—guess you could get there by following this here road, then turn at the rotten stump and cross Holler Bridge. Funny thing about that bridge—"

"I'll find it. Thanks." Luke descended the weathered steps, then paused and glanced over his shoulder. "The woman in the picture—was she all right when you saw her?"

The storekeeper shrugged. "Couldn't rightly say. Didn't see much, don'tcha' know. She stayed in the car, kinda like your lady there." He punctuated the last statement with a curt nod toward Luke's pickup truck.

Gazing through the drizzle, Luke saw the blurred outline of Kelsey's bowed head through the passenger window. Re- calling the bullet he'd found in Ridenour's apartment, he again wished that he hadn't allowed her to come, but after the incident at the motel, he'd realized that he couldn't leave her alone.

The memory of Kelsey's anguished scream still sawed at Luke's heart, because even though she'd refused to discuss her terrifying nightmare, he understood what she'd been through. For over a year, he'd been haunted by the same nightmare, and had wanted to share that, to comfort his wife with the knowledge that she wasn't alone in her grief and her pain.

He'd wanted to, but he hadn't. He flat didn't know how.

Now Luke wiped a strand of wet hair from his eyes, ab- sently thanked the storekeeper again, and joined Kelsey in the truck.

Without looking up when Luke slid into the driver's seat, Kelsey continued to stare at her lap as though intrigued by the shape of her own neatly folded hands. In the hour since they'd left the motel, she hadn't spoken except for an oc- casional, monosyllabic reply.

Luke inserted the key into the ignition and slanted a wor- ried glance to his right. "Are you going to get through this okay?"

Her lip quivered, then tightened with determination. "Please don't worry about me, Luke. Ruth should be our primary concern." As though to fortify that statement,

Kelsey raised her head and stared out the windshield. "Has the store owner seen them?"

"Yeah."

Her head snapped around and her eyes widened. "They actually came up here? I mean, I'd hoped—but it was such a wild hunch."

Turning on the engine, Luke shrugged. "We're not there yet." Without mentioning the storekeeper's warning, he shoved the truck into gear and allowed the truck to idle loosely in place. "Kelsey?"

She waited without reply as he gathered his thoughts.

Finally, he swallowed hard and tried to spit out the word. "I just wanted to say that . . . I know."

A strange expression crossed her face. "You know what?"

"I know and—" he coughed away the choking sensation "—I'm sorry."

She frowned, seeming baffled. After a strained moment, she started to speak, then apparently thought better of it and turned away. "We should get started."

Nodding, Luke released the clutch and drove onto the narrow mountain highway. There was nothing else to say. Kelsey had withdrawn from him now, as she'd done after their child's death. Only this time, he couldn't retreat from her silent accusation.

Pattie's death hadn't been his fault.

At least, that's what he'd told himself every minute of every day for over a year. Too bad he didn't believe it.

Although he hadn't wanted Kelsey to hand their tiny daughter over to strangers, if he'd been able to provide what his family had needed, she wouldn't have taken that damned job in the first place.

Luke knew that. So did Kelsey.

That's what hurt the most. The guilt, the gut-tearing realization that if he'd been half the man his family deserved, his baby daughter might still be alive.

Chapter 9

"Good Lord," Kelsey muttered, as the truck stopped beside a muddy path winding into the forest. "That looks more like a deer trail than a road. Are you sure this is the right way?"

Luke pulled the emergency brake, then left the idling truck and grimly gestured toward the massive clump of rotting wood that had once been a magnificent tree. "The storekeeper said to turn at the stump."

"There must be dozens of stumps around here," Kelsey offered, nervously eyeing the pair of puddled ruts. "Maybe this isn't the right one."

Without disputing her, Luke walked the first hundred feet of road, testing the depth of the puddles and the softness of the surface mud. He didn't look happy, but when he returned to the truck Kelsey recognized the stubborn crease of his forehead and realized that argument would be futile.

To her surprise, Luke didn't immediately reenter the truck. Instead, he squatted by the left front tire and fiddled with something—Kelsey couldn't see what—then moved around to the right tire.

She rolled down her window and noticed that he was twisting a huge bolt in the middle of the wheel. "What are you doing?"

"Changing to four-wheel drive."

"Do you think the truck can get through?"

Standing, Luke wiped his muddy palms on his jeans. "Maybe."

That was not the definitive assurance Kelsey had been hoping for. When Luke entered the cab and shoved the pickup in gear, she cleared her throat nervously. "What if we get stuck?"

"There's a winch in the back," he replied, as though that information explained everything.

Easing up on the clutch, he guided the truck onto the mounded center and edge of the road, avoiding the puddled groves. Kelsey grabbed the shoulder strap of her seat belt and held on. As the truck whined and lurched through the forest, Kelsey stared at the blur of pine and black oak, remembering a similar adventure fifteen months ago.

It had been one of those rare spring afternoons with dumpling clouds floating through a cornflower-blue sky. The Sontag family had headed up Azusa Boulevard to the San Gabriel Canyon, then Luke had turned off onto a rugged logging road.

Strapped in her car seat between them, five-month-old Pattie had squealed with delight as the truck bounced like a Disneyland ride.

Kelsey had been less enthralled. "Where on earth are we going?"

Luke's eyes crinkled mischievously. "On a picnic."

"The park is back that way." Kelsey pointed toward the paved highway behind them.

"Park's too crowded," Luke replied cheerfully. "Besides, I promised Pattie that she could feed the ducks."

On cue, Pattie squeaked, whacked her chubby hands on the tray of her car seat and emitted a wet, drooling bubble. Kelsey couldn't help but smile. "Just where do you plan to find these hungry ducks?"

Luke grinned smugly. "You'll see."

Two minutes later, Luke pulled off the road into a large clearing that bordered a beautiful body of water that could have been described as a small lake or a very large pond. The sapphire-colored water was encrusted by a thick forest of emerald greenery, a sparkling jeweled broach in the wilderness. Its glassy blue surface was alive with waterfowl of every size, color and description, and the serene beauty took Kelsey's breath away.

"Oh," she whispered, opening the door and breathing the clean, scented air. "How did you ever find such a place?"

Unfastening the tiny straps, Luke lifted Pattie from her car seat. "My grandfather took me fishing here when I was a kid."

Holding his baby daughter, Luke walked to the edge of the lake and squatted down, pointing at the feathered flurry of activity that their presence had created. "See there, princess? Those are snow geese, and mallards, and these little black guys are coots."

Pattie's little arms flailed in excitement. Luke tenderly kissed the baby's silky hair, and a lump of pure happiness wedged in Kelsey's throat.

Then Luke stood and announced that he was going to teach his daughter how to fish. Placing the baby in her secondhand infant carrier, he sat cross-legged on the ground and carefully explained the fine art of worming a hook.

Kelsey denounced the demonstration as disgusting; Pattie tried to eat the bait. Later, when Luke proudly displayed his catch, the baby squealed with delight, then promptly clamped a fat fist around the wriggling minnow and only Luke's quick action kept her from shoving the slimy thing into her mouth.

While he pulled a cloth from the diaper bag and wiped Pattie's fishy little hands, Kelsey laughed so hard that she nearly choked.

"I think she's hungry," Luke muttered, tossing the rag over his shoulder. "Maybe we'd better have lunch."

Wiping her damp eyes, Kelsey agreed, so they laid an old blanket beneath the shade of a black oak tree and spread their meager feast.

An hour later, Pattie slept on her father's lap while Kelsey repacked the empty soda cans, baby bottles and discarded sandwich bags. The afternoon would have been perfect, except for the gnawing concern that Kelsey had suppressed all weekend. Dreading a confrontation, she'd put off telling Luke; now, the relaxed atmosphere boosted her courage.

Skimming a glance toward the spot where Luke sat propped against the gnarled trunk, Kelsey broached the subject as though it were an afterthought. "By the way, do you remember that bond sale I told you about last month?"

Shifting slightly, Luke laid a protective hand on his sleeping daughter's back. He emitted a sound that Kelsey interpreted as meaning that he did indeed remember but couldn't have cared less.

Forcing a casual tone, she continued as though he'd expressed interest. "Anyway, the deadline is this week and everyone's pushing to get all the stats together for the financial prospectus." She paused. He said nothing. Since her courage was rapidly shrinking, she blurted out the coup de grace. "I'll probably be working kind of late next week."

That got his attention. "How late?"

She managed a nonchalant shrug. "A few hours."

A covert glance confirmed his obstinate frown. "No."

Disappointed, Kelsey sighed and absently touched her forehead. "I wasn't asking permission. Overtime isn't optional—it's mandatory. If I don't work, I could be fired."

"Good."

"That isn't fair. I like my job, and besides, we need the money."

"We do *not* need the damned money," Luke snapped, then glanced at the sleeping child in his lap and lowered his voice. "I don't want my daughter to be raised by strangers. You're gone all day as it is—now you don't even want to come home in time to put your own child to bed."

"Me? You're a fine one to talk. I can't even remember the last time you got home before ten at night...."

The image faded as the pickup hit a rock, forcing Kelsey to steady herself by grabbing the dash. She stared out the window again, still reminiscing about that afternoon at the lake.

The argument that had followed her announcement was redundant and all too predictable. Luke had hated the fact that Kelsey had gone to work against his wishes. When she'd returned from maternity leave and been offered a permanent position, he had nearly exploded. Kelsey had let him rant, then accepted the position anyway.

Over the next few months, Kelsey's job had been a raw nerve, in their relationship, a sore point that couldn't be discussed in a civilized manner, so was rarely discussed at all. Bringing up the sensitive subject during the family outing had ruined their picnic and cast a pall over the entire day.

The following night, Kelsey had arrived home—late, of course—to find Luke paying the sitter. Ignoring his sullen glare, she'd dropped her briefcase on the kitchen table and tiptoed across the living room to check on Pattie.

What she had found would haunt her the rest of her life.

There'd been a scream—her own, she thought—and then the memory blurred. Kelsey dimly recalled blue-and-red lights strobing outside the apartment window, and uniformed EMS personnel clustered around the bassinet. There had been chaos. There had been terror.

At the hospital, a young physician had sympathetically explained that there was nothing he could do. Their cherished child had simply stopped breathing. SIDS, the doctor told them, Sudden Infant Death Syndrome. The cause was unknown.

Although medical personnel had offered repeated reassurance that no one was to blame for Pattie's death, Luke's stricken expression conveyed that he hadn't accepted that. Kelsey hadn't, either. How could a perfectly healthy, happy five-month-old baby suddenly forget how to breathe? It hadn't made any sense to Kelsey then, and it still didn't. If she hadn't worked late that night, maybe—

Suppressing useless conjecture, Kelsey absently kneaded the burning knot in her stomach. She would happily have sacrificed her own life to bring their baby back, but it was too late. She'd already failed the most sacred duty of motherhood—that of protecting her beloved child.

Pattie was gone.

Kelsey squeezed her eyes shut and shook her head, as though the slight movement could exorcise her inner demons. Inhaling deeply, she tried to focus on their current predicament.

Looking out the window, she noted with some dismay that the forest had fallen away, plunging down a brushy embankment into a deep tree-studded ravine. The muddy path was now clinging tenuously to the mountainside, and she was unnerved by the drastic change in terrain.

A quick glance at Luke's intense expression confirmed that he was well aware of their precarious situation. The path was so narrow that the truck's left fender scraped the mountain wall, and prickly branches grated against the steel cab. A shower of pebbles bounced from the cliff above, bouncing from the pickup's hood onto the windshield in a series of stinging pops.

Kelsey bit her lip nervously and the fire in her belly swelled into a raging inferno. There was a roll of antacids in her purse, so she reached toward the floor, but was restrained by her shoulder harness. Unbuckling the seat belt, she scooted forward and had just touched the leather handle when Luke shouted a sharp warning.

Instantly she straightened in time to see the flood of large rocks cascade down the embankment and rumble across the road. Luke hit the brake pedal, and a rock the size of a basketball crunched the hood, then rolled into the ravine on their right.

An ominous vibration shook the ground, and a massive boulder thundered over the cliff. Luke yanked the wheel and swerved left. The tires climbed the embankment and pivoted, then the entire truck wobbled backwards and pitched into the ravine. The passenger door flew open. Luke swore. Kelsey screamed.

A wet wind hit her face, and sharp branches clawed at her as she fell. She was rolling, bouncing, sliding out of control into the yawning mouth of the mountain slope. Then she crashed into something huge and hard. Consciousness faded.

* * *

She was floating. It was a nice sensation.

There were clouds, and a bright warm light. She felt cherished and secure.

"Kelsey?"

She squinted into the light. "Luke? What are you doing here?"

"I came to be with you."

Kelsey couldn't see his face, but she felt his presence and smiled. "I'm glad. I've missed you."

"I missed you, too, honey. I love you."

"You do?"

"Yeah."

"I...never knew that." Kelsey felt an overwhelming rush of warmth. "Say it again, please. I need to hear it. I need to know—"

"I love you, Kelsey. I love you. I love..."

"Kelsey?" Luke gently cradled Kelsey's neck and touched her bruised face. Responding to his voice, she moaned slightly and oddly enough, she smiled. "Are you okay, honey?"

Turning her head, she grimaced and slowly opened her eyes. "Luke?"

The surge of relief left him limp. "Yeah."

She gazed up vapidly. "What are you doing here?"

"I came to get you," he replied gently, examining the oozing wound on her forehead.

"I'm glad." She slurred the words slightly. "I've missed you."

"Do you know where you are?"

Pursing her lips, she considered the question, then her eyes focused with increased clarity. "What happened?"

"You fell down the hill."

"Oh." She frowned, seeming strangely disappointed, then touched her head and winced.

"Easy, honey. You took a nasty bump."

Since she was already struggling to sit up, Luke pressed the trembling woman to his chest and laid his cheek on her wet head. His own hands were shaking uncontrollably and he needed a couple of seconds to jump-start his heart.

When he'd heard Kelsey scream and seen her disappear over the edge, his terror had been indescribable.

If he'd lost her, too—

He couldn't complete the hideous thought.

Kelsey stirred, pressing her cheek against his ribs. "Your heart is beating so fast."

After the scare she'd just given him, Luke considered himself lucky that the damned thing hadn't stopped altogether. He plucked a twig from her matted hair, allowing his hand to linger briefly in a tender caress.

When she questioned him with a look, he moved his hand to the relative safety of her shoulder. "Can you walk?" The question was harsher than he'd intended.

Kelsey averted her gaze, and supported herself against a branch. "I won't hold you back, if that's what you mean."

That wasn't what he meant at all, but he didn't correct her errant assumption. He stood and braced himself by digging one sneakered foot into the side of the slope, then cupped his hands under her arms. She was a mess. Her torn pantsuit was saturated with red mud, and her sweater hung from her shoulders like a wad of soggy green moss.

Kelsey found her feet, then swayed slightly.

Luke was instantly alarmed. "Are you dizzy?"

"A little," she admitted, and proved it by slipping on the slick blanket of pine needles. She steadied herself against his chest.

"You could have a concussion," Luke announced tightly, scanning the steep climb above them and wondering how far it was to the nearest hospital.

"I don't think so." Flinching delicately, she rotated her shoulders and flexed her arms. "I'm fine, really, just a little sore."

The icy wind whipped through the forest canopy, and she shivered violently. Luke embraced her shoulders, trying vainly to warm her. The temperature was dropping like a rock and the turbulent sky darkened. Their situation had just gone from bad to worse.

Fifty yards above them, the truck was half pitched-over the embankment, and if the vehicle couldn't be winched onto the road before the storm broke, their only means of transportation would wash down the canyon. They wouldn't be much help to Ruth if they were stranded in this godforsaken wilderness, locked in their own desperate fight for survival.

Ruth. Luke was worried sick about his sister, wondered if they were even on the right track. Intuitively, he felt that she was nearby, but reasoned that the obscure cabin could be anywhere, if the damned thing existed at all. There was no creek. Hell, they hadn't even glimpsed a lake. In fact, the only water they'd seen were the massive puddles inundating the sloppy ribbon of mud they'd been navigating for the past hour.

Deep down, Luke secretly hoped they *had* taken a wrong turn, since there seemed no way to continue their journey. The rock slide had completely blocked the road, and if Ruth were beyond the barrier of boulders she would be hopelessly trapped.

Kelsey shivered again, and Luke forced his attention back to more immediate concerns. Bracing himself with a sturdy branch, Luke used his free hand to grasp her elbow. "Step up onto the rock, then hug that tree and wait until I get above you."

Her head bobbed in what could have been either an indication that she understood or an uncontrollable shudder.

She found a sturdy foothold in the cracked granite and hoisted herself into position.

"Good," Luke mumbled. "Now stay there."

Eyes wide, Kelsey clung to the rough bark of a sugar pine as though it were her best friend. Her lips were white and her jaw muscles twitched. A swirling gust lifted a tiny funnel of wet leaves, and above them, the wind rushed through the forest canopy, whistling a warning of the impending storm.

Luke climbed a few feet higher then grasped Kelsey's frigid fingers and urged her to follow. Slowly, painfully, they half climbed, half crawled up the embankment through the icy drizzle.

As they neared the crest, Luke saw the truck, still listing over the precipice with its passenger tire dangling over the edge. He scanned the area, searching for a location to tie off the winch pulleys.

Anxiety made him careless, and he stepped flat-footed onto a sloping blanket of slick pine needles. In less than a heartbeat, he was airborne. Before he could so much as mutter a one-syllable oath, he hit the wet ground and skidded as though his belly were a bobsled.

Spinning out of control, Luke reached blindly out and frantically grabbed at a low branch. It snapped off in his hand. He plunged downward with Kelsey's horrified scream ringing in his ears. Something sharp ripped his shirt and stung his chest. His head clipped a rock and he grunted in pain. Still he kept sliding, spinning, plummeting into the bowels of the ravine while clawed forest fingers tore at his flesh.

A distant roar grew louder, like a thousand high-performance engines revving all at once. The din surrounded him, swallowing him whole.

Trying to focus, Luke saw an oddly angled tree that jutted from the edge into an empty cavern of air. He was heading right for it.

The impact jarred his teeth and emptied his lungs. He wrapped around the massive trunk and stuck like a human staple. Paralyzed and unable to breathe, he was nonetheless aware of an immense roar just beneath him and felt an icy spray in his face. That was odd, he thought fuzzily. Rain was supposed to fall down, not up. Although dazed, he realized that his arms and legs were dangling in midair and thought it odd that this particular tree had grown horizontally.

Over the deafening noise, Luke heard a strained wheezing sound and realized that it was coming from him. He felt like a deflated tire. Again, he tried to suck air through his teeth but the life-giving oxygen backed up in his throat. The forest was spinning, growing darker. The pressure increased until he was certain that his rib cage had collapsed and his entire body would implode.

He didn't feel cold anymore. He didn't feel anything.

Hell of a way to go, squashed around a tree trunk like so much lichen. He fuzzily wondered if Kelsey would miss him.

At that moment, it would have been easy to give in to the numbing blackness. But he couldn't. Although he hadn't thought much about living for the past year, he simply wasn't ready to die.

He rolled slightly to one side, not much, but enough to ease the lethal pressure on his chest, then sucked a gurgling gulp of oxygen into his starving lungs. A stabbing pain encircled his torso but he took a deeper breath, then another. His head cleared. The spinning forest gradually slowed, then rocked to a stop.

"Luke!"

The frantic call came from above him. He painfully twisted his head and gazed blearily up the slope. Kelsey was on her knees, hanging onto a limb with one hand and reaching futilely out with the other. Luke wanted to warn her, but his faint croak drowned out by the rushing roar. He gestured weakly, trying to wave her away, but it was too late. She was on her way down.

When she reached the base of the tree, she stared over the edge, her eyes enormous. Below them, a boiling mass of white water gouged the earth in a frenzied rush down the mountain. The ancient oak to which Luke was so tenuously clinging had not grown horizontally. It had been seriously undermined by the flood and was cantilevered over the running water that continued to chew great chunks from the fragile embankment.

"Oh my God," Kelsey whispered. "If it hadn't been for that tree—" When her voice broke, she grabbed the waistband of Luke's jeans and tried to drag him to safety.

Spurred by the horror of imagining her swept to a watery grave, Luke found his voice. "Get . . . back."

"Not without you." She gritted her teeth, wedged her feet against the massive root ball that was emerging from the base of the listing oak and pulled for all she was worth.

Terrified that she'd fall into the churning creek, Luke tried to swat her insistent hands away. "Wait."

Kelsey stopped yanking, but didn't release her grip.

Luke struggled to position his hands on either side of his chest, then painfully raised his upper body, but couldn't hoist his knee high enough to straddle the log. Silently comparing his position to that of a bug pinned in a display case, Luke decided on a desperate move that would either lead to freedom or disaster.

When he sharply commanded Kelsey to turn loose of him, she was startled enough to comply. Then, using the tree as a gymnast might use a parallel bar, Luke pivoted his torso forward, swung his leg over and scooted to safety.

Panting and grunting in pain, he flopped onto the saturated earth and let the freezing rain pelt his face. Kelsey knelt and examined him anxiously. Emotion thickened her voice. "Are you all right?"

Grimacing under the force of yet another stabbing pain, Luke swallowed a groan. "Yeah." That wasn't a complete lie, he reasoned, deciding that he was as well as could be expected with a chest full of cracked ribs.

There was a bright side to this near disaster, however. The raging torrent that had almost sealed Luke's fate had turned out to be the sign he was looking for. The water was rushing downstream from a northeasterly direction that, by his calculations, must have intersected the road a few hundred feet beyond the rock slide.

If this swollen waterway was actually Martha's Creek— and Luke had convinced himself that it was—then the bridge and Ridenour's cabin was less than a mile away.

All he had to do now was haul his broken, battered body up this stinking cliff, hoist a three-ton truck out of the ravine, then hike through a freaking hurricane and rescue his pregnant sister. Hey, no problem.

So what if the whole damned mountain was a solid wall of water. He'd just park Ruth and Kelsey in the truck, clamp a towrope in his teeth and swim for it. He was a man, after all. There were no limits to his strength, no end to his endurance.

That was the credo with which he'd been raised, yet even having recognized the stupidity of that macho myth, Luke had no choice but to fulfill it or to die trying.

* * *

Standing by the bridge, Kelsey felt her heart leap and sink at the same time. Beyond the churning creek, the unmistakable outline of a peaked roof was wedged between stands of thick ponderosa pine, and a slow curl of smoke wafted above the treetops. It had to be Ridenour's cabin. They had made it. Well, almost.

The bridge presented a frightening challenge. The swollen waters were already lapping over the flimsy wooden structure, and although Kelsey couldn't see the strength of its supporting pillars she doubted that any engineering marvel could hold up to the punishing current much longer. The steady rainfall ensured that, at least for a while, the waters would continue to rise. Although the creek bed was only about fifty feet wide, the turbulent current was a force to be reckoned with.

Beside her, Luke shaded his eyes against the stinging rain and scanned the area beyond the bridge.

"Do you think we can make it across?"

Shielding his chest with one arm, Luke surveyed the undulating handrail. "I can. You stay here."

She sighed, tired of the constant argument. You'd think that he'd have realized by now that she didn't respond well to canine commands like "sit" and "stay." Without replying, she brushed past him to take a few tentative steps toward the mouth of the bridge. Luke grabbed her arm.

Kelsey whirled, prepared for bloody battle, then instantly sobered when he doubled up. "Oh Lord, you're hurt. Why didn't you tell me?"

During their exhausting climb out of the ravine, she had chalked Luke's stiff movements up to expected soreness from his long slide down the embankment. After all, her own muscles felt like pounded beefsteak. Throughout the grueling chore of hauling the truck safely out of the ravine, she had paid little attention to Luke's occasional grunts.

Now she could kick herself for having been so blind. "Stand up—let me see."

Partially straightening, he sidestepped her concern with a feeble gesture. "Never mind. It's nothing."

Ignoring his protest, she gently touched his collarbone then slid her fingers lightly over his chest. He moaned and stepped away.

He had always been a tower of strength, ignoring injuries that would have grounded most men. Kelsey remembered how Ruth had once described the way Luke acquired the curving scar on his forearm. Apparently he'd interrupted an armed robbery and been badly knifed. After having subdued the thugs by smacking their skulls together, he had returned home and nonchalantly sutured a four-inch gash on his own arm with sewing thread. Or so Ruth had said.

At the time, Kelsey thought the story had to be a gross exaggeration by a proud sister who worshiped the ground Luke walked on. After living with this man for over a year, however, Kelsey had no doubt that the facts were accurate.

There had been a time, in fact, that Kelsey had thought this powerful man was invincible. The past few hours had changed that assessment dramatically. When Luke had been dangling half-conscious over the white-water death trap, she'd realized that he was all too mortal. Life was fragile, a fleeting gift that could be repossessed without warning. Kelsey had already lost her precious baby; if anything happened to Luke, she wouldn't want to live.

Dear God, she still loved him—deeply, irrevocably, with every ounce of her heart and her soul.

The unwelcome revelation shocked her to the core, but there was no time to dissect the dire implications, because Luke suddenly reached into his pocket and flipped a key ring in her direction. Caught by surprise, she automatically shied away and the keys plopped into the mud.

As she bent to scoop them up, Luke started across the deteriorating bridge. He spoke over his shoulder. "If Ruth is in the cabin, I'll signal with a wave, then you can take the truck and get help."

Kelsey pocketed the keys and hesitantly stepped onto the first wooden plank. A thin sheet of water flowed over the surface, swirling around her ankles with surprising force. "I'm going with you."

"Damn it, Kelsey, the creek is still rising."

Grabbing the splintered rail, Kelsey braved the stinging rain and displayed a confidence that she certainly didn't feel. "Then you'd better hurry, or we'll both end up as floating fish food."

Hesitating, Luke's steely gaze evaporated into one of total frustration, then he grabbed Kelsey's wrist and quickly pulled her across the inundated structure.

When they were on the other side, she warily inspected their new terrain. A muddy driveway climbed upward, then flattened into the small clearing in which the cedar-clad cabin had been built.

Luke silently signaled that they should avoid the path, so Kelsey followed as he blazed a trail through the maze of brush and trees that extended right up to the cabin's covered porch.

The house was small but less rustic than she had expected. A natural stone chimney dominated the north wall, which faced the creek, and a covered porch encircled the remaining structure.

Like the Ridenours' Santa Barbara home, the cabin had been badly neglected. The split cedar clapboards had weathered to a mottled gray, and the white New England-style trim was stained by the iron-rich mud dripping from the composite roof and peeling eaves. The quaint little place must have been quite lovely once, although its style was more suited to a Maine fishing village than to a Sierra mountain retreat.

Kelsey's visual inspection ended when Luke touched her shoulder, then pointed beyond to a spot beyond the cabin where the trees formed a shallow natural arch. A glimmer of slate blue amid the greenery caught her attention. It was the trunk of a car, and the license plate read JOE III. She started to speak, but Luke silenced her by placing one finger on his lips.

Since the cabin was barely ten feet away, Kelsey nodded, then stealthily followed him up the wooden steps. In spite of their caution, the old planks creaked and they both froze, listening to the drumming rain. At that moment there was no sound emanating from inside, just an amber glow that spilled from the nearby window, illuminating the gloomy porch.

Flattening against the clapboards, they sidled quietly toward the lighted window. Luke's hand signals beseeched Kelsey to stay put while he moved to the other side. This time she offered no argument. He crouched below the sill and crossed silently. Straightening, he angled a glance inside the room and his expression hardened.

With her back pressed against the uneven clapboards, Kelsey sidestepped to the window and peered through the smeared glass. At one end of the compact parlor was an open doorway. Beyond it stood a sturdy old icebox and the corner of a kitchen table. The living area was sparsely furnished, with a plaid sofa beneath the window where Kelsey stood, and a murky oil lamp glowing atop the small coffee table in the center of the room.

Then Kelsey saw her and nearly cried out in joy.

In front of the blazing fireplace, Ruth was seated stiffly in a high-backed rocking chair, her hands clasping the polished wooden arms as though they were lifelines. She looked exhausted and frightened but very much alive.

Then a shadow crossed Ruth's face and Kelsey heard the sound of muffled footsteps through the thin glass. Joseph was in the room, too, and he had a gun.

Chapter 10

Paralyzed with fear, Kelsey watched the hideous scene unfold.

Joseph's normally neat blond hair was disheveled, and his white-lashed eyes were colder than the frigid mountain rain as he lifted the snub-nosed revolver, then inspected the cartridge chamber. Apparently satisfied, he calmly spun the cylinder and snapped it back into place. He smiled unpleasantly, caressing the weapon with perverse affection.

In the stiff wooden chair, Ruth paled slightly and her lips thinned, but she made no other indication that she'd noticed what her husband was doing. Dwarfed by the tent-like maternity garment, she seemed incredibly fragile, her shadowed eyes reflecting the vacuous stare of a shell-shocked soldier.

"It would be so easy," Joseph murmured, stroking the blue metal as though it were a living thing. "No one would ever know."

Ruth stared straight ahead without responding.

Raising the weapon, Joseph brushed the steel barrel against his own cheek, then moved slowly behind his rigid wife. His free hand caressed her hair as he positioned the gun barrel against her temple. Ruth quivered slightly.

Still holding the revolver in its deadly pose, Joseph leaned over and brushed his lips across Ruth's dark curls. "I'll bury you in the woods, my love, deep enough so the coyotes won't find you." He straightened, his mouth contorted cruelly. "The animals can't have you either, Ruthie. You're mine, don't you understand? You belong to me."

His wife blinked at the graphic threat, and moved one hand protectively across her swollen belly.

Suddenly Joseph's sinister countenance changed as his cold eyes melted and filled with tears. Inexplicably, he dropped to his knees. "I love you, Ruthie, don't you know that? I can't let you leave me. We belong together."

Still clutching the weapon in his right hand, he laid his head in his wife's lap and sobbed. Ruth continued to gaze blankly across the room, as though the blubbering man didn't exist.

After a moment, he raised his reddened eyes and spoke in a childish whine. "Remember how happy we used to be, Ruthie? It can be like that again. My parents will take the kid and we can go back to the way things were. I can't bear to be alone, you know that. It was very mean of you to leave me."

Punctuating the last sentence with an infantile pout, Joseph stood and paced the lacquered pine floor, becoming more agitated with every step. "Haven't I been a good husband? I've given you everything you could want, but it's never been enough, has it? You ungrateful slut."

Tensing, Ruth dug her fingers into the rocking chair's curved wooden arms and bent her head forward until her chin touched her chest. Eyes closed, her taut shoulders shuddered and she swayed slightly.

Joseph's tirade continued to build and he shook a fist at Ruth's curled body. "You're nothing but a gold-digging whore, a cheap ghetto tramp. You should be on your knees, groveling with gratitude and begging my forgiveness."

In two steps, he was beside the rocker, then dug his fingers in his wife's hair and viciously yanked her head up. Her lips fell apart in a silent gasp, her eyes widened in quiet horror.

"On your knees, bitch," Joseph growled, using the handful of hair to drag Ruth from the chair. "Beg for your life."

Kelsey's horrified scream was smothered by a powerful hand, and she vaguely realized that Luke had returned to her side of the window.

"Shh," he whispered against her ear, but Kelsey continued to struggle, too terrified to understand that revealing their presence would increase Ruth's peril.

Eyes wide, Kelsey went rigid and watched as Joseph suddenly released Ruth, who curled forward and slumped to the floor.

Absently scratching his head with the gun barrel, Joseph gazed down at his prostrate wife with no more emotion than if he'd been watching a wounded insect. "Are you hungry?" he asked softly. "I could make you some soup."

The scene disappeared as Kelsey, still silenced by the pressure of Luke's callused palm against her mouth, was dragged away from the window. The thrumming rain on the porch roof concealed the sound of their movements, and Luke hauled Kelsey down the steps to the scant protection of a nearby tree.

When he released her, the pent-up terror spilled out in a horrified rush. "He's insane, Luke! Did you see what he did? My God, he's going to kill her! We have to do something, we have to stop him—" A sob bubbled into her throat and she pressed her knuckles against her lips to keep from screaming.

Luke's eyes were colder than Ridenour's blue steel revolver, but his tone was measured and calm. "If we blow in there without a plan, he'll pick us off with two shots."

"But he's going to *shoot* Ruth—"

Touching his fingertip to her lips, Luke stifled her protest. "No he won't—at least not now. He's having too much fun terrorizing her."

Bewildered, Kelsey wiped the rain from her eyes and tried to digest this alien concept. "Do you mean that this is all some kind of sick mind game?"

Luke was too engrossed in studying the cabin layout to respond to her question. "Wait here," he whispered tightly, then slipped around the porch and disappeared behind the cabin.

Hugging herself, Kelsey sagged against a tree trunk. It was true, she realized quickly. By trapping Ruth in a controlled situation, Joseph was reinforcing his dominance and power. He could be kind, he could be cruel, depending on whether or not his wife's response pleased him. Joseph was training Ruth as though she were a disobedient animal. It was the ultimate degradation, and witnessing such abuse turned Kelsey's stomach.

Stumbling further into the forest, she retched violently and was physically ill. Afterward, she knelt in the mud and shook like a feather in the wind.

In a moment, Luke returned and crouched beside her. "Are you okay?"

She nodded weakly. "Did you find anything?"

"The bedroom window has been nailed shut," he replied grimly.

Feebly wiping her dripping bangs out of her eyes, Kelsey met Luke's bleak gaze with bewildered desperation. "Is there anything we can do?"

"Sure," Luke replied simply, but the glint in his eye belied his calm tone.

Kelsey was instantly alert. "What?"

His jaw twitched and he glanced toward the cabin. "I'm going in through the kitchen."

"What about the gun?"

"I'll take it away."

For a moment, Kelsey was certain that she'd misheard. "Are you out of your mind? You can't just walk in and confront an armed lunatic. Good Lord, Luke, your ribs are all crunched and you're in so much pain that you can barely stand up straight."

"Do you have a better idea?"

She swallowed. "No."

Bracing himself against the tree, he stood slowly, glancing around the clutter of forest debris until he spotted a sturdy branch half hidden in a quagmire of rotting leaves. He lifted the limb and wiped off the mucky coating. "Now I have a weapon. Feel better?"

"Oh yes," she replied dryly. "That nasty old gun won't have a chance against that great big twig."

"I don't care if the bastard has an AK-7 in his back pocket and a mortar under his arm." Luke's dark expression scared Kelsey half to death. "When I get through with that cowardly maggot, he'll wish to God that he'd never laid a hand on my sister."

Kelsey did not doubt that statement in the least. Armed or not, Joseph was no match for Luke Sontag; few men were. But Luke was hurt, and although Kelsey didn't know how serious his injuries were, she realized that they would have an averse affect on his ability to safely disarm Joseph.

The mere thought of what could happen to Luke if he charged into that madman's lair scared Kelsey spitless. She laid a pleading hand on his arm. "You are the strongest and bravest man that I've ever known, Luke Sontag, but please, *please* don't go in there alone."

Luke's eyes softened, then he looked away. "Stay hidden until it's over. Ruthie will need you then. If things go wrong, get to the truck and go for help."

As he started toward the kitchen porch, Kelsey blocked his path. "Joseph will see you. The living room has a clear view of the entire kitchen, including the back door."

Since Luke's veiled eyes reflected no surprise at that observation, Kelsey ascertained that he was well aware of the risks. He caressed her cheek with his fingertip. "I suppose you have another one of your famous plans."

She managed a weak smile. "As a matter of fact, I do."

As she mounted the front porch steps, Kelsey's heart was in her throat and her pulse beat so erratically that she feared she might faint. She bit her lip and squared her shoulders, forcing herself forward. Somehow, she'd carry this off. Ruth's life—and Luke's—depended on it.

With a deep breath, she pasted on a stiff-but-cheerful grin and pounded on the living-room door. Silence greeted her. She swallowed, and knocked again. "Yoo-hoo," she called. "Anyone home?"

After an eternal moment, she heard footsteps. Then the door swung open and there stood Joseph, gawking as though he'd just witnessed the descent of a messiah.

It's show time, Kelsey told herself and threw her arms around the stunned man's shoulders.

"Joseph!" she squeaked. "How wonderful to see you again!"

Even the brief contact with this despicable person turned Kelsey's stomach, but the hug allowed her to scan the room behind him. In the rocking chair, Ruth leaned forward, her mouth open and her eyes round with astonishment.

Glancing toward the kitchen, Kelsey watched the back door swing open. When Luke was safely inside, she stepped back and captured Joseph's attention with a renewed round of chatter.

"This is just a charming place," Kelsey cooed with saccharine delight. "I'm so glad you two made up—marital squabbles are such a drag, don't you think? Anyway, I was in the area on business because my company has an affiliate out of Modesto—such a quaint little town—and I decided to drop in and return Ruth's credit card."

Kelsey took a breath and from the corner of her eyes, noticed that Joseph was holding his right hand behind his back. Ruth had started to rise from the chair and Kelsey quickly motioned her to remain seated. "Don't get up, Ruthie—I can only stay a minute. Goodness, this mountain air has done wonders for your complexion."

Beyond the rocking chair, Luke peered from the kitchen doorway, so when Joseph started to turn, Kelsey immediately snagged his arm and hauled him around. "Say, you've dropped a few pounds, haven't you? You're looking very sleek. Have you been working out?" Kelsey pumped his bicep and emitted a low whistle, trying to keep her eyes from following Luke's stealthy movements through the living room. "Hot stuff, Joe. No wonder Ruth missed you so much."

Yanking his arm from her grasp, Joseph stumbled back and eyed Kelsey with undisguised suspicion. "What in hell are you doing here?"

Behind Joseph, Luke had reached the rocking chair and was signaling his sister to be quiet.

"I told you," Kelsey replied, sidestepping to the left so that Joseph would follow her movements. "Ruth's credit card. I have it here in my purse . . . oh darn. I left my purse in the car." Backing toward the front door, Kelsey reached behind and fumbled for the knob. "I'll just run and get it—"

"No you don't," Joseph growled, slamming the door with his left hand. His right hand emerged, holding the revolver.

The whistle of split air issued a brief warning, then the branch bludgeoned Joseph's arm. He howled and the gun clattered to the pine floor. Whirling, Joseph's eyes widened in recognition an instant before Luke's fist caught his jaw. The burly blond staggered backward, hit a wall, then pitched forward and crumpled to the hardwood floor.

Panting, Luke winced, dropped the branch and cradled his ribs. Joseph moaned weakly. Kelsey exhaled, relieved that the confrontation was over so quickly, then saw that Ruth was curled in the chair, one hand clinging to the wood arm, the other clutching at her belly. Dashing across the room, Kelsey embraced Ruth, brushing the damp hair from her pale face and whispering encouragement. "It's all over," she murmured. "You're going to be all right now."

Dazed and bewildered, Ruth looked up. "Kelsey? Is it really you?"

"Yes, sweetie." Kelsey hugged her fiercely. "Everything's going to be fine, just fine."

As Kelsey helped Ruth lean back into the chair, Ruth stared across the room, then her eyes widened. "Luke—"

Kelsey followed Ruth's frantic gesture in time to see Joseph reach across the floor and grab the gun. Luke spun around and planted a foot on the struggling man's wrist, then bent to retrieve the weapon. As Luke leaned forward, Joseph swung his free arm upward into Luke's midsection. Grunting, Luke doubled up and staggered backward, allowing his opponent free access to the revolver.

With a sharp cry, Kelsey ran across the room, and as Joseph rose to his feet she grabbed his wrist and tried to wrestle the gun away. There was a loud noise, and the acrid odor of sulfur stung her nose. Smoke wafted from the blue steel barrel. Luke was on the floor.

Screaming, Kelsey reached toward Luke, but something had a cruel grip on her elbow and she couldn't move.

Joseph spun Kelsey around, slammed her against a nearby wall, then pinned her in place by wrapping his fingers brutally around her throat. "Shut up," he snarled, his face inches from hers. "Or you'll get the same thing." With that, Joseph leveled the .38 until the deadly barrel was aimed at the middle of Kelsey's face.

"Let her go."

The weak request caught Joseph's attention and he glanced over his shoulder.

Ruth had crossed the room and was bracing herself against the sofa. Straightening, she took a few unsteady steps. "I'll go with you, Joseph, anywhere you want. I promise that I'll never leave you. Never. Please . . . let Kelsey go now."

Joseph hesitated, then jerked the gun toward Luke's motionless body. "What about him?"

Ruth barely blinked. "He can't hurt us anymore."

Grief and panic surged into Kelsey's throat, and only the brutal pressure of Joseph's hand kept her from crying out. Tears spilled over her cheeks, silent testament to the depth of her anguish.

Luke was curled on his side, facing away from her, but Kelsey hadn't noted the slightest movement, not even the shudder of a final breath. Ruth was standing on the other side of her brother's prone body. She could see Luke's face. She knew. Oh God. Ruth knew that Luke was gone.

Heartbroken, Kelsey went limp, sagging into the brutal pressure that was obstructing her airway. She couldn't breathe but didn't care. Anything would be better than the agony of life without her beloved husband.

Joseph suddenly released Kelsey, and she slid heavily down the wall. Oxygen flooded her lungs and her blurred vision cleared.

Agitated, Joseph raked his mass of white-gold hair and stared down at Luke's crumpled body. "What about the cops, Ruthie? What am I going to do?"

"We'll leave the country," Ruth said soothingly. "No one will find us."

Chewing his lip like a recalcitrant child, Joseph nervously tugged at the collar of his knit golf shirt. "Do you love me, Ruthie? I need to know that you love me."

Ruth's eyes softened with pain and, Kelsey thought, with pity. "You are my husband. I have always loved you."

Having recognized Ruth's willingness to sacrifice herself, Kelsey took advantage of Joseph's momentary distraction and stumbled forward. "Don't do it, Ruth," she croaked, holding her bruised throat. "For God's sake, don't go with h—"

"Quiet!" Joseph boomed, catching the side of Kelsey's face with a vicious backhanded slap.

Kelsey's head snapped around, she spun, then fell facefirst against the wall. Joseph uttered a sharp oath. Holding one palm against her stinging cheek, Kelsey turned just as the burly blond tripped and lurched forward. It took a moment to realize that Luke was hanging on to one of Joseph's ankles.

The moment the startled man hit the floor, Luke sprang to his feet, teeth bared and eyes flashing with a fury hot enough to sear human flesh. He grabbed Joseph's collar, hauled the dazed man partially upright, then flattened him with a measured blow. Joseph gurgled and covered his face with his hands, but the scant protection was useless against Luke's savage wrath.

Dazed, Kelsey glanced from the sweaty tangle of male bodies to Ruth, who clutched the revolver as though it were a sword and watched the melee without visible emotion.

Still bewildered by the puzzling turn of events, Kelsey looked back toward the struggling men and tried to gather her thoughts. Luke was alive. Thank God, he was alive.

But he was killing Joseph.

Horrified, Kelsey suddenly realized that Luke was out of control. Joseph's eyes had rolled back into his skull and blood ran from between his slack lips, yet Luke straddled the semi-conscious man and continued to pummel him weakly. If Luke's strength hadn't already been sapped by his previous ordeal, Kelsey had no doubt but that Ruth's husband would already be dead.

Grabbing a handful of the bloodied knit shirt, Luke hoisted the blonde's lolling head off the floor and managed to land a limp, glancing blow. "That was for my sister." Panting, Luke used both hands to again yank Joseph's battered head off the floor. "And this is for my wife."

When Luke's elbow arched, Kelsey snagged his arm. "No, Luke, don't. He's not worth it. Please, you're going to kill him."

"Good," Luke mumbled between shallow breaths, yet making no effort to shake off Kelsey's restraining hand. "The rat . . . deserves . . . to die."

"Luke—listen to me."

The desperation in Kelsey's voice reached a tiny shard of rational thought deep in Luke's brain.

"If Joseph dies, you'll never forgive yourself. Please. Your sister needs you now."

That got Luke's attention. He had no sympathy for Ridenour—only pure exhaustion kept Luke from spitting in the guy's bloodied face—but Kelsey was right. Luke wasn't a killer, and the fact that he'd been the width of an eyelash from committing murder was sobering.

Panting, Luke slid off Ridenour's limp body and allowed Kelsey to help him stand, wincing as each shallow breath tortured his fractured ribs. He drooped against the wall and felt gentle fingers brush his cheek, skimming the swollen bruises with infinite care.

"I thought you were dead," Kelsey whispered brokenly. A single tear slid down her face, and the poignant moment touched Luke to the core.

Capturing her hand, he turned his face and nuzzled her soft palm. He used his thumb to brush a teardrop from her lashes, then traced the ugly red handprint smeared across her beautiful skin. A renewed surge of anger bubbled in his belly, and apparently spilled into his expression because Kelsey's eyes widened before she touched her fingertip to his lips.

"I'm all right," she assured him huskily. "He didn't hurt me. But Ruth—" Kelsey's eyes widened as though she'd momentarily forgotten the sister whose safety had been the sole purpose of their quest. Whirling around, she saw poor Ruth standing ramrod-straight, clutching the gun in a dual-handed death grip. "Ruth? Sweetie, are you all right?"

Ruth's bewildered gaze traveled from Kelsey to her brother and back again. "Luke called you his wife."

In two steps, Kelsey was beside Luke. "It's a long story," she told the confused woman. "We'll talk about it soon."

Pushing himself away from the supporting wall, Luke masked a grimace and managed to cross the room "First, we have to get out of here." Luke pried the weapon from his sister's convulsive grip, then tucked it in the denim waistband at the small of his back. "Do you have any rope around here?"

Ruth's benumbed expression nearly broke Luke's heart. "Why... do you need it?"

Grimly eyeing the moaning man on the floor, Luke automatically flexed his fists. "Don't worry. I'm not going to hang him."

The idea did have a certain appeal, although Luke kept that to himself. Actually, he planned to hog-tie Ridenour's carcass behind the pickup truck and drag his rotten butt to the nearest police station, but rather than graphically describe that satisfying scenario, Luke chose a more diplomatic response. "Let's just say that I'd be more comfortable if he was, uh, restrained."

Stumbling back a step, Ruth put one hand to her belly. She looked as though Luke had suggested cutting the guy's ears off. "You can't do that to Joseph. He's hurt."

The unexpected response stunned the hell out of Luke. "*He's* hurt? How can you defend that sleaze-ball after everything he's done to you?"

Instead of replying, Ruth knelt beside her husband and used the hem of her skirt to wipe his bloodied face. After a moment, she bowed her head, then turned and met her brother's astonished gaze with one of infinite sadness. "He doesn't mean to be evil."

Feeling gut-punched, Luke turned helplessly toward Kelsey and was surprised that her dark eyes reflected understanding rather than shock at Ruth's statement.

Laying a pleading hand on Luke's arm, Kelsey shrugged. "Love isn't always logical." Before Luke could digest that cryptic message, Kelsey was assisting Ruth to her feet. "What Joseph did was wrong. You know that, don't you?"

Chewing her lower lip, Ruth squeezed her eyelids shut and nodded miserably. She hugged her belly, rocking slightly, and her jaw tightened perceptibly. After a moment, she took a shallow breath and without raising her gaze, whispered, "There's rope in the shed, around back."

Squeezing Ruth's frail shoulders, Kelsey guided her toward the hallway that led to the bedroom. "We're going to take you home soon, sweetie, but maybe you should lie down and get some rest until we're ready to leave."

Still holding his throbbing ribs, Luke exhaled, pressing air through his teeth with a tight whistle. This was too much to comprehend. He couldn't believe that his sister could actually love such a brutal man, particularly in light of their own mother's suffering.

Although physical abuse had never been part of their parents' relationship, Ruth could certainly recall the emotional cruelty and the neglect. During her teen years, Ruth had frequently commented that when she grew up, no man would ever push her around.

Luke had always assumed that his sister had been referring to their overbearing father. It now occurred to him that Ruth's sullen proclamations usually arrived on the heels of a disagreement between the two of them, most commonly one in which Luke had been exercising a measure of reasonable control over her activities. The logical extension of that thought was discomfiting.

Still, Luke would have severed his own arm rather than hurt his sister and had never, to his recollection, said anything crueler to her than the word "no." He was completely puzzled as to why Ruth would have tolerated brutality from any man, even her own husband.

Love isn't always logical.

Kelsey's simple statement carried one hell of a punch. Ridenour had wounded Ruth deeply, yet she loved the guy. If Luke wanted to understand that, he had only to look at his own marriage. He and Kelsey had repeatedly hurt each other, and yet he still loved her. God help him, he always would.

The realization shook Luke to the soles of his feet, but there was no denying what he'd felt when Ridenour's cruel fingers dug into his wife's delicate flesh. A rage had overtaken Luke, a fury so savage that he'd wanted to kill the bastard with his bare hands—and he nearly had.

Luke's contemplation was interrupted as Kelsey returned to the parlor.

"Ruth is exhausted," she announced. "And quite frankly, she doesn't look well. I think we should take her to the nearest hospital, just to be safe."

Luke had no argument with that. He, too, had noted his sister's pale complexion and the bluish coloration beneath her eyes. Besides, the left side of Ruth's face was swollen and red, evidence that her sadistic husband had slapped her around.

Ridenour groaned and rolled slightly. It was all Luke could do to keep from stomping his slimy throat. A man who'd beat a pregnant woman was the lowest form of animal. If Luke didn't get out of that cabin in the next thirty seconds, he wouldn't be able to control his murderous urge.

Reaching behind his back, Luke extracted the revolver and handed it to Kelsey. "I'm going to the shed. If the bastard tries to get up, shoot him."

Kelsey held the weapon as though it were a snake. "Luke?"

Pausing with his hand on the knob, Luke glanced over his shoulder.

Eyes darting toward the bedroom where Ruth was resting, Kelsey nervously wet her lips. "Hurry," she whispered.

Luke nodded tightly and went out to the windswept porch. The bellowing storm was whipping the rain into slanted sheets that pelted his unprotected body with punishing force. Bending into the wind, Luke used his forearm as a shield and sloughed up the southern embankment in the direction that Ruth had indicated.

Pausing, he glanced into Ridenour's slate-blue sedan. A few wadded papers littered the floor, along with an empty soft-drink cup and a few fast-food wrappers. Luke pocketed the ignition keys and looked into the back seat. There was a man's jacket wadded over a pair of hiking boots and a barrel-shaped canvas duffel. Since Luke was curious about the bag's contents, he took it, then continued climbing the slope to the shed.

When he reached the crest, a distant hint of blue caught his attention. "Well what do you know," he muttered aloud. "There really is a lake."

Whitecaps marred the water's surface, offering a depressing reality check on the storm's growing ferocity. A sense of urgency propelled Luke to the shed door, where he dispatched the flimsy padlock with customary ease, then searched the dank and cluttered interior. There was the usual assortment of rusty tools, pruning saws and the like. He found a small hatchet and a pair of wire cutters, but set them aside when he located a fat coil of rope. It was a bit thick for the intended purpose, and couldn't be tied as securely as could a thinner strand but it would have to do.

Still, he didn't feel like dragging a hundred feet of rope back to the cabin so he sawed off a ten-foot length with his pocket knife, then relocked the shed door and headed down the slippery slope. He glanced beyond the cabin toward the creek, hoping the water had receded. It hadn't. In fact, only the support posts were visible above the rushing wall of water. The bridge was now impassable.

Luke's stomach twisted into a knot of frustration. Even if the rotting planks hadn't been destroyed by the churning creek, anyone foolish enough to step into that swirling current would be instantly swept away. Luke considered using Ridenour's car, then discarded the notion. Attempting to navigate that rickety structure would be suicidal.

They were trapped.

Swearing bitterly, Luke returned to the cabin and burst through the front door. When Kelsey appeared in the hallway, wringing her empty hands, he flung the rope on the floor. "Where's the damned gun?"

"On the nightstand." Obviously distracted, she gazed toward the bedroom without challenging his abrupt tone. "We have to leave now."

Luke grunted and shook his wet hair. "The bridge is out."

She sucked in a quick breath and held it, then clasped her knotted fists beneath her chin. After a long moment, she exhaled all at once. "You're joking."

"Do I look amused?" Luke knelt beside Ridenour, rolled the groaning man on his stomach and roughly pinned his hands in the small of his back. "We can't cross until the creek recedes."

"When will that be?" Kelsey demanded, her voice rising in panic.

Although Luke knew that the bridge could be permanently destroyed, he didn't see the need to worry her further. He secured the rope around Ridenour's wrists with a square knot, then stood. "When the storm is over, the creek level should go down. That might happen tonight, or tomorrow or the day after for all I know."

Eyes wild, Kelsey frantically clutched at Luke's arm. "That's too late! We have to get out of here, Luke, we have to get out now!"

The irrational outburst surprised the hell out of him. Kelsey had always been calm and reasonable, even in the face of adversity. This frenzied behavior wasn't like her. "Look, honey, I know this isn't the best situation in the world, but—"

"You don't understand!" Kelsey blurted, then covered her face with her hands and turned away. Shoulders quivering, she struggled to control herself, then faced Luke, clear-eyed and deadly serious. "Ruth is in labor."

Chapter 11

Luke's body vibrated as though he'd been shot. "You're putting me on."

"Ruth's water broke some time last night—she doesn't remember exactly when. The contractions aren't regular yet, but they're getting stronger." Kelsey cooled her face with her palms and tried to get hold of herself. The situation was desperate, but panic wouldn't help so she struggled to control a spiraling sense of dread. Lowering her hands, she took a calming breath and hugged herself to quell the involuntary tremor. "What are we going to do?"

Luke gawked dumbly, his expression flickering between disbelief and raw terror, then he brushed past Kelsey and strode into the cabin's small bedroom.

As Kelsey turned to follow, a scratching noise caught her attention. Joseph was struggling to sit up, an impossible effort since his hands were bound behind his back.

Kelsey's first inclination was to let him flop around like a beached carp, but compassion took over. Grabbing his upper arm, she levered him into a sitting position. Joseph bent his knees and used his feet to propel himself, awkwardly scooting back until his shoulders rested against the foyer wall. Cocking his bruised head, he focused the eye that was not swollen shut.

Shuddering inside, Kelsey felt an unwanted sympathy for the vanquished man. His nose veered off at a peculiar angle, his shirt was spattered with blood and his split lips were swollen to nearly twice their normal size.

The grossly distorted mouth moved. "I want Ruthie."

"She's busy," Kelsey replied tartly, then started down the hall. After two steps, she paused and glanced over her shoulder. Cursing her inability to ignore the stabbing guilt, Kelsey went into the tiny bathroom, dampened a washcloth, then returned to sponge Joseph's battered face. She'd found a bottle of aspirin in the medicine cabinet and held two of the tablets to his lips, along with a glass of tap water. "Can you swallow these? They might help."

Struggling, he choked for a moment, then managed to consume the pills. When he looked at Kelsey again, there was no gratitude in his gaze, only the accusing stare of a petulant child.

"You spoiled everything." Joseph's words were slurred and his whining tone grated her nerves. Without responding, Kelsey straightened and went to Ruth's bedroom.

The cramped quarters contained a wooden chair, a small pine dresser and a full-sized bed that had been pushed beneath the window. Outside, the dark day was evolving into an even darker night and the room's dim illumination was provided by an oil lamp on the nightstand. Luke was sitting on the edge of the mattress and Ruth was in bed, propped up with pillows. She fiercely clutched at her brother's hand and if her petrified expression were any clue, Kelsey guessed that Luke had already explained their dilemma. She stepped quietly into the room.

Alerted by the movement, Ruth's head jerked around and tears filled her eyes. "We can't get out?"

Somehow, Kelsey managed a reassuring smile and a light reply. "Not at the moment, but now that the rain has stopped we'll be leaving soon."

Licking her lips, Ruth turned beseechingly to her brother. "How soon?"

Luke didn't even try to fake it. "I don't know."

"What about my baby?" Silence greeted Ruth's whispered question as Luke and Kelsey shared a telling look. The panicked woman's voice was heightened by mounting hysteria. "I can't have my baby here! Luke, please do something. You can't let me have my baby here!"

"Shh, Ruthie." Luke gathered his sobbing sister in his arms. "Everything is going to be all right. Kelsey and I will take care of you." Luke lifted her trembling chin with his thumb. "I'm not going to let anything happen to you or your baby, hear?"

Ruth's chest heaved. "But—"

"No buts," Luke interjected firmly. "Have I ever lied to you?"

She shook her head weakly.

"Then trust me, Ruthie." Luke kissed the top of her curly head. "Besides, this kid is a Sontag. If he wants out, he's damned well going to come out, so we might as well get ready for the big event, okay?"

"I don't know how to have a a baby," Ruth said miserably, feebly plucking at the bedclothes.

Luke patted her hand and stood. "It's a piece of cake, right, Kel?"

Kelsey blinked, but recognized the bleak plea in Luke's eyes. "Sure. Nothing to it."

Ruth cocked her head skeptically. "How do you know?"

Luke's stoic demeanor nearly crumbled then. He coughed, took a deep breath, then mumbled, "Kelsey will tell you," and strode out of the room.

Kelsey felt as though she'd swallowed a rock. Discussing Pattie Sue's birth was the last thing she wanted to do, and she seriously doubted that the information would console Ruth. Pattie had been born with breathing difficulties that might have been fatal, if not for the prompt attention of trained personnel and modern medical equipment.

Of course, Kelsey would never be so insensitive as to relay that kind of information to a woman about to give birth, but even if she withheld those details, she'd still be faced with explaining why their daughter was no longer with them. Ruth was suffering enough emotional trauma without being reminded that lives, especially tiny lives, are fragile.

"Kel—!"

The frightened cry broke Kelsey's reverie. Instantly, she was at Ruth's side, murmuring words of encouragement as the contraction peaked, then subsided. Ruth collapsed against the pillows and her eyelids fluttered. "I'm scared."

"I know." Willing herself not to cry, Kelsey touched Ruth's colorless cheek. "I'm right here, sweetie. I'll be with you every step of the way, and so will Luke."

"Luke," Ruth whispered, frowning slightly. "He called you his wife." Kelsey looked away, but Ruth tugged insistently on her hand. "I've been away for a long time, but not long enough that I can't recognize the kind of looks you two give each other. Tell me, Kel." She managed a wan smile. "I want all the juicy details, just like when we were in college, remember?"

In spite of the tense situation, Kelsey laughed softly. "I remember. You got such a thrill out of hearing about my dates, that sometimes I tried to make things up, just so you wouldn't be disappointed."

"You didn't." Weakly shaking her head, Ruth lightly slapped Kelsey's arm. "What about the time you went skinny-dipping with that French foreign exchange student?"

Shrugging, Kelsey slid Ruth a sheepish glance. "I, uh, accidentally fell into the pool—fully clothed, mind you—and Maurice was chivalrous enough to dive in and rescue me."

Ruth's tinkling laughter warmed Kelsey's heart. "You silly twit, why didn't you tell me that?"

"What, and sound not only boring but clumsy to boot? I had an image to maintain. Besides, you were so naive about men...." The words trailed away, the laughter died and both women averted their eyes. After a moment, Kelsey took Ruth's hand. "What happened with Joseph? You two seemed so right for each other—where did it all go wrong?"

Shrugging her dark brows, Ruth sighed. "I honestly don't know. At first, he was so protective and attentive that he kind of reminded me of Luke. I thought that because he worried about me so much, he must really love me. Gradually, I began to change my life to please him. I wouldn't go out during the day, because he'd be so upset if I wasn't home when he called. Eventually I realized that staying in the house had become an edict, and Joseph's subtle controls were becoming more blatant.''

''What do you mean?''

Obviously uncomfortable, Ruth fidgeted briefly, then stared out the dark window. ''The first couple of months, Joseph analyzed the telephone bills and questioned every call I'd made. He'd get angry, calling me greedy and selfish for spending so much money. After a couple of months, he put a lock on the telephone.''

''What?'' Kelsey couldn't believe that Ruth would have tolerated that, and said so.

''I felt guilty, don't you see?'' Ruth gestured helplessly, then allowed her hand to fall back into her lap. ''It was Joseph's money, and I believed that he had a right to dictate how it was spent. I loved him so much, and I wanted to make him happy. It's hard to explain, Kelsey. Sometimes I don't even understand myself.''

Oddly enough, Kelsey could relate to that and conveyed empathy by squeezing her friend's icy hand. After a moment, she faced Ruth boldly. ''When did Joseph start beating you?''

Ruth flinched and studied the wrinkled bedclothes. ''One night, after we'd been married about a year, Joseph came home in a horrible mood. We argued about something, then he ... hit me. It was the first time.''

''Why didn't you leave then?''

''Because he didn't mean to do it. He'd had a really bad day and I'd nagged at him about something.... Afterward, he was so sorry. He cried.'' Ruth swallowed hard. ''He didn't do it again for a long time.''

''But he *did* do it again, didn't he?''

''Yes.'' The whispered word was almost inaudible. ''When he found out about the baby.''

''Oh God.'' Kelsey stood, and unable to quell her mounting agitation, mumbled an explicit description as to what should be done with a certain part of the rotten cad's anatomy.

"It wasn't totally his fault," Ruth declared fervently. "We hadn't planned to have children yet. Joseph's business wasn't going well, and he had some gambling debts, so naturally he was upset."

Astounded by this defense of the indefensible, Kelsey could barely speak. "So he had a right to beat you? Ruth, you can't believe that. I mean, unless biology has taken a drastic turn in the past year, pregnancy requires a joint effort."

"Yes, but I was on birth-control pills, so we never expected that this would happen." Suddenly Ruth sobered and she closed her eyes, depleted by recounting her hellish ordeal. "Joseph accused me of deliberately getting pregnant. He wanted me to have an abortion. I refused, so he—" Her voice quivered and she covered her face, unable to continue.

She didn't have to. Kelsey got the message loud and clear, and it made her sick. "He decided to beat the baby out of you, didn't he?"

"I can't believe that's what he meant to do." Squeezing her eyelids shut, Ruth took a shuddering breath. "He apologized again and was so charming and sweet ... but I realized that Joseph might never be able to control his temper. I knew that I had to leave, for the baby's sake. Joseph simply couldn't handle life's disappointments and frustrations, because deep inside, he is just a child himself. I always knew that, but I also knew why. When Joseph was a little boy, there was a neighbor who did ... disgusting things to him. He never recovered from that experience. It warped him."

Exhaling slowly, Kelsey considered that. "So you believed that the love of a good woman could turn this poor, abused soul around?"

"Something like that," Ruth replied blandly. "But over the past few months, I realized that I couldn't handle his problems. Eventually he sensed that I was going to leave and became even more irrational and cruel. I was afraid of him, but he threatened that if I left, he'd find me and—" She sighed. "And he did."

Blinking back tears, Kelsey could only whisper. "You're safe now. Luke and I won't let him hurt you ever again."

Ruth nodded, but her expression held no conviction. Suddenly, she looked up and smiled weakly. "So, what about you and my brother?"

"Are you sure you want to hear about this now?"

Leaning forward as much as her swollen stomach would allow, Ruth deflected Kelsey's concern with forced cheer. "Absolutely. After all, it's going to be a long night and what else have we got to do? Except have a baby, of course."

Kelsey's heart swelled with admiration. "You're really something special."

Ruth's feeble smile faded. "No, I'm not. I need to think about something besides what's going on with my body. Please, Kel."

The poignant plea touched Kelsey, and she decided that as long as she avoided the subject of her own pregnancy, a bit of chatty girl-talk might relax the demoralized woman and keep her mind off their precarious situation, at least for a few minutes.

"Scoot over." Kelsey slid onto the bed and slipped an arm around Ruth's shoulders. "Do you remember the afternoon I drove to the shop planning to tell your tyrannical brother what I thought of him? Well, I never admitted this to you, but things turned out a little differently than I'd planned...."

Luke piled the torn sheets on the kitchen table and checked his inventory: scissors, sewing thread, blankets, makeshift bandages and/or diapers, the sterilized eyedropper from a bottle of nasal decongestant scrounged from the minuscule bathroom medicine cabinet, and a waffle-weave, thermal blanket that had been cut into three-foot, infant-sized squares. A cooking pot of water along with their meager stash of towels had already been taken to the bedroom that would soon serve as an improvised maternity ward.

So that was that. It was 2:00 a.m., nine hours after the initial chaos of their arrival at the cabin, and Luke couldn't think of anything else to do. Pulling out one of the turned-maple chairs, he sat heavily, slumping forward in utter dismay. During the evening, Ruth's contractions had regulated to five-minute intervals and now lasted a sixty grueling seconds apiece.

From the bedroom, the velocity of her moans increased and Luke heard Kelsey's soothing voice encouraging short, shallow breaths. A sharp scream stung Luke's ears, and he leaped to his feet, then paced the cramped kitchen, wondering if he should take a flashlight and check the creek again.

The exercise was futile. It would take hours, perhaps days, for the flood to subside. Luke knew that, but a walk in the cold night air helped him breathe and boosted his energy so he could deal with his scheduled shift with Ruth.

Grabbing the flashlight, Luke entered the living room and paused by the sofa, where Ridenour was slouched between the wooden arm and the end cushion. Joseph glared up with undisguised malevolence and on a hunch, Luke pulled the big blond forward and examined the bindings. His instinct paid off. The overly-thick rope had loosened considerably, so Luke set the flashlight beside the flickering oil lamp and remedied the problem.

Ridenour protested. "That's too tight."

"Then you should be thankful that it's not around your neck." Luke shoved him back against the cushion.

Joseph's good eye narrowed. "I'm thirsty."

Although Luke would have liked to brush off the statement without a twinge of guilt, even a dog deserved a drink. Returning to the kitchen, Luke tried to fill a plastic tumbler, but the faucet dribbled weakly, then stopped altogether. Great, Luke thought. What next?

He took the half-filled glass into the living room and Ridenour sat up, eyeing the liquid eagerly as Luke held the glass to the man's swollen mouth.

Joseph drained the glass, then requested more.

"There isn't anymore," Luke replied impatiently. "The faucet won't work."

Ridenour didn't seem particularly surprised by that news. "The tank's empty. There's a generator out back."

At first the cryptic message meant nothing, then Luke realized that since the remote cabin had no electricity, the water supply was apparently pumped by generator from an underground well into a pressurized tank, which supplied the cabin. That was good news, since a supply of fresh water would become even more crucial when the baby arrived.

Luke put down the tumbler and reached for the flashlight. "I'll check it out."

"It fires up like a lawn mower." Ridenour shifted uncomfortably, twisting to ease the awkward position. "As soon as the juice is flowing, you'll hear the pump go on."

Luke indicated that he understood, then left the cabin. Rounding the north corner, he noticed the cylindrical propane tank situated about thirty feet from the cabin, and absently wondered if it held enough gas to fuel the cookstove for a couple of days. A huge woodpile had been stacked against the cabin, and he also made a mental note to bring in an armload of cut logs, since the fireplace provided the cabin's heat.

Beside the woodpile, the rusty generator was situated beneath a makeshift lean-to. A steel pipe emerged from the generator's electrical plug, stretched up the slope behind the cabin, then disappeared into a small square vault that Luke recognized as the well-housing. Stiff 220-volt wire had been strung sloppily through the hollow rod and the excess wire was wadded into an untidy heap beside the generator. All in all, the cabin's utilities could handle an occasional weekend visit but were woefully inadequate for long-term use.

Still, the accommodations were better than a pup tent and a can of Sterno, so Luke fiddled with the starter, yanked the pull cord and the engine sputtered to life. When the water tank had been refilled, he shut off the generator, scooped an armful of logs and returned to the cabin.

As he entered the parlor, Joseph jerked as though startled by the intrusion. Luke dropped the firewood and started to re-check Ridenour's wrist bindings when Ruth cried out, emitting a long agonized scream that faded into a series of tormented sobs.

Shaken, Luke sat on the rocking chair and hoped that he wouldn't pass out.

"Is Ruthie having the kid?" Joseph asked bluntly.

Disgusted by the stupidity of such a question, Luke simply folded his arms and stared across the room.

"Maybe I should go in there. I mean, she *is* my wife."

Luke couldn't believe the guy's chutzpah. "If you get within ten feet of my sister, I'll rip your lungs out."

After a few silent moments, Ridenour tried another tactic. "Look, man, I can see that you're ticked off about all this, but you don't know the whole story."

Massaging his aching head, Luke stared at his own knees, tempted by a sudden urge to use the creep's liver as a doorstop.

Unable to take the hint, Ridenour apparently misread Luke's silence as interest and continued to defend his position. "How would you feel if your wife was out tooling around, God knows where? The streets are full of weirdos and drunks. Hell, she could have cracked up the car or been mugged or something. I mean, how can you take care of your wife if you don't know where in hell she is? You can understand that, can't you?"

Unfortunately, Luke *could* understand it but brushed off the twisted rationale as irrelevant to his personal authoritarian philosophy. After all, Ridenour was a deranged SOB who had abused and imprisoned his own wife, and was trying to justify those despicable actions as the normal, protective concern a man feels toward his loved ones. That kind of behavior had nothing to do with Luke. Nothing.

Ridenour readjusted his shoulders against the sofa cushions. "Okay, maybe I did get mad and go a little overboard, but I didn't know what else to do. I had to convince Ruthie that she couldn't just run off any time she wanted to. A wife belongs with her husband, doesn't she?"

Luke balled his fists. "Shut up or I'll break your freaking neck."

Joseph's face reddened. "This is none of your damned business, Sontag. Ruth is *my* wife—she belongs to *me*."

As Luke listened with growing horror, Ridenour's tirade continued, exposing the demented demagoguery and destructive possessiveness caused by insecurity and fear of loss. The concept was grossly distorted but sickeningly familiar. Suddenly, Luke recognized Ridenour's perverse, irrational fury as a mirror to his own soul, and he recoiled at the reflection.

Before Luke could ponder this disturbing revelation, Kelsey entered the room, raking her tousled hair and looking completely whipped.

Luke stood, instantly alarmed. "Is something wrong?"

She slid a wary glance at Joseph, then signaled for Luke to come into the hall. When he'd complied, Kelsey gestured toward the closed bedroom door and whispered, "Ruth's cervix is dilating, but I can't really tell whether she's halfway there, or nearly home. Would you check her, please?"

Certain that the shocking request was some kind of cruel joke, Luke tested his voice twice before the broken words finally emerged. "Me? What in hell do I know about it?"

"More than I do," Kelsey replied patiently. "If I recall this part of the process correctly, your vantage point was considerably better than mine."

"No way." Luke crossed his stiff hands as though warding off a vampire. "She's my sister, for crissake. I can't just violate her privacy like that."

Wearily rubbing her eyes, Kelsey was unimpressed by Luke's vehemence. "At this point, Ruth wouldn't be embarrassed if the eyewitness news team rolled in and set up a satellite feed on the foot of her bed. She's so worn out that she can't even keep her eyes open between pains."

When Luke continued to balk, Kelsey placed her hands on her hips, confronting him with a gutsy brashness that she hadn't displayed in quite a while. "Now you listen to me, Luke Sontag—I don't have the time or the patience to deal with your squeamish sensibilities. Ruth's contractions are brutal. She doesn't have much strength left. If, based on what you observed during Pattie's birth, you can give me some idea of how close she is to delivering, we might all have a clue as to how much longer this ordeal will last. Now, are you going to help me out here or not?"

In spite of himself, Luke smiled. He'd always liked the old spit-in-your-eye Kelsey, and it was good to see her again.

Although her request flat scared the pants off him, Luke reluctantly agreed to give it a try. Bringing his heels together, he took a deep breath, offered a lazy salute and sauntered down the hall.

When he'd disappeared into the bedroom, Kelsey emptied her lungs and sagged against the wall. This entire situation was too weird for words. She was frightened to death, not only for Ruth's safety but for that of the unborn child. Feeling inept and unworthy, the effort of concealing those doubts in front of her courageous patient had all but eaten Kelsey alive.

A low moan filtered from the room, then escalated into a series of guttural screams. After a small eternity, Ruth's cries subsided and the hall was silent.

The momentary calm, however, offered scant solace and Kelsey was worried sick. Ruth was depending on her and Luke, trusting her life and that of her child's to their very incapable hands. It was a disconcerting—no, a horrifying thought, and one which Kelsey was still mulling when Luke exited the bedroom, looking pale and grim.

"How is she?" Kelsey asked anxiously.

"I'm no expert . . ."

When he paused, Kelsey's impatience flared. "Forget the disclaimer. How far do you think she has to go?"

Luke rubbed the back of his neck. "Let's put it this way. The kid is bald."

Kelsey covered her solar plexus and blinked rapidly. "You can see the baby's head?"

"Only during a contraction. She doesn't have the urge to bear down yet, but it shouldn't be very long. I don't know for sure, but I think the cervical dilation is nearly complete." Luke jammed his hands in his pockets. "I guess it's a good thing you talked me into those Lamaze classes after all."

Kelsey smiled wistfully. "You were a great coach."

And a magnificent father, she added silently.

Luke's eyes warmed. "We made a good team, didn't we?"

If Kelsey's throat hadn't suddenly clogged with a rush of conflicting emotion, she would have agreed. Luke lifted her hand, pressing her palm against his and their fingers auto matically intertwined so tightly that an observer would be unable to note where one touch ended and the other began.

Their eyes met, each gazing deep into the reflected soul of the other, seeking that which neither could identify, but which each needed so desperately to find. The outside world, with its tragedy and pain, dissipated into a vague background blur, and for a brief but cherished moment hands touched, hearts melded, and two wounded souls were healed.

"K-K-Kel— Ahhh..."

The anguished cry shattered the spiritual silence and they sprang apart, momentarily stunned by the unexpected urgency of the scream. Kelsey moved first, nearly tripping in her haste to reach the bedroom.

Ruth was coiled forward like a gate spring, the bedclothes so tightly wound in her convulsing fists that the mattress had been partially exposed. Teeth bared, eyes crushed shut, Ruth's face was horribly contorted by the immense pressure enveloping her rigid body.

Instantly Kelsey dashed to her side, crooning encouragement while supporting Ruth's straining torso and wiping wet hair from the quivering woman's forehead.

Eventually Ruth fell back against the pillows, limp and too depleted to open her eyes. Panting, her pale lips slackened and with great effort, she lifted her eyelids far enough to peek out from beneath the fringe of dark lashes. "Something is happening."

At that moment Luke tripped into the bedroom carrying an armful of torn towels and other odd paraphernalia. He dumped the items on the dresser, then rounded the bed and supported his sister's slender shoulders. "Listen, Ruthie, do you remember what we talked about a few hours ago?"

"Umm." Ruth's eyelids fluttered shut again and she mumbled weakly, "Focus."

"That's right, honey. Focus on the sound of my voice okay?" Accepting her soft hiss as an affirmative reply, Luke continued to speak with a firm confidence that conflicted with the stark panic in his eyes. "Remember that story you used to love as a kid—the one about the little engine trying to climb a mountain? That's our focus—''

Ruth took several quick breaths and moaned, her hands thrashing in the tousled covers.

''Breathe, Ruthie, that's good.''

As the contraction strengthened, Kelsey issued a silent prayer and moved into position to assist with the birth. Her trembling hands testified to her terror, but she took courage from the sound of Luke's cool, confident voice.

''Focus now! *I think I can, I think I can* . . . breathe, breathe . . .''

With a strangled cry, Ruth's body catapulted forward and curled into a vibrating knot.

''*I think I can,* good, Ruthie, you're doing fine . . . breathe, breathe . . .''

Kelsey gasped as something resembling a soggy, elongated melon appeared. ''I can see him. Ruth, I can see your baby!'' The infant's wet head turned to reveal a scrunched little face, complete with pouting lips and quivering eyelids. ''Oh God,'' Kelsey breathed, awed by the tiny human miracle. ''His head is out, Ruthie. Push hard next time, as hard as you can.''

The only response was a quiet gurgle.

Alarmed, Kelsey looked up and saw Ruth lying limply against Luke's arm, her head lolling as if she were unconscious. A renewed surge of icy fear coursed through Kelsey's veins as she watched Luke try to regain Ruth's attention.

''Come on, honey, it's nearly over. I know you're tired, but your baby needs you.'' Tenderly lifting his sister's head, Luke used his free hand to rub her chalky cheeks. ''Remember how tired the little engine was, Ruthie? Remember how you cried, because he wanted to give up? But he didn't give up, honey, and neither will you. You're a Sontag. You're a fighter.''

But when the next contraction came, Ruth was too weak to push, or even to scream. She simply went rigid, shaking as though she'd been electrocuted, while the intense pressure rolled through her fragile body.

When the pain subsided, Luke looked anxiously at Kelsey, his eyes questioning whether the infant had further emerged. Swallowing her own disappointment and fear, Kelsey simply shook her head. Luke's expectant expression faded, and he returned his attention to Ruth, wiping her wet face and murmuring encouragement.

Kelsey dipped a washcloth in the cool water and carefully sponged mucus from the infant's gaping little mouth. The baby's head was moving, stretching slowly to the side as though trying to unbind itself, but he made no sound, not even a faint whoosh.

Of course, the baby couldn't emit any sound. His tiny lungs were compressed in the tight confines of the birth canal. Kelsey fought an overwhelming urge to grasp his little head and pull the child to safety and had enough command of her faculties to realize that any maneuver evoked by panic could be deadly.

Besides, there was no time to dwell on such ominous possibilities because another contraction had begun.

Luke's voice filled the room. "Focus, Ruthie . . . *I think I can, I think I can* . . . breathe, breathe . . ."

Somehow Ruth gathered the strength to bear down, and one tiny shoulder emerged.

Kelsey looked up sharply and caught Luke's eye. He nodded, then added a variation to the rhythmic mantra. "*I know I can, I know I can*. . . You're at the crest, Ruthie, just one more push. The mountaintop is right in front of you. Picture the little engine—he's almost there, and so are you."

With the next contraction, Ruth's head fell back and she emitted a strangled cry as the infant squirted into Kelsey's waiting hands. Tears blurred Kelsey's vision, but she could feel the slippery baby squirming in her grasp.

Instantly Luke was by Kelsey's side, and she was amazed when he expertly tied the umbilical, then used the scissors to cut the pulsing cord.

The infant's arms jerked, expressing his instinctive fear of falling, and his little eyelids stretched open to reveal two perfect, gray-blue irises.

Cursing her trembling fingers, Kelsey struggled to wash he baby's face, paying careful attention to his mouth and he tiny nostrils still plugged with uterine fluid.

"Here, try this." Luke dropped a slender glass tube opped with a rubber bulb into Kelsey's palm. "They used omething like this on Pattie."

Grateful for Luke's foresight, Kelsey used the eyedropper to gently extract the fluid first from the infant's mouth, hen from each little nostril. Afterward, Luke took a towel nd briskly rubbed the baby's discolored torso while Kelsey ought intrusive memories of her own daughter's birth.

And then it happened. The baby sucked a gulp of cleansing oxygen, then emptied his lungs with a forceful wail. Kelsey bit back tears of joy as she gently wrapped the qualling child in the trimmed blanket.

Alternately laughing and crying, Ruth accepted the bundled baby. Then she kissed the infant's soft head and welomed her son into the world.

Chapter 12

After the placenta had been delivered, Ruth and her new born infant were temporarily moved to the bedside chair while Kelsey stripped the wet linens from the saturated mattress.

Luke gathered the soiled bedclothes. "I'll take these out side."

"There's a vinyl cloth on the kitchen table," Kelsey said. "Would you mind bringing it back with you? Otherwise, the clean sheets will be soaked as soon as I put them on."

Nodding brusquely, Luke left the room and Kelsey turned her attention to the new mother. "How are you feeling?"

Seeming loath to tear her gaze from her baby's sleeping face, Ruth managed to meet Kelsey's eyes long enough to be polite. "A little tired, but wonderful."

The poignant sight of Ruth and her child was difficult for Kelsey, and she looked away, feigning interest in unfolding the fresh linens. "You should try to sleep. The sun won't be up for a while, and your son looks like he could use a bit of shut-eye, too."

"Umm." Ruth carefully unwrapped one corner of the blanket, extracted a tiny hand and, for the fifth time, care

fully opened the teensy fist and touched each little finger.
"Kel?"

"Yes?"

"How are we going to get out of here?"

Shaking out a pillowcase, Kelsey managed a casual response. "As soon as the creek goes down a bit, we'll take
Joseph's car across the bridge. The road is blocked about a
half mile down, but Luke's pickup is parked on the other
side, so we'll just sashay around the rocks, hop in the truck
and buzz to the nearest hospital."

"Hospital?"

"Just a precaution," Kelsey added quickly. "I'd feel
better if you and the baby had a checkup before we start the
long drive home. . . ." Kelsey's voice trailed off as Luke entered the room. He quietly lifted the revolver from the
nightstand, then left without speaking.

Kelsey dropped the pillow she'd been sheathing, relieved
that Ruth had been too enthralled with her baby to notice
Luke's ominous action. "I'll be back in a minute, okay?"

Still gazing at her infant's face, Ruth replied with a nondescript hum and Kelsey instantly left the room.

She found Luke at the parlor window, clutching the revolver while he peered out at the dark forest. His grim expression was chilling, and Kelsey was instantly alarmed.
"What's going on?"

Without breaking his gaze, Luke nodded sharply toward
the sofa.

Kelsey followed the gesture, but saw nothing. "I don't—
Oh, God."

She saw nothing because nothing was there. Joseph was
gone.

The moonless night settled like puddled ink and even with
the .38 nested in his palm, Luke felt like a sitting duck.
Ridenour was out there somewhere, waiting and watching,
but unless the rat had night goggles, Luke's flashlight offered a minuscule advantage. Of course, it also offered a
glaring beacon to his own location, but that was a chance he
had to take.

Since the utensil drawer had been left open, Joseph was no doubt armed with an assortment of kitchen knives. It was up to Luke to make certain that his adversary acquired no further weapons.

Sloughing through the mud bog surrounding the parked sedan, Luke noted that two of the doors were yawning open and assumed that Ridenour had probably planned on using the vehicle to escape. The stupid fool. There was no way short of levitation to get a vehicle out of this swamp, but Luke was still grateful that he'd had the foresight to snag the car keys because Ridenour was apparently untutored in the fine art of hot-wiring. Those preppie schools *did* have their limitations.

Shining the flashlight beam into the sedan's interior, Luke saw that the boots and jacket were missing, then circled the vehicle and noticed that the trunk lid was ajar. The jack compartment had been opened and the heavy tire iron was missing.

Damn. Luke could have kicked himself halfway to Georgia for not realizing that this particular model had a trunk latch under the dash. He slammed the compartment shut and cursed himself six ways from Sunday. Now Ridenour had added a nifty skull-cracker to his arsenal. Even worse, Luke didn't have a clue as to what other formidable weapons might have been in the trunk, but the possibilities were unnerving.

It wasn't like Luke to be this sloppy. Without excusing the carelessness, he focused on his mission and was determined not to repeat his stupidity.

As he moved up the embankment, Luke swept the flashlight beam through the surrounding forest at irregular intervals, searching for anything that seemed out of place. His ears were attuned to the slightest sound whispering through the post-storm silence. When a rustling noise caught his attention, he simultaneously aimed both the flashlight and the gun but saw nothing but a mulch of wet leaves and broken twigs. In spite of the predawn chill, Luke started to sweat. He didn't like leaving the women alone.

As soon as he reached the shed, he picked the padlock and went inside, relieved to note that nothing seemed to be missing. Working quickly, Luke gathered up the hefty coil of rope and the wire cutters, a wood saw and a small ax, anything that they could use to escape—or that Ridenour could use as a weapon—then he re-locked the shed and returned to the cabin.

Silently entering through the kitchen, a sweet humming greeted Luke and a peculiar tingle numbed his spine. The tune was hauntingly familiar and his heart suddenly ached as though it had been squeezed. He froze, listening. The quiet humming stopped, and he felt oddly bereft.

Moving quietly, Luke unloaded the shed items on the kitchen table, then stepped to the doorway. What he saw raised a lump the size of Wyoming in his throat.

Kelsey sat in the living-room chair with Ruth's baby on her lap, moving her knees sideways in a slow rocking motion as she caressed the infant with exquisite tenderness. Eyes glowing, Kelsey's beautiful face seemed illuminated from within, and she gazed at the sleeping child with an expression of ethereal love.

The touching sight jarred Luke to his toes, and he barely stepped back into the kitchen before his knees buckled. Leaning heavily against the wall, he squeezed his eyes shut and fought the emotional surge. Blood pounded through his veins, rushing to his brain with the power of a storm-whipped surf.

Then Kelsey started to sing softly. The lilting melody eased the crashing roar in Luke's skull and the sweet lyrics enveloped his soul.

"Above the clouds where angels cling
And fairies glide on golden wing,
Love dwells amidst eternal spring,
Bluebells chime, and butterflies sing."

It was the haunting melody of his dreams, and Luke shook uncontrollably as resurgent memories overwhelmed suppressed grief. He covered his ears, unable to endure the sound of Kelsey's sweet voice, crooning the poignant cradlesong that she had once sung to their beloved baby daughter.

"So come with me and we will fly
To a happy place up in the sky
Where clouds of magic butterflies
Sing baby's bedtime lullaby."

Choking on repressed sorrow, Luke was powerless to halt the encroaching flood of memories. He remembered the hopeless days and endless nights following Pattie's death. He remembered how, in her interminable grief, Kelsey had reached out to him and he had turned away, so that his stoic countenance would not be shattered by her bereaved touch.

And he remembered the pain, the internalized anguish of self-recrimination, drowned out by a mutual barrage of castigation and blame.

The final breakup of their marriage hadn't been a sudden, violent thing. It had been insidious, a creeping plague of silence and unshared sorrow, a wordless emotional retreat that Luke had been helpless to reverse. Eventually, he'd simply moved the last of his things back to the shabby trailer behind his auto shop, thereby rejecting that which he couldn't control.

Now, with Kelsey's delicate voice caressing his ears, Luke reexamined those hideous days, and all that had come before, and was chagrined to realize how closely his behavior had paralleled that of his controlling, emotionally isolated father. Kelsey had tried to expose this fatal flaw, but Luke had been too arrogant to listen.

All of Kelsey's accusations had been true. The independence that Luke had purported to want for his sister he had denied to his own wife; then he'd abandoned Kelsey, as his own father had abandoned his mother. Luke had become that which he most despised.

The revelation was shattering.

Through the emotional miasma of the past year, Luke had stubbornly refused to acknowledge the vulnerability of his sorrow. As the bittersweet lullaby peeled the protective shroud from his heart, the masculine mystique cracked like a broken promise and Luke was unable to stem the choking tide of grief. Once, he had cried in celebration of his daughter's birth.

Now Luke bowed his head, and wept to mourn her loss.

"Luke?" Kelsey stepped into the darkened kitchen and laid a hand on his shoulder. "Are you all right?"

"Wha—?" Bolting upright, his eyes darted warily around the room, then he rubbed his face.

Kelsey wanted to reach out and stroke the curling mass of dark hair from his creased brow. Instead, she pulled out a chair and sat beside him. "I didn't mean to wake you, but you went to check the shed half an hour ago, and I didn't hear you come back. Is everything all right?"

"Yeah." Shuddering, Luke covered his eyes and took a deep breath. "What time is it?"

"Four-thirty. It should be daylight in a couple of hours." Chewing her lower lip, Kelsey stared out the small mullioned window at the hated darkness. "Did you see any sign of Joseph?"

Luke rolled his neck, wincing as though the effort was painful. "No, but he's out there."

That was not the news Kelsey was hoping for. "I thought he might have hiked down to the lake. Ruth told me that Joseph is an accomplished rock climber. The south face of the mountain is fairly steep, but she believes he might be able to make it."

Not seeming impressed by that information, Luke stood and stretched. "How is Ruth?"

"She's sleeping, and don't change the subject."

Swiveling around, Kelsey watched Luke draw a glass of water and take a long drink. Still holding the tumbler, he gazed blankly out the window. "I guess Ridenour could have walked out."

"But you don't think so, do you?"

Turning, Luke propped one hip against the counter. "No."

Swallowing a knot of fear, Kelsey folded her hands primly in her lap. "Why not?"

"Because he has a debt to settle."

"With Ruth?"

"With all of us." Luke drained the glass, then set it in the sink. "The way Ridenour sees it, we've stolen something that belongs to him. His ego isn't about to let us get away with that.''

"Do you mean that he's actually...*stalking* us?" She couldn't suppress an annoying squeak of panic. "What can we do?"

Luke shrugged. "Until he makes a move, there's not much we *can* do."

"Well, we can't just sit here like trapped prey. Ruth is barely able to stand without help and the baby—" Without finishing the sentence, Kelsey quickly stood and paced the small kitchen. "There must be some way to protect them from that lunatic."

Luke's jaw twitched and his eyes reflected fearsome determination. "I'll take care of Ridenour."

At that moment, Kelsey had no doubt in her mind that if given half a chance, Luke would do just that. She shivered, rubbed her cold arms, then turned to leave. An odd glow in the distance caught her attention."

"What's that?" she asked, pointing out the window.

Following her gesture, Luke looked over her shoulder. "What's what?"

"That pink light." Standing on tiptoe, she strained for a better look, but the source of the illumination was behind the cabin, beyond her view.

Luke took Kelsey's shoulders and moved her aside. He looked at the peculiar reddish aurora for a moment, then slammed his fist on the counter and swore violently.

As he headed toward the back door, Kelsey grabbed his arm. "What is it, Luke?"

He whipped the revolver from his waistband and slapped the weapon in Kelsey's palm. "Lock the door behind me. Take Ruth and the baby into the hallway, then get down on the floor."

Before Kelsey could question him, Luke flung the door open and the kitchen was bathed by the eerie glow. Kelsey stared out, stunned by the bizarre sight. About thirty feet from the cabin, several slender bolts of spitting color sizzled beneath what appeared to be a large metal cylinder. Resembling fireworks, the sparking rods were perversely beautiful, although she was confused and vaguely perturbed by the peculiar phenomenon.

Luke roughly shook her shoulder and snapped, "Hurry!" Crouching, he zigzagged toward the metal cylinder as though crossing an enemy battlefield.

Suddenly, Kelsey realized that the metal cylinder was a propane tank, and the sparkling rods weren't fireworks at all; they were road flares, and if the searing heat from those flares ignited the propane gas, the entire cabin could be leveled by the ensuing blast.

The metallic taste of fear flooded her mouth, and she slammed the kitchen door, fighting the encroaching nausea. It was her duty to protect Ruth, but Kelsey was torn by conflict. Her husband was out there, unarmed. Joseph could be lurking in the dark, having lured Kelsey into a fatal trap.

The paralysis of indecision was broken by a terrified scream, followed by the sharp sound of shattering glass.

Ruth.

Adrenaline spurted through Kelsey's veins and, still grasping the revolver, she sprinted into the parlor. There was another crash and another bloodcurdling scream. Dashing toward the hallway she collided with the wall, spun to the left, then stumbled forward to the bedroom door and was horrified by what she saw.

With his grotesquely swollen face contorted in rage, Joseph was outside the bedroom window, smashing away the glass with a long metal bar. Ruth was on the bed, screaming and holding her hand up as a shield against the rain of jagged shards.

When Joseph saw Kelsey, he dropped the bar and lunged through the empty window frame clutching a serrated steak knife in his raised fist. He snarled a venomous threat to slice out his wife's vital organs, then wildly slashed air a few inches above Ruth's cowering body.

Curled protectively around her infant, Ruth tried to roll to safety, but Joseph managed to grab the back of her gown and drag her toward the window.

Kelsey's knees buckled so she leaned against the door frame for support. Gripping the revolver with both hands, she leveled the weapon and spoke in a voice so deadly that she even surprised herself. "Let her go or i il shoot."

Startled, Joseph paused, just for a moment, then regarded Kelsey with a menacing grin. Quickly grabbing a clump of his wife's dark hair, he yanked Ruth's head back and laid the serrated blade on her throat.

Somehow Kelsey managed to maintain both eye contact and a determined tone. "Don't make me kill you, Joseph."

With an unpleasant laugh, Joseph demonstrated his lack of concern by twisting Ruth's head and pressing the knife tip against her throat. "Would you enjoy watching her bleed?"

The baby started to fuss and Joseph stared disdainfully at the infant.

Kelsey's mouth was dry and she suppressed the urge to moisten her lips, knowing that Joseph would recognize the nervous gesture. In spite of the weapon she held, Kelsey realized that he didn't consider her as a legitimate threat. Since Ruth's safety depended on persuading him otherwise, Kelsey raised the revolver and pumped a single bullet into the wall above the window. The explosive percussion vibrated in the room.

Ducking instinctively, Joseph swore sharply, then twisted and stared up to inspect the punctured panel. With his fingers still knotted in Ruth's matted curls, the startled man regarded Kelsey with increased caution.

Taking advantage of his uncertainty, Kelsey cocked the weapon with false confidence. "I'm an excellent shot," she lied. "The next bullet will ruin your whole day."

Joseph hesitated, then eased the blade from his wife's throat and released her hair. Ruth immediately hugged the wailing infant to her breast, scooted awkwardly across the mattress, then dropped to her knees beside the bed and was hidden from her husband's psychopathic gaze.

Suppressing a premature sigh of relief, Kelsey maintained the tenuous bluff, aiming the revolver as though she'd done so all her life. Joseph's good eye was riveted on the gun barrel as he levered his torso back through the broken window.

Once outside, the thwarted man glared at Kelsey with a black fury that chilled her to the bone and hissed a vile threat about what happened to women like her. Before the disgusting words had left his puffy blue mouth, Joseph emitted a grunt of pain and lurched sideways. A blurred figure passed the window, followed by the distinctive sounds of struggle.

Kelsey quickly knelt beside Ruth. "Are you hurt?"

The dazed woman shook her head and commenced an anxious examination of the baby who was now screaming with lusty indignation.

Tugging on Ruth's arm, Kelsey urged her up. "Go into the hall. It's safer there."

Something crashed into the cabin wall and a low moan filtered from outside. Ruth paused at the doorway, fearfully glancing toward the open window. "What about Joseph?"

"Luke's taking care of him," Kelsey replied tightly, hoping that the optimistic statement was accurate.

When Ruth and the baby were safely out of the room, Kelsey circled the bed, ignoring the crunch of broken glass beneath her feet and she leaned across the mattress. "Luke?" She saw nothing, no pink glow, no tussling bodies—just the quiet blackness of the forest. *"Luke!"*

Then she heard the whistling of air sucked through clamped teeth. Luke staggered to the window and hunched over the frame. "Ruth?"

Kelsey reached through the opening and touched his slumped shoulder. "She's fine and so is the baby. Where's Joseph?"

Luke's mouth thinned. "He got away."

Suppressing her disappointment, Kelsey brushed a dark strand of dripping hair from Luke's forehead. "Don't look so grim. Since I haven't heard a big boom, the propane tank has obviously not exploded. You've saved our lives—again."

With a snort, Luke flicked away her gratitude with a limp wave. "All I did was douse the flares in mud. Besides, the whole damned thing was nothing but a ploy to get me out of the cabin, and it worked." He cocked his head, eyeing Kelsey as though seeing her for the first time. "I guess Ridenour didn't figure that a mere woman would give him a problem."

Kelsey shrugged, too shaken to take credit for their narrow victory, yet unwilling to let Luke know how truly terrified she had been. "A misconception he regrets, I imagine."

An amused smile played one corner of Luke's mouth, then faded as he sharply scanned the forest perimeter. "Keep everyone in the living room. It's the most defensible area of the cabin."

As Luke moved away, Kelsey was instantly alarmed, "Where are you going?"

"To pull some plywood off the generator lean-to and board up this window."

"Do you think that will keep him out?"

"No, but it will slow him down and eliminate the advantage of surprise. If he decides on another assault, he'll probably come through the kitchen or living room."

Another assault. Kelsey felt ill, as the truth of their deadly situation hit home. This was the stuff-and-nonsense of adventure movies; never in her wildest imagination had Kelsey believed that such things actually happened to real people.

Yet it *was* happening. They were unwilling combatants in an escalating war zone, mapping out battle strategies against an enemy's lethal intent. The siege had just begun.

Dawn cast a gray pall over the mountain. Luke stretched painfully, then returned his attention to the jumble of cut wire cluttering the kitchen table.

Ruth appeared in the doorway. "May I come in?"

Standing quickly, Luke set the rusted wire cutters aside and pulled out a chair. "You should be resting."

Taking the chair he offered, Ruth lowered herself slowly. "Still telling me what to do, big brother?"

Feeling a flush crawl up his neck, Luke reseated himself and managed a sheepish smile. "I guess I deserved that."

She touched his hand. "What you deserve is a commendation for valor, but all I can give is my gratitude."

Luke turned away, feeling that he deserved neither. There was so much he wanted to tell his sister, yet the words massed into an immutable lump of silence.

After a moment, Ruth flinched and shifted painfully then picked up one of several hastily scratched drawings scattered across the table. "What are you working on?"

"An E-ticket ride."

Ruth didn't smile, and Luke knew that she hadn't been misled by his casual reply. She somberly studied the sketches. "What are these?"

"Plans for the harness." He pointed to the wire sculpture propped against a wall by the table.

Turning in her chair, Ruth winced slightly, then examined the object without getting up. "It looks like a floppy, oversized tennis racket. What on earth are you going to do with it?"

Leaning back in the chair, Luke considered whether he should explain his idea in advance, or wait until the moment had arrived, when any protest would be silenced by shock.

Luke regarded the wire contraption warily. The design seemed sound enough on paper, but he was a bit nervous about implementing the bold plan. It would be dangerous, he knew, but remaining in the cabin posed a more immediate risk.

Ruth propped her elbows on the table. "I know that expression, Luke. I saw it every time I asked about something that you considered to be none of my female business."

Luke was stung that his sister had misinterpreted his protective silence. "I never said that."

"You didn't have to. I'm not a child, Luke."

"I know that."

"Do you?"

"Yeah." Against his better judgment, he took a blank sheet of paper and sketched a rough outline of the nearby terrain. "Okay, here we go. This square represents the cabin, and these parallel lines are the creek. We have to string the rope here, where the creek narrows—" he pointed to a spot about twenty feet from the bridge "—then hook up the safety harness and pull ourselves across."

Ruth's already pale complexion faded to the color of library paste. "I don't think I'm strong enough to do that."

"That's why I've created your own private carriage for the trip." Luke stood and helped Ruth out of her chair, then lifted the harness, pointing to the four-foot wire handle that had been looped at the tip and secured with a series of corkscrew twists. "The guide rope will be threaded through this eyelet so the harness can slide freely from one side of the creek to the other."

A two-foot wire hoop was attached halfway down the handle, and Ruth touched it gingerly. "What does this do?"

"It slips over your head and under your arms, like this."

Ruth reluctantly allowed him to demonstrate. When the hoop encircled her chest, she looked over her shoulder and peered down at the flat round piece dangling against her backside. "Why has that one got all those criss-crossed wires woven through it, and why is a belt hanging in the middle of it?"

"That's the harness seat, and the belt will be pulled up between your knees and buckled to the top hoop, here." Luke didn't complete the process, since the harness was designed to be suspended in midair. His poor sister didn't need to be folded in half in order to understand the essence of the prototype's function.

Judging by Ruth's pained expression, she understood perfectly and wasn't particularly pleased by the prospect. "Sort of like a grown-up car seat."

"Actually, since we'll be crossing from low side to high side, the concept is based on the principle of a working ski lift."

Raising her arms, she allowed Luke to lift the hoop carefully over her head, then returned to her chair and seated herself with great care. "Well, at least you didn't make one of those upside T-things, where the skier holds on to the pole and dangles his legs over two little brackets. My bottom isn't up to that."

Luke winced at the thought of how painful that would be for a woman a few hours after childbirth. Besides, Ruth wouldn't have enough strength to hang on while swinging over the creek, and Kelsey would need her hands free to hold the infant, so he'd had no choice but to use a harness system.

Ruth drummed the tabletop with her finger. "Why can't we stay here?"

"You know why."

"But Joseph is just one man, and he's injured. Surely the three of us can hold him off until the creek goes down."

"Maybe, but there's no food left and no gasoline to run the generator, so the water will only last another day. Besides, the bridge is history and we could die waiting for someone to stumble across this isolated place."

Ruth was white as a sheet and obviously scared to death, so Luke attempted to soothe her fears with feigned bravado. "There's nothing to worry about, Ruthie. We'll have a towline attached to the harness, and I'll pull you up from the other side. Besides, this 220-volt wire is almost as strong as steel cable. It'll be a piece of cake."

With a disgruntled sigh, Ruth leveled a reproachful gaze at Luke, and he realized that instead of easing her fears, he'd been belittling her intelligence. The crossing would be hazardous and they both knew it.

"There are risks," he admitted finally. "But we don't have any other choice."

To his surprise, Ruth acknowledged that without flinching. "I know, but I'm worried about you."

"Me?"

"How do you plan to get the rope to the other side?"

Luke puffed his cheeks, then exhaled slowly. "About a half mile downstream, there's a tree listing over a narrow part of the creek. I should be able to lasso one of the branches and swing across."

Deepening stress lines bracketed Ruth's mouth. She started to speak, but the words evaporated into a regretful sigh and she absently scratched at a small burn hole on the laminated tabletop.

Interpreting Ruth's troubled expression as fear, Luke wanted desperately to reassure her but didn't quite know how. He would give his life to protect his sister and her child but realized that given the gravity of their situation, even that ultimate sacrifice might be futile.

In the past, he would have tried to buoy Ruth's spirits with false humor. Now, Luke finally realized that the old methods had insulted her intelligence. It was difficult for him to believe that the gawky, timid girl he had raised had evolved into this beautiful and courageous young woman. Even as his heart swelled with pride, it ached with regret. He wanted to hold his sister and blurt out his feelings, but personal revelation still didn't come easily to a man for whom emotional isolation had always been a shield.

Luke rearranged his body in the stiff wooden chair. "Is Kelsey asleep?"

Lifting one neat eyebrow, Ruth indicated that she'd noted a revealing huskiness in his tone. "Yes, she and Eric are both dozing peacefully."

"Eric?"

Maternal pride illuminated Ruth's dusty blue eyes. "Eric Michael Ridenour. Has a nice ring to it, don't you think?"

"Eric Michael, huh." Luke considered it. "Yeah. I like it, but I don't suppose you could drop that last part."

Ruth's eyes clouded. Luke could have kicked himself for his insensitivity. Since he couldn't take back the stupid remark, he said nothing.

Ruth broke the thick silence. "When I realized that I was going into labor, I was certain that my baby and I would both die. You and Kelsey saved our lives."

Luke shifted uncomfortably. "You would have done fine without us. Babies have a way of being born whether the rest of us are ready or not."

Studying him with perceptive intensity, Ruth absently rubbed her fingertip against her lower lip. "I've been thinking about what happened during the delivery. You both seemed so—I don't know—experienced, but you were the one that surprised me most. The way you tied the umbilical and massaged my stomach...it was almost as though you'd delivered a dozen babies by candlelight."

"God forbid," he mumbled.

"But where did you learn those techniques?" Ruth insisted. "Have you ever delivered a baby before?"

The mere thought made Luke shudder. "Hell, no. I was just a glorified cheerleader when Pattie was born, and that role suits me fine."

Ruth nodded as though she understood perfectly. "Who's Pattie?"

A noise outside caught Luke's attention. "Our daughter," he answered absently. After realizing that the sound was a trilling bird, he turned back toward Ruth.

Her lips fell apart. "You and Kelsey . . . have a baby?"

Feeling suddenly uncomfortable with the conversational direction, Luke frowned. "I thought Kelsey filled you in about all this."

Ruth slowly shook her head. "She told me that you'd been married and that it hadn't worked out. There was no mention of a child."

Considering the fact that Kelsey would never have married a man like him had it not been for the pregnancy, Luke was momentarily confused by the glaring omission. Suddenly a thought struck him. "Kelsey had a rough time when Pattie was born. Since you were getting ready to have your own kid, she probably just didn't want to upset you."

"But that still doesn't make any sense. I mean, she could have told me the basics without getting into gory details." Suddenly excited, Ruth leaned forward. "I can't believe that I have a niece. Tell me all about her. How old is she? Who does she look like? This is wonderful. Eric has a cousin! They can grow up together and— What's wrong? You look sick."

Sucking his lips between his teeth, Luke waited until he could speak without shaking. "Our baby . . . didn't make it."

Ruth's smile evaporated and she seemed bewildered by the cryptic statement. After a stunned moment, her eyes filled with horror.

Unable to endure his sister's pity, Luke looked away. "Maybe I should start from the beginning."

By the time Luke had finished his story, he was emotionally drained, and Ruth stared across the room like a colorless zombie. Neither spoke for several minutes, then Ruth closed her eyes and bowed her head.

When she looked up, her eyes were shining with unshed tears. "It must be torture for you both, seeing my son and remembering your own beautiful child. You have suffered so much for me, endured such sacrifice, and after everything I've done to you, Luke, I honestly don't understand why you bothered, but—" Her voice broke and tears beaded her lower lashes. Wiping her eyes, she sniffed and raised her trembling chin. "I'm just so very grateful."

"What *you* have done to *me?* Do you mean when you married Ridenour?"

"No, before that, when I was a little girl."

Now Luke was totally baffled. "What in the devil are you talking about?"

Staring into her lap, Ruth twisted a swatch of her cotton robe into a tight spear. "Even though I was spoiled and ungrateful, you always treated me well. I was such a burden to you—and apparently still am—yet you never complained. You gave up everything to take care of me, and I rewarded you by being spiteful and defiant. The worst part is that I don't even know why. Perhaps, in my own misbegotten manner, I was trying to get out of your way, hoping that after having lost so much because of me, you could recover at least some of your life."

Luke could barely speak. "Dear God, Ruthie, you could never be a burden to me. You are my *sister.* I have—" He turned away so she wouldn't see the humiliating redness in his eyes, and his voice faded to a whisper. "I have always loved you."

Ruth's head snapped up and she stared at him in open-mouthed astonishment. Finally, she stammered, "You've never told me that before."

Luke discreetly wiped a knuckle beneath his lashes. "You knew how I felt."

"I knew you cared about my welfare, but I also knew that you had this enormous sense of responsibility." Crying openly now, Ruth touched her brother's arm. "You never told me anything else. I never knew—"

A deep sob shattered Ruth's final words and she fell into Luke's waiting arms. As he held his weeping sister, comforting her as he'd always done, Luke's thoughts were in complete disarray. It was true, he realized, that he'd never specifically told Ruth that he loved her, but it had never occurred to him that she hadn't known. Every day, he'd shown her how much he cared, by worrying about her, by providing for her, by supporting her as a person.

But Luke had also been harsh and unyielding, with others and with himself. Because he'd equated compassion with weakness, his sister had been afraid to turn to him in times of need, and his wife had been left to drift in her own sorrow.

Kelsey. Luke's scalp prickled ominously. As with Ruth, he'd never actually spoken the words, but surely she must have known deeply he'd loved her. Was it possible that Kelsey, too, had misunderstood his feelings?

Luke dismissed that troubling concept. She had to know. He'd *married* her, for crissake. Sure, she'd been pregnant, but he certainly could have taken financial responsibility for the child without a lifetime commitment. Surely Kelsey understood that.

Luke's mind reeled as black-and-white issues boggled into muddy shades of gray. Kelsey must have known that he loved her—but what if she hadn't? The implications were staggering.

Chapter 13

Bending into a chilly gust, Kelsey hefted the roll of knotted bed sheets that would be used as a towline and headed toward the creek. Behind her, an engine roared to life. The noise was startling, although she knew that Luke was moving Ridenour's car down to the crossing so that the rear bumper could be used as one tie-off point for the thick guide rope. At least, that was Luke's plan.

Luke's plan. Kelsey shuddered at the thought of the harrowing strategy. After Luke's matter-of-fact briefing, her first reaction had been horror, followed by repulsion and, finally, resignation. There seemed no other option. The rain had stopped nearly twelve hours ago, yet the creek had subsided only a couple of inches, barely enough to observe that the brutal current had washed several bridge piers off their foundations. Even after the water receded to normal levels, the rickety structure would be impassable.

That hazard, however, paled in comparison to the imminent threat of being stalked by a homicidal psychopath. Although there had been no further assaults on the cabin, neither Kelsey nor Luke believed that Joseph had withdrawn completely. He was out there somewhere, waiting for an opportunity. Kelsey could feel his sinister presence.

Joseph wasn't a fool. He probably hadn't been concerned about Ruth lodging a police complaint, since domestic disputes have a disgustingly low priority with law enforcement agencies. Besides, between the word of an upstanding, well-pedigreed businessman and an ex-barrio housewife, the deck had definitely been stacked in his favor.

When Luke and Kelsey had shown up, the odds had taken a dramatic turn, and by now Joseph had apparently concluded that eliminating witnesses was the only way to avoid criminal prosecution.

The droning car engine grew closer and Kelsey automatically stepped aside. As Luke backed the vehicle slowly down the spongy driveway, one tire flung a sloppy stream of mud over her already-ruined slacks and crusted, once-white sneakers. Kelsey ignored the newest coating of filth. The clothes she'd worn for the past two days felt like they had fused to her skin. If by some miracle they survived this ordeal, she planned to burn the grungy garments, then draw a hot bath and soak until her bones melted.

Dismissing the delicious image, Kelsey swept the surrounding forest with a wary gaze, then continued down the driveway. A few feet from the parked sedan, the empty duffel—which had contained nothing but men's socks and underwear—was draped on a rock, along with two neatly folded blanket squares. Ruth slumped against a nearby tree, holding the bundled infant against her shoulder. She shivered. Along with the maternity slacks she'd been wearing when kidnapped, she wore one of her brother's plaid shirts, courtesy of the laundry stash, but the long-sleeved flannel was scant protection against the chill wind.

Luke positioned the blue sedan a safe distance from the flooded creek bed, then pulled the emergency brake and exited the car. He pulled the wire harness from the vehicle, then reached inside for the fat coil of rope.

Kelsey extended the roll of knotted fabric. "What shall I do with this?"

Luke slipped the coil over his head and left shoulder, so that the rope wound diagonally around his body like a soldier's cartridge belt. "Double-tie one end where the upper hoop is attached to the harness handle. Are you sure it's long enough?''

"It's a little over sixty feet," Kelsey said, kneeling beside the harness. Since Luke had figured the creek to be about fifty feet across, the towline had to span that distance and allow enough slack for a firm grip on the other side. However, the length of strips of knotted yardage seemed flimsy in comparison with the sturdy hemp rope, and Kelsey said so.

Luke extracted the hatchet from the car, and tucked the handle though one of his belt loops. "The towline doesn't need as much tensile strength as the guide rope. Besides, there's barely enough of the heavy stuff to stretch a line across the creek, and I'm still not sure we won't come up short when we try to tie it off."

Reaching behind his back, Luke pulled the revolver from his waistband and, after checking the load with a quick spin of the cylinder, he handed the weapon to Kelsey. She hesitated only a moment, then accepted the gun and pretended that the feel of cold metal didn't make her feel as if she'd just chewed tinfoil.

Ruth gazed warily across the expansive clearing to where the concealing forest swallowed the cabin a hundred yards away. "Do you think Joseph's watching us?"

"Let him watch," Luke growled. "Once Ridenour sets foot into the clearing, he becomes a can't-miss target. He underestimated Kelsey once—I don't think the jerk is brainless enough to do it again."

Shifting the restless infant, Ruth chewed her lip nervously, then verbalized the painful thought that had silently nagged at Kelsey. "If he *is* out there, he knows that Kelsey has the gun, so he also realizes that you aren't armed, Luke. What if he follows you downstream?"

Luke's smile wasn't particularly pleasant. "I hope he does."

Instantly riled by the he-man display, Kelsey whirled and confronted him angrily. "That would be just swell, wouldn't it? You two gorillas could cut each other's throat, then gurgle your way to macho heaven and leave us at the mercy of this godforsaken wilderness. That kind of masculine Rambo complex is what got us into this mess in the first place."

The gender-thumping tirade wasn't fair and Kelsey knew it, but was too stressed out for rational thought. Luke would be a half mile down stream performing a Tarzan power play where the slightest mistake would result in a horrible death, while Kelsey waited helplessly. That was bad enough; realizing that a lunatic might try to ensure Luke's fate was the final blow for Kelsey's strained composure.

Rising to her full five-foot six-inch height, she wagged a finger in front of Luke's stunned face. "How dare you take our life so lightly? If anything happens to you, Luke Sontag—if you do anything stupid—you'll go to your grave knowing that I will never forgive you, do you understand? *Never.*"

The final word ended with a broken cry as Kelsey spun away. The gun hung loosely at her side and she propped her sagging head with her free hand, fighting to conceal the full extent of her terror. It was a fruitless attempt. As her chest heaved with silent sobs, she felt Luke's presence close behind her, then his warm arms encircled her.

His unshaven cheek brushed her hair, the stubble snagging a flyaway strand. "Nothing's going to happen to me, honey. I promise."

She trembled, wanting to believe, yet remembering other promises, promises to love and to cherish, until death—

Closing her eyes, she shook off the despicable thought. "Keeping promises isn't your strong suit."

Luke went rigid and, after a long moment, he stepped away, avoiding her gaze by scanning the periphery of the quiet forest. "It should take about a half hour to make the crossing and get to the other side."

Readjusting the heavy rope coil, he slanted a glance at Kelsey, then strode toward the point where the turbulent creek disappeared into a tangled mass of foliage.

A moment before he disappeared into the foreboding woods, Kelsey reached out, as though vicariously touching him for the last time. "Luke!"

He turned expectantly.

Words clogged in her throat, all the things she wanted to say, the feelings that she'd been too proud, too stubborn, to reveal. "Be safe," she finally whispered.

With a jerky nod and a lingering glance, he was gone.

But in her mind, Kelsey still saw him, moving through the forest like a green-eyed jungle cat, drawing strength from danger and a courageous spirit that had been repeatedly cracked, yet never shattered. God, how she loved him. Her heart ached; her chest throbbed so forcefully that she feared she might explode under the billowing force of the bittersweet emotional assault.

She would die if she lost Luke; and yet, in all ways that mattered, she'd lost him long ago. When Luke had left her, he'd taken more than a suitcase of dreams. An intrinsic part of Kelsey had been destroyed, too, leaving a rift in her soul that had forever changed the woman she was, and the woman she would become. She'd been stronger, but she'd been hollow inside. Over the past few days, Luke's warmth had filled that void; Kelsey could never endure that emptiness again.

Ruth offered quiet reassurance. "Luke will be all right, Kel. My brother has always been a fighter."

An icy gust whipped Kelsey's hair, and she impatiently brushed a strand from her face. "Of course he will."

Distracted by a soft mewing sound, Kelsey automatically raised the revolver, quickly scanning the clearing before she realized that the pitiful fussing had come from the blanketed bundle in Ruth's arms.

Stepping over the deepest puddles, Kelsey crossed the short distance from where the vehicle was parked to the large rock where Ruth was nervously examining the fretting infant. As Kelsey approached, she gazed up apprehensively. "Do you think he's sick?"

The blanket had been folded to protect the newborn, and Kelsey gently lifted the corner, using her own body to block the unrelenting wind. Eric's tiny face contorted as he fitfully squirmed against his restraints and wailed weakly. He was so precious that Kelsey wanted to cuddle him until he squeaked. Fighting a surge of maternal instinct, she gently caressed his silky cheek with her fingertip. Instantly, the infant twisted his greedy little mouth toward her touch.

"Oh, so you're finally ready for breakfast, are you?" Kelsey murmured, sliding her finger up to brush the silky fuzz of his head. Eric twisted awkwardly, his tiny bow mouth trying to follow the movement. Kelsey smiled.

Ruth's forehead puckered with concern. "I tried to nurse him earlier, but he didn't seem to know what to do."

"He's only a few hours old. It takes time for a fellow to get his juices going, right, little guy?"

Eric's beet-red face crumpled and he responded with a brief, lusty wail that unnerved his mother. "I should probably try again, but..." Ruth's voice trailed away as she glanced apprehensively toward the cabin and surrounding forest.

Kelsey followed her gaze, and when satisfied that nothing seemed amiss, patted Ruth's hand sympathetically. "Are your breasts terribly sore?"

"A little," she admitted. "I'm just afraid that Eric will starve because I don't know how to feed him."

"Instinct will guide you both." Since the new mother was quite naturally inexperienced with this maternal process, Kelsey offered reassurance. "Just relax. There's plenty of time and, believe me, once Eric locates the luncheon buffet, you'll wonder why you ever worried about his appetite." As Kelsey spoke, she arranged a blanket over Ruth's shoulder, allowing the protective shield to drape over the infant. "That should keep the wind out of his face. Now just brush the nipple against his lips... that's right. Aha!"

Ruth laughed as the baby clamped on, sucking hungrily. After a moment, Eric lost his grip and wailed before his mother managed to guide his frenzied little mouth back to the proper spot. Ruth was beside herself with excitement and both women laughed aloud with delight.

When the infant's frantic gulping made the nipple pop out of his mouth again, Kelsey grinned broadly. "Goodness, such impatience. I remember that Pattie used to get so excited, she'd—"

Ruth's smile faded and as she quickly glanced up, her eyes softened with pity.

Standing, Kelsey silently announced her return to guard duty by checking the weapon, then adopting an alert stance. The forest was silent, except for the whistling wind and the noisy suckling of the nursing child, but Kelsey stared blindly, trying to exhume the intrusive memories.

After a moment, Ruth spoke. "Luke told me about your daughter."

Without turning, Kelsey faced the wind and nodded. She could do nothing more.

"I . . . God, Kelsey, I'm so sorry."

Kelsey moistened her lips. "Thank you."

"I can't imagine how difficult this must be for you, reliving your loss through the birth of my son. If the situation had been reversed, I don't know if I could have done the same."

"You could have." Kelsey faced her then, allowing the tears to fall without shame. "And you would have."

Ruth was crying too. "I feel so helpless, Kel. You and Luke have always been there for me. Then, when both of you needed me most, I abandoned you. How can you ever forgive me?"

"There's nothing to forgive. I love you, Ruthie, and so does your brother. What happened was beyond your control, but you've escaped now. That took great courage." Wiping the back of her hand across her cheek, Kelsey took a deep breath. "No matter what went on between Luke and me, each of us will always be there for you. You know that, don't you?"

Sniffing, Ruth's head bobbed and she delicately dabbed her eyes with the corner of the blanket. "Luke loves you."

Hearing those precious words vacuumed every ounce of oxygen from Kelsey's lungs. When she could speak, she stammered, "I don't think so."

"I know my brother," Ruth insisted. "I see how he looks at you. He loves you, Kelsey. I think that he always will."

There was no need to dispute Ruth's heartfelt statement. Luke had never loved Kelsey, but even if he had, those feelings would have been destroyed by all that happened. There had been too much pain between them, too much loss.

Love wasn't a panacea, the conquering salvation of a sick and cruel world. Ruth of all people knew that. She, too, had loved a man, a man who was trying to destroy her. Love hurt. That was the bitter secret of life's sweetest illusion, and both women knew it well.

"Kelsey, look!"

Swinging her head around, Kelsey followed Ruth's excited gesture and squinted at the trees on the far side of the creek. Something moved, then disappeared behind a wall of foliage. A branch wiggled. A twig cracked. Leaves crunched.

Luke emerged, staggering with exhaustion. Dragging the heavy rope coil over his head, he collapsed on the gravel road and rested his forehead on his knees.

Kelsey pressed her knuckles against her lips to keep from screaming with blessed relief. He was filthy, wet from the waist down, and his spattered jacket hung off his slumped shoulders like shredded blue cabbage, but he was alive.

Finally he took a heaving breath, lifted his head and wiped the sweat from his eyes as he blinked across the swirling waters that separated them. "Is...everything...all right?" He took a gasp of air between each strained word.

The pounding of Kelsey's heart obscured her own response. "Yes. Are you okay?"

He nodded weakly and gazed at the clearing beyond the two women. When he'd caught his breath, he carried the rope to the tree that had been designated as the tie-off point. He wrapped a length twice around the trunk and fastened the end with a series of knots. He glanced across the creek. "Are you two ready?"

Dropping the gun into her jacket pocket, Kelsey replied that they were as ready as they'd ever be, then watched Luke secure the hatchet to the free end of the rope. She'd expected that. It was part of the plan, the details of which they had painstakingly rehashed in the early morning light.

Having completed his task, Luke tested the weighted end, then circled his arm in a windmill pattern, allowing the hatchet to orbit with increasing velocity. "Heads up," he called, then released his grip.

The rope arched over the crevasse as the hatchet smoothly cleared the rift and buried itself in the mud on the other side. Kelsey quickly retrieved it. Her fingers shook as she untied the knots, then laid the hatchet aside and dragged the heavy rope toward Ridenour's sedan.

First, she threaded the rope through the eyelet noose of the harness handle, then draped a loop of rope around the vehicle's back bumper. Wedging her foot against the bumper, she threw her weight backwards and pulled the rope as taut as she possibly could. Maintaining her awkward stance, she glanced over her shoulder and saw a disheartening sag in the middle of the fifty-foot span.

Luke cupped his mouth with his hands. "Can you pull it tighter?"

Levered backward, she was nearly horizontal to the ground and dismayed to realize that she would be unable to stretch the rope tight enough. This step was crucial, since during the crossing, the guide rope would obviously sag beneath their weight; if the line were too loose, it would dip its human cargo into the turbulent waters below.

Twisting her grip, Kelsey jumped and braced both feet on the bumper, straining backwards until the rope gave a satisfying slip. It wasn't enough, but it was something. Now, however, she was trapped. She felt like a spring-loaded doorstop, jutting in midair with both feet stuck to the bumper.

From the corner of her eye, she saw Ruth busily tucking little Eric into the padded duffel that would serve as an infant carrier for the hazardous crossing. After carefully placing the canvas crib between two rocks, she ran to help Kelsey.

Gripping the rope just in front of Kelsey's hands, Ruth braced herself and added her weight to leverage the rope. It wasn't working.

"Wait a minute." Panting, Kelsey eased off and Ruth stood back. "I have an idea." Allowing the rope to droop loosely, Kelsey knotted the rope around the bumper, then pulled the car keys from her pocket. "Let me know when it's tight enough, okay?"

Ruth nodded and moved into position as Kelsey slid into the driver's seat. She started the engine and inched the car forward until Ruth signaled to her that the rope had been pulled taut.

Kelsey stepped out of the car and both women eyed the result of their efforts. The guide rope began its ascent on the cabin side of the creek about ten feet above the surface, then angled upward to the top of the embankment where Luke was waiting. At that point, the rope was suspended a harrowing twenty feet above the turbulent waters.

The ascent was steeper than Kelsey had expected, and she mentally replayed Luke's game plan. After Ruth was secured in the harness, Luke would use the knotted linen towline to haul his sister up the guide rope, then return the empty harness to her for the next crossing.

The plan seemed simple, but so did Einstein's theory.

Kelsey was unnerved by the entire scene. In comparison to the turbulent rapids, the half-inch-thick rope looked amazingly fragile, like a sewing thread strung over Niagara Falls. The harness dangled near the car bumper, a limp tangle of wire that seemed frighteningly unsuited for the enormity of its task.

All of a sudden the actual risk involved in executing this dicey strategy hit Kelsey like a body blow. A planning session complete with practice runs had been one thing, but this was real. The pounding current and deadly rocks bore mute witness to the life-or-death consequence of this perilous crossing. There was no net. There would be no second chance.

And Ruth would be first.

Shivering uncontrollably, Kelsey gripped Ruth's slender arm and felt her friend's involuntary shudder. One look at Ruth's ashen face confirmed that she was absolutely terrified. Kelsey simply couldn't bear to let her go.

Taking the revolver from her pocket, Kelsey pressed the cold steel against Ruth's limp palm. "You stand guard. I'll go first."

Ruth gazed numbly at the weapon. "I . . . can't use this."

"There's nothing to it. Just cock this hammer and pull the trigger."

Squeezing her eyes shut, Ruth moaned and shook her head miserably. "No. I couldn't shoot Joseph, no matter what he did. I just can't." She returned the gun to Kelsey and shivered. "Besides, everything has been planned. I have to cross first—then, if everything goes well, Luke will send the harness back and you will bring Eric."

If everything goes well . . .

The implication of what could happen if things didn't go well made Kelsey ill. She absently replaced the revolver into her blazer pocket, watching Ruth lift the canvas duffel and gaze down at her baby with an expression of reverence that nearly tore Kelsey's heart out.

"The towline," Luke called loudly. "Throw the towline across."

Shading her eyes, Kelsey tried to concentrate. Towline? For a moment, the request meant nothing, then she realized that Luke was referring to the knotted length of sheets that was fastened to the harness. Kelsey was supposed to tie the hatchet to the loose end and fling it back across the creek, as Luke had done with the guide rope. Kelsey, however, had the added burden of attaining sufficient height to hit an uphill target on the other side.

Although her fingers numbed by the frigid wind, Kelsey managed to secure the hatchet to the knotted linen, then swung the weighted towline around her head and threw it as hard as she could.

The first attempt fell short, and she was horrified as the hatchet bounced off a rock, then plunged into the roaring creek. Instantly the towline yanked taut, dragging the harness along the rope until Kelsey managed to wrap one hand around one wire hoop, stopping its ascent. The force of current dragging the knotted linens nearly jerked her off her feet before she fished out the towline, and thankfully, the hatchet was still attached.

"Try again!" Luke looked a bit paler and considerably less confident. "This time, build more speed before the release."

Gritting her teeth, Kelsey swung the damned hatchet around her head until it whistled like a sailor, then she grunted and let loose, holding her breath as the weighted sheet-rope arched across the stream and landed at Luke's feet.

She breathed a sigh of relief as Luke untied and discarded the hatchet, then wrapped the linen strips firmly around his hand. He stared tensely across the creek at Kelsey, his gaze meeting hers with telling intensity. He filled his lungs. "Let's do it."

Kelsey swallowed and looked at Ruth, who had become visibly rigid. After a moment, she lifted the duffel and bent to kiss her newborn infant, lingering only a moment, as though savoring the sight. Then she shuddered, carefully replaced the bag between the protective rocks, and held her head high as she went to meet her fate.

Kelsey held the wire to prevent the harness from sliding out of reach. As the stoic woman approached, Kelsey extended her free hand to her helplessly. "Ruthie—"

Ruth held up her palm, silencing Kelsey's protest, then moved into position and slipped the upper hoop down over her head. The harness handle paralleled Ruth's spine, extending upward between her shoulder blades to the eyelet loop through which the guide rope had been threaded.

Struggling, Ruth slid one arm through the upper hoop, but the other arm was trapped against her side. "Can you give me a hand with this thing, Kel?"

Kelsey held the wire loose, allowing Ruth to extract her arm. When the hoop encircled her friend's torso, Kelsey threaded the leather belt from top hoop, between Ruth's knees to the seat of the harness. When Kelsey had secured the belt, Ruth's feet lifted off the ground and she dangled in the wind.

Ruth managed a wan smile. "Just like a man to design this kind of a corset, isn't it?"

Not daring to speak, Kelsey simply stared in horror as the guide rope dipped under the strain of Ruth's meager weight. She looked across at Luke, her eyes signaling alarm, but he simply nodded. "Is she ready?"

"I...don't know." Torn, Kelsey's agitated gaze darted from Ruth to Luke and back again.

Finally, Ruth signaled her brother, then touched Kelsey's hand, which still held the wire harness with a convulsive grip. "Turn loose, Kel."

All Kelsey could do was to shake her head and grasp the wire even tighter. Eric suddenly began to fuss as though concerned by his mother's plight.

Ruth bit her lower lip. "Please. If I don't get this over with, I'm going to be sick."

Kelsey realized that postponing the inevitable was merely prolonging Ruth's agony. With a strangled sob, she released the harness and Ruth swung out over the turbulent water.

Luke wrapped the knotted-sheet rope around his hand and pulled. The harness slowly ascended. Kelsey held her breath as the rope steadily sagged and Ruth's feet nearly touched the boiling water. Straining, Luke backed up and pulled again. The harness jerked a few feet higher, then began to sway in the blustery wind.

Gasping, Ruth raised both hands over her head and clamped onto the harness handle in a death grip.

Kelsey covered her mouth and prayed.

Again and again, Luke braced himself and heaved, moving his sister's weight slowly up the steep incline. After what seemed an eternity, he reached out and grasped the harness hoop, then hauled her to the safety of solid ground.

After tying the towline to a branch, Luke unfastened the harness belt and slipped the hoop over Ruth's head. She shakily stepped away from the contraption into her brother's waiting arms.

From Kelsey's vantage point, she recognized Luke's expression of agony mingled with relief as he caressed his sister's hair and hugged her so tightly that it was a wonder the poor woman didn't pop. Reluctantly releasing her, Luke helped Ruth to a spot where she could rest while Kelsey and the baby came across. When the exhausted woman was seated beneath a tree, Luke bent and spoke to her. Kelsey couldn't hear his words over the roar of the creek, but they had an obvious impact on Ruth, who stiffened and glanced anxiously toward Kelsey.

Luke retrieved the harness, loosened the towline and, to Kelsey's shock, slid the hoop over his body, grabbed the harness handle and leaped off the steep embankment, sliding down the guide rope at a frightening speed.

As he reached the cabin side of the creek, he extended his feet in an attempt to slow his descent. His sneakers hit the ground and left two mud grooves as he rammed into the car trunk with a sickening thud.

Kelsey ran to him. "Are you all right?"

"Yeah." He lifted the hoop over his head and scrutinized the surroundings.

"What on earth is going on here?" Kelsey was bewildered by the entire episode. "You were supposed to send the harness for Eric and me, not come zooming over like a carnival act. How are we supposed to get across now?"

Focusing narrowed eyes on the surrounding woods, Luke ignored her questions and posed one of his own. "Where's the gun?"

Kelsey didn't like the look on his face. "In my pocket."

"Give it to me."

She complied, baffled and unnerved by Luke's strange behavior. When he turned his face to scrutinize the far side of the clearing, Kelsey noted an ugly abrasion extending from the side of his forehead into his scalp. "Good Lord, Luke, what happened?"

As he secured the towline to the car bumper, his lips tightened into a grim line and he spoke through clamped teeth. "I ran into a little trouble crossing the creek."

A chill ran down her spine. "Joseph?"

"Unless bears throw rocks."

"Oh, God." Kelsey's knees vibrated and she steadied herself against the car. She didn't need to ask what had happened. Joseph must have followed Luke, then tried to knock him off the rope while he was suspended over the water. "How did you— Never mind. I don't want to know."

"Good, because there isn't time." Luke hauled the harness into position and studied the guide rope's brutal incline. "Ruth is too weak to pull the harness. Can you haul yourself up?"

For a moment, Kelsey wasn't certain what Luke meant, then she realized that he wanted her to do a hand-over-hand crawl up that damned rope. "Talk to me, Luke. We're obviously implementing Plan B here, and I don't have a clue as to what that entails."

Luke glanced at the sleeping infant tucked inside the padded duffel. "This gun is the only thing keeping Joseph at bay. If the gun, and whoever is holding it, is dangling over the creek—"

Luke didn't have to complete the statement for Kelsey to get the message. The final person to cross would be unprotected and most vulnerable to attack. Luke planned to stand guard while Kelsey carried the baby across, assuming that she had enough strength to pull herself over.

As though reading her mind, Luke asked, "Can you do it?"

She honestly didn't know. "There's one way to find out. I'll do a test run... without the baby."

Luke frowned. "We don't have a lot of time here."

"Look, if I can get halfway up, I'll know whether or not it's safe to try it with the baby."

Since she was adamant on that point, Luke had no choice but to buckle her into the harness and let her try. He held the knotted towline so it wouldn't fall into the water and be dragged by the current, increasing the effort needed for the climb. Then he signaled Kelsey with a look.

Reaching over her head, Kelsey grabbed the fat guide rope and pulled. The effort was more intense than she'd imagined and as she inched over the creek, she forced her gaze upward, away from the rapids below. Sweat beaded her brow and her leaden arms began to quiver with the exertion. God, she couldn't do it. As she moved one hand in front of the other, her grip slipped and she plummeted back down the line. Luke caught her, but the force of her descent nearly knocked him over.

Breathless and shaking, Kelsey meekly allowed Luke to unfasten the belt and lift the hoop over her head. "Now what?"

He handed her the gun, and she nodded somberly. Luke would take Eric across, then Kelsey would be on her own. There was no choice now, and both knew it.

In a few moments, Luke had draped the duffel's soft handles around his neck and was firmly strapped into the harness. Since Kelsey now assumed that Joseph was indeed watching them, she made a point of holding the revolver in both hands, hoping that an unobstructed view of the weapon would continue to discourage any plan he might have to stop their escape.

Using a hand-over-hand movement, Luke hauled himself up the guide rope, but Kelsey noted that even his superior strength was tested by the grueling manual ascent.

On the other side, Ruth stood at the edge of the precipice, wringing her hands while her brother and his precious cargo inched painfully across the ravine.

Finally, Luke reached the embankment, released the harness and gave his sister the canvas carrier that contained her newborn son. Instantly Ruth cradled the duffel in her arms and turned away, her shoulders shaking as though wracked by intermittent sobs.

There was no time for Kelsey to savor the victory. Luke had grounded the harness and was pulling the knotted rope to his side in preparation for the final crossing. When he'd finished, he straightened and repositioned the harness on the guide rope. "Stand back."

Kelsey dodged the harness's free fall down to the downhill position. With a wary glance around the clearing, Kelsey pocketed the revolver and strapped herself in. She took a deep breath, then grasped the handle extending above her head and signaled that she was ready.

Immediately she felt a distressing jerk and Luke pulled the towline. Below her, the muddy ground fell away and she felt queasy. A gust of wind buffeted the harness, making it sway uncontrollably. She fought an onrush of nausea. Closing her eyes made her even queasier, but by the time she was halfway across, she decided that watching was even worse, so she squeezed her eyelids together and clung to the rigid wire handle.

Ruth suddenly screamed. "Joseph, no!"

Snapping her head around, Kelsey looked back toward the clearing and nearly fainted. Joseph stood beside the car bumper, grimly sawing at the guide rope with the knife.

Above her, Kelsey heard Luke swear and Ruth scream again, and the harness was jerked forward with more urgency.

The gun.

Kelsey struggled to retrieve the weapon, but the jacket was bunched around her waist and she had difficulty locating the pocket. When she finally felt the cold steel against her palm, she fought to extract the revolver from the wadded fabric. Just as she freed the gun, the harness jerked erratically. The revolver slipped from her frigid fingers, then plunged into the swirling creek.

From the cliff above, Ruth again pleaded with her husband. "Joseph, stop...please, you can't do this." She enforced that entreaty by flinging a small rock across the ravine.

Joseph barely blinked as the harmless projectile bounced off his shoulder. Displaying neither maniacal glee nor a victorious smirk, he continued his deadly task with a calm resignation that chilled Kelsey to the bone.

Spinning in the harness, Kelsey saw that she was still fifteen to twenty feet away from solid ground and prayed that Luke could haul her to safety before Joseph cut through the rope.

Suddenly Ruth reappeared at the precipice and cocked her arm.

Luke shouted. "Ruth, don't—"

It was too late. The hatchet arched over Kelsey's head and Joseph sidestepped it, allowing the weapon to land harmlessly in the mud. With a menacing smile, he hoisted the hatchet and looked straight at Kelsey before severing the rope with a single chop.

Kelsey screamed as the harness tipped, then plummeted her downward. Bile surged into her throat as she somersaulted, then jerked to a stop.

For a moment, Kelsey thought she was dead, then she felt the icy spray on her face and opened her eyes. She was hanging upside down just above the rapids while the dismembered rope twisted in the current like a drowning snake.

Although dazed, Kelsey realized that somehow Luke had maintained a grip on the knotted towline. Still buckled into the harness, she dangled helplessly and was immensely relieved to see the rushing creek grow smaller and smaller as Luke painfully hauled her up.

When Luke's strong fingers finally grasped her shoulder, Kelsey nearly wept with relief. He dragged her a few feet from the edge, then quickly unfastened the harness and pulled her into his arms. He was shaking. So was she.

Ruth appeared, clutching her infant and sobbing hysterically. "I'm sorry, oh God, Kel, I never realized that he could use the hatchet—"

"Shh." With one arm still wound around Luke's neck, Kelsey reached out with her free hand and hugged the weeping woman. "I know, sweetie. It's okay now."

At least, Kelsey hoped that it was okay. Her heart was still pounding wildly and she looked quickly across the ravine just as Joseph limped into the woods.

Luke's choked voice captured her attention. "Are you all right?"

Kelsey nodded.

Closing his eyes, Luke swallowed hard and seemed on the verge of collapse. Fear and exertion had sapped his remaining strength. The transformation frightened Kelsey. His sunken eyes reflected vulnerability, and his strong jaw, now bruised and shadowed with stubble, had lost its usual jaunty, defiant tilt.

Her heart went out to him.

Suddenly Ruth blurted, "Joseph is getting away."

"He won't get far." Keeping one arm around Kelsey's waist, Luke pulled his sister into the protective circle.

They all huddled together, foreheads touching, each silently contemplating the disaster they had so narrowly escaped.

Finally, Luke raised his head and his reddened eyes again displayed his trademark courage. "Let's go home." Then he led the battered human convoy up the road toward the rock slide, the pickup truck and freedom.

Chapter 14

"Kel—honey, wake up."

Kelsey whimpered and burrowed deeper into the comforting pillow of human flesh cradling her head. A gentle hand caressed her face, and she painfully opened one eye. "Where are we?"

"In front of your apartment," Luke replied. "A hot bath and soft bed are just a few steps away."

Yawning, Kelsey propped herself on one elbow and squinted into the darkness. She was momentarily confused before realizing that they were in the cab of Luke's truck, and she'd been blissfully sleeping with her head nestled in his lap. Every fiber in her body wanted to curl back into a fetal position, pressed against the warm solace of her husband's body. Instead, she painfully sat up and rubbed her eyes. "What time is it?"

"Around midnight."

Kelsey massaged her stiff neck and winced as her abused muscles rebelled at the minute movement. The past fifteen hours had been a nightmarish blur of hospitals and police stations. After their escape, they'd driven straight to the nearest telephone. Two hours later, Ruth and her newborn infant had been examined at a Modesto hospital while detectives had grilled Luke and Kelsey with annoying fervor and obvious skepticism.

Eventually the police had located and arrested Joseph, who'd immediately requested his lawyer, then sullenly refused further comment.

After making arrangements to transfer Ruth and Eric to a Los Angeles medical facility, Luke and Kelsey had climbed back into the pickup and started their long journey home.

One ordeal had ended, but for Kelsey, another had begun. Past heartache, long suppressed yet never healed, had reopened into an emotional wound more debilitating than any physical damage she'd suffered over the past few days.

Luke had broken Kelsey's heart when he'd left her, but she still loved him. Her discovery of that emotional frailty had been devastating. How could she pick up the pieces of her life, when that which gave her life meaning continued to elude her?

Beside her, Luke shifted restlessly, then opened the truck door. "I'll walk you up."

"You're not staying?"

He seemed surprised, perhaps by the tremor in her voice, or the realization that she hadn't expected him to leave. Moistening her lips, she veiled the irrational panic. "I mean, it's so late and it's such a long drive back to south-central and, ah, your trailer doesn't even have a shower."

Propping one elbow on the steering wheel, Luke rested his chin in his palm and regarded her thoughtfully. "Would you rather not be alone?"

Actually, being alone had nothing to do with what she was feeling. A tiny voice deep inside told her that if Luke left now, Kelsey would never see him again. The thought was unbearable. "I'd feel better if you stayed."

After a moment, he looked out the windshield, seeming fascinated by the glow of a nearby street lamp. "Then I'll stay."

His pensive expression cut Kelsey to the core. Their entire relationship had been one of unintended coercion on her part, from the initial pregnancy to this final, pressured chapter. She should set him free, but she couldn't. Perhaps she'd be stronger tomorrow.

Deep inside, Kelsey knew that she'd never be strong enough to let Luke go. Considering the disastrous consequence of Joseph's warped obsession, that was the saddest irony of all.

Stepping out of the draining tub, Kelsey toweled her wet head and marveled at the wondrous sensation of simply feeling clean again. She slipped a warm robe over her bare skin and combed her hair with her fingers. For the first time in days, she felt human.

Kelsey draped the towel around her neck, then went into the living room. Luke was sitting on the sofa. He held something in his hand, but she couldn't identify the object that he was so wistfully examining.

Luke looked up as Kelsey entered. "Are you feeling better?" he asked, closing his hand over the item as though it were a small book.

"Yes." She crossed the room, hesitated, then sat beside him on the sofa and saw the folded black leather object in his hands. She wondered why he'd been studying his wallet with such reverence, but chose not to ask. "I thought you'd be asleep by now."

"I got enough sleep while you were driving." He combed his fingers through his damp hair. "Thanks for letting me shower first."

"It was purely selfish. I wouldn't have been able to enjoy the luxury of a thirty-minute soak knowing that you were still crusted in mountain mud."

He nodded with a weak smile, but stress lines marred his handsome face and he seemed unduly tense. Avoiding Kelsey's concerned gaze, Luke stared blankly across the room. "Do you have any pictures of Pattie?"

The question nearly took Kelsey's breath away but she managed to stammer that she did.

"Where do you keep them?"

"They're...put away." She stood, upset that Luke would bring up such a painful subject.

Apparently oblivious to her distress, he opened his wallet and extracted a small snapshot that had been carefully trimmed to fit the clear plastic sleeve. "I only have this one."

Kelsey's gaze was inexplicably drawn to the picture cradled in his palm. She bit her lip, recognizing the photograph as one Ernie had taken of her, along with Luke and Pattie, on Mother's Day. "I didn't realize that you had that picture."

"Yeah." Luke replaced the photograph and tucked the wallet into the back pocket of his clean denim jeans. "I don't know why I kept it."

Kelsey looked away as bitter memories resurfaced. "Neither do I. You made it quite clear that you didn't want any reminders of the time we spent together."

"That's not true."

"Then why did I return from Pattie's funeral to an apartment that had been wiped clean, purged of evidence that my daughter had even existed?"

Luke started to speak, then stood up and walked across the room. After a moment, he faced Kelsey with exquisite sadness. "I told myself that I was doing it for you, because I didn't want you to be constantly reminded that our baby was gone. I guess I was doing it for me. I couldn't stand seeing Pattie's bassinet or her toys... hell, I couldn't even stand seeing the couch where I'd changed her diapers, or the kitchen table, where she'd sat in her little carrier—" Luke's voice broke. Concealing the frailty with a sharp curse, he covered his face with one hand and slumped against the wall.

Kelsey was stunned by the depth of her husband's anguish. After their daughter's death, Luke had refused even to speak Pattie's name aloud, as though pretending that she'd never existed would erase the pain of her loss. Kelsey had interpreted his silence as accusation and his withdrawal of emotional support as punishment. Now, for the first time, she recognized that this staunch and stalwart man had been immersed in his own personal hell.

"I never realized," she whispered. "I'm so sorry."

After a moment, Luke lowered his hand to his hip and regarded Kelsey thoughtfully. "You needed to talk about Pattie, didn't you?"

Tears stung her eyes. "Yes."

He nodded, then stared across the room with a faraway expression. Suddenly, he smiled. It was a sad smile, perhaps no more than a gentle curve of his lips, but it was a smile nonetheless. "Do you remember when the kid got her first taste of real food? What was that mush, anyway—bananas?"

"Cereal." Kelsey cleared her throat and wiped her eyes. "Rice cereal. She loved it."

"Yeah, that was it." Luke pursed his lips pensively. "By the time I got home, she looked like she'd taken a bath in the stuff."

Kelsey sniffed and laughed softly, remembering how Pattie's hair had poked out in sticky, cereal-coated spikes. "That's because I got so excited when she swallowed her first bite that I dropped the whole bowl on her tummy."

"Hell of a mess," Luke mused. "Pretty funny, though, and you were in worse shape than Pattie."

"Only because she sneezed with her mouth full. I'm basically a very tidy person." As warm memories washed over her, she recalled how gentle and loving Luke had been with his tiny offspring, taking to fatherhood with ease and profound devotion. One image in particular stood out in her mind. "Do you remember the afternoon you propped Pattie in front of the television and described the play-by-play defense of a stupid football game?"

Luke looked stung. "It was the NFL championship."

"Whatever." Kelsey waved off the information as insignificant. "The point is that Pattie was only three months old."

"So what? She liked football."

"Umm." Kelsey smiled, recalling how he had held their bright-eyed daughter in front of the screen during the most exciting moments, then declared firmly that no kid of his would lack an appropriate education in such crucial matters. "You were a wonderful father," she murmured, without realizing that her thoughts had been spoken aloud.

Luke's smile faded. "And you were a good mother, Kel. The best."

Hugging herself, Kelsey tried to still her body's sudden tremor. Moisture gathered on her lower lashes, then splashed down her face in an unrelenting flood. She turned away, knowing how Luke despised seeing anyone cry. In the past, he'd always left the room in disgust at the first sign of a tear. Tonight, however, he didn't leave. Instead, he came up behind her, locked his arms around her chest and laid his cheek on her bowed head.

"I know, honey," he murmured. "I know."

Finally, a year after their devastating loss, Luke was able to console his grieving wife. As sobs wracked Kelsey's body, Luke simply held her, smoothing her hair and offering silent solace. After several wrenching minutes, Kelsey took a shuddering breath and turned in the circle of his arms.

She laid her palms on his chest and looked deeply into the soulful emerald eyes that had stolen her heart so long ago. When she started to speak, Luke silenced her with a slow, sweet kiss.

Raising his lips, he hesitated, holding his mouth mere inches from hers, then stepped away, seeming agitated and bewildered. He rubbed the back of his neck and stared at the floor. "I'm no good with words, so I don't know how this is going to come out. It's just that—" His jaw twitched and he raised his head, staring over her shoulder in frustration. "I never meant to hurt you."

Perplexed and unsettled herself, Kelsey absently touched her tight stomach. "Luke, I—"

Raising his palm, he stifled her protest and continued. "After... it happened, I tried to tell myself that everything was your fault, that if you'd stayed at home, Pattie would have been okay because you'd have taken care of her. I knew it was a cop-out, but I just couldn't admit that my daughter was gone because her daddy couldn't give her a decent place to live. I don't expect you to forgive me, but I just wanted you to know that I wish things had been different, that's all."

Kelsey couldn't breathe. Her mind must have been playing tricks on her. Surely she hadn't just heard Luke blame himself for Pattie's death.

His anguished expression revealed otherwise, and as he turned to leave, Kelsey took hold of his arm. He stopped but made no attempt to look at her and she stood stupidly, hanging on to his elbow, not knowing what to do or say to alleviate the feelings of inadequacy that he'd so carefully concealed behind that wall of rage. "There's nothing to forgive, Luke."

"I said awful things to you."

"You didn't say anything half as hurtful as what I had already said to myself." Kelsey hesitated, then decided that if she shared her own secret guilt Luke might take some comfort in knowing he was not alone. Still, it was difficult, and her voice wavered. "A mother is supposed to cherish and protect her child. Regardless of the reason, I had failed to do that, so you were right all along—"

Before the words had completely left Kelsey's mouth, Luke dragged her into his arms and kissed her with an urgency that took her breath away. Kelsey responded instinctively, wrapping her arms around her husband's neck and pressing him closer. She craved his touch, his warmth, the strength of his body.

Luke groaned and buried his face in her wet hair. "What have I done to you?"

Framing his face in her hands, she brushed her lips against his mouth. "You made me love you."

Luke couldn't have looked more stunned if she'd gut-punched him. The silence unnerved her and she kissed him again, harder this time, with an intensity born of desperation. His response was gratifying. Cupping her head tenderly, his free hand glided to her throat, caressing and embracing as he deepened the kiss with intimate strokes that lit a bonfire in Kelsey's awakening soul.

God, how she needed him. Her body throbbed with desire, a passion to touch and to heal and to share that soared beyond the physical into the etherealized plane of infinity.

Luke slid his hand downward, tracing the line of her collarbone to where it disappeared inside the thick furry robe. When his fingers hesitated, lingering just inside the open collar, the exquisite anticipation weakened her knees. Her breasts ached impatiently, and she urged his hand downward until his palm closed around the tingling mound of warm flesh. While the heel of his hand supported the soft weight, his thumb and forefinger teased the erect nipple until she nearly cried out with the joy of it all.

Fumbling with the knot at her waist, she loosened the belt and the robe fell open, displaying her nudity for his pleasure. He stood back, gazing at her body as though it were a temple, then reached out and simultaneously caressed both breasts until her head rolled back in ecstasy. Sparks arced from her nipples to that most private part of her, sending heat waves coursing like molten lava through her veins.

His fingers reluctantly left her breasts, moving upward to sweep the robe from her shoulders. The furred fabric pooled at her feet, and she stood before him naked and unashamed.

With a soft gasp, Luke fell to his knees, embracing her hips as he laid his face against her softly rounded belly. "You're so beautiful, so perfect," he whispered, as though the shimmering white stretch marks merely added to her allure.

"You make me beautiful," she murmured, smoothing his wildly tangled hair. "Your touch gives me life."

Luke crossed his arms, grasped the hem of his T-shirt and shrugged the garment over his head. He tossed the shirt aside, and Kelsey heard the metallic hum of a zipper. In a moment, Luke simultaneously shoved his jeans and briefs down his tempered thighs and, lifting one knee at a time, rolled the denim over each calf to fully reveal his magnificence.

As her husband knelt before her, ugly scratches and purple flesh marring his perfection, the reminder of what he had endured made him all the more dear. Kelsey methodically traced each scar and bruise as though her delicate fingertips were healing wands.

Pressing him against her aching abdomen, Kelsey reveled in the feel of his freshly shaven cheek rubbing her bare flesh. She urged his head slightly back, then lowered one breast into his waiting mouth. When his tongue touched her sensitive nipple, she sucked air through her teeth and whimpered with pure joy.

As his lips and mouth worked their magic, his fingers caressed her buttocks, then brushed her inner thighs until Kelsey was so frantic with need that she could no longer stand. She wondered if people could die of such agonizing pleasure. Her legs weakened, then buckled and she, too, was kneeling.

Cupping his face, Kelsey covered Luke's mouth with frenzied kisses, allowing him to part her thighs, then waited breathlessly for his gentle fingers to find the secret place that most craved his touch. Completely overwhelmed by the sweet homage of Luke's intimate caress, she cried out and fell back against her heels, and her convulsing torso was propped upright only by the waning strength of her rigid arms.

A split second before the tiny spasms could engulf her, Luke pulled Kelsey forward and lifted her, suspending her writhing body over his aroused flesh. She wrapped her legs around his waist and clung to his shoulders, posed for the completion that she so desperately craved.

But Luke made no move toward that completion. Instead, he held her firmly in place and fixed her with an unnervingly lucid gaze. "I need you, more than I need my next breath," he said quietly. "But I don't want you to look in the mirror tomorrow and see regret looking back at you. Are you sure this is what you want?"

Kelsey licked her dry lips. Since she was half mad with passion and wound around him like a feeding octopus, the question seemed ludicrous. "I love you, Luke Sontag. I have always loved you. That is the one thing in my life that I have never regretted."

Luke closed his eyes as though her words pained him, then he slowly lowered her, shuddering when their bodies joined.

Kelsey was overwhelmed by the profound beauty of their ultimate intimacy and by the reemergence of that which had been so elusive—joy in today, hope for tomorrow and love that would last a lifetime.

"Hey, man." Ernie glanced up from the partially dismantled engine compartment, then extracted his lanky torso from under the hood. "Where the hell you been? We got cars stacked from here to Christmas, bill collectors been buggin' the crap outta me, and that toadstool-sucking jock you hired to do smog checks got himself busted."

"Busted?" The other significance of the word escaped Luke, since his mind was still focused on the haunting image of the sleeping woman he'd just left. "Busted for what?"

Whipping a grease rag from his back pocket, Ernie wiped his hands, crossed his ankles and propped one skinny hip against the fender. "The boozed-up fool made wee-wee in the middle of Figueroa Boulevard."

Luke shook his head in disgust. "So he spent the night in a drunk tank and he'll be out later, right?"

"A damn sight later. The cops pulled six rocks outta his shorts."

"Cocaine? He's a freaking crackhead?" Luke was outraged by what he considered to be a personal betrayal. "Fire him. If that junkie ever sets foot in this garage again, he'll wish to God he was still in jail."

Ernie shrugged. "Don't break a sweat, man. He's already history. Everyone around here knows the rules."

Furious, Luke snatched the clipboard of repair orders from a wall hook, quickly scanned the backlog, then muttered a curt oath. "Put out the word. Entry-level position—dopers need not apply."

"You got it." Ernie pursed his lips and eyed Luke warily. "If those are tread marks on your face, it must have been one hell of a truck. That ain't no mouse under your eye—it's a freaking rat. What gives?"

Not up for a blow-by-blow description of war wounds, Luke replied with an annoyed grunt.

"So, does the other guy look worse, or what?"

The image of Joseph's ugly battered face come to mind, and Luke couldn't conceal his satisfied expression. "Let's just say that my nose doesn't look like a squashed bug and I still have all my teeth."

A flash of white teeth signified Ernie's pleasure. "That's my man. Did you find Ruthie?"

"Yeah." Luke made a production of studying the repair orders, hoping Ernie would let the subject drop.

No such luck.

"Was she back home making sweet talk with her old man, or what?" With a maddening grin, Ernie twisted the bill of his blue baseball cap, then folded his arms. "Spill it, bro'. I ain't heard no good stuff all week."

Well, hell. Luke rubbed his neck and realized that Ernie wouldn't do a lick of work unless his legendary curiosity was mollified. With a resigned sigh, Luke dropped the clipboard on the workbench and offered an abbreviated version of events without mentioning any personal interaction between himself and Kelsey.

Afterward, Ernie's dark complexion was faded to ash gray. "Are you shuckin' me, man?"

Since the question was purely rhetorical, Luke didn't bother to reply. Ernie's somber expression clearly conveyed that he'd believed every word and besides, Luke wasn't known as a kidder.

With a low whistle, Ernie lifted his hat and scratched his cropped scalp. "Poor little Ruthie. What's she gonna do?"

"She and the baby will stay with Kelsey for a while. After that, I don't know. It's up to Ruth."

Ernie hiked one thick brow. "Is this you talking?"

The perceptive question was discomfiting, and Luke felt a slow flush creep up his neck. There had been a time when Luke had taken charge of his sister's life based solely on his judgment of what was best for her. Obviously, Ernie considered Luke's concession to Ruth's wishes as a banner event and not without reason. Still, he was irritated. "Yeah. You got a problem with that?"

"Not me." Holding his palms up, Ernie made a judicious retreat and abruptly switched subjects. "Can I do anything to help? I mean, does Ruthie need stuff for the kid, like diapers and such?"

"Thanks, but I can take care of that."

"You sure? Those rug rats can really suck up the cash."

"Yeah, I know." Smiling, Luke slapped his friend's shoulder. "You say that every time your wife gets pregnant, right before you hit me up for a raise."

"Kids are great, but you got to do right by them." Ernie regarded Luke thoughtfully. "Worst part is letting go when the time is right. It's tough, but if you love 'em, you got to do it. Otherwise, you got nothing but a two-legged dog on a leash."

"Yeah, right." Luke frowned as a queasiness settled in the pit of his stomach. "Are you going to put that engine back together sometime today?"

With an amiable grin, Ernie resettled himself under the yawning hood, then suddenly snapped his fingers. "I almost forgot—that city dude wants you to call."

Luke frowned. "The guy from the redevelopment agency who wants to turn this building into an employment office?"

"Yeah, that's the one. Hey, man, maybe we're gonna get outta this rathole and move uptown after all." That said, Ernie returned to work and Luke went into the small shop office.

Since Luke had given serious thought to relocating the shop in a more lucrative area, a potential buyer for the crumbling brick garage structure was good news. He should be pleased about the city's interest, but at the moment he was too distracted to work up much enthusiasm.

After spreading paperwork over the dented metal desktop, Luke pretended to concentrate, but the handwritten figures blurred beneath his vapid stare. All he could think about was Kelsey, and what they had shared last night. They'd made love in the living room—on the floor, for crissake—and that had only been the beginning. Later he'd carried her to bed, where they'd made love again, and, finally, as dawn crept over the rumpled sheets, their unquenchable thirst for each other had been sated a third time.

Last night had been a turning point for Luke, and not because of any world-record sexual prowess. Last night, Kelsey had said that she loved him. That had been astounding enough, but the most amazing part was that he'd actually believed her. It was a stunning development. Never in his widest fantasy had Luke ever considered that Kelsey could love a man like him, but in her own words, "Love isn't always logical."

So logical or not, they loved each other. Part of him longed to proclaim the joyous news from the rooftops; another part warned him to slow the hell down. Kelsey hadn't said anything about living together as man and wife, which wasn't surprising since Luke's financial situation had changed little in the past year. In fact, all the evening's events had actually revealed was that they cared deeply for each other and their extraordinary physical attraction hadn't diminished.

But things were different now. Luke was different. It was as though he'd seen a mirror for the first time and realized that his face was covered with warts. It hurt to judge his own past, but Luke now realized that his marriage to Kelsey hadn't failed; he had killed it. Afterward, he'd hovered on the edge of her life, tying her with an invisible cord that, if she'd strayed too far, would become a merciless choke collar around her beautiful throat.

. . . Like a two-legged dog on a leash.

Luke pondered the full implications of Ernie's unsettling remark, and his scalp bristled.

Worst part is letting go when the time is right. . .if you love 'em, you got to do it.

The literal interpretation of that subliminal message was chilling. He pushed the unsettling thought aside.

. . . If you love 'em . . .

"Damn." Luke grabbed a pencil and concentrated on an indecipherable column of revenue estimates.

. . . Got to do it.

Ignoring the repetitious call of his conscience, he pressed on the pencil with enough force to snap the lead. He swore and jammed the pencil into the electric sharpener.

. . . Got to do it
. . . Got to do it
. . . Got to—

He angrily extracted the pencil and flung it against the wall, where the pointed tip pierced the plaster as surely as the anguished decision had pierced his heart.

Kelsey meant more to Luke than his own life did, yet he could offer her nothing of value, except that which he'd taken away. Deep down, Luke knew what had to be done, and his shoulders slumped with silent acquiescence. He would do it, because he loved her. But it would damn near kill him.

Ruth stepped into the sunny living room, then shifted the sleeping child in her arms. "I feel like we're really putting you out, Kel."

"Nonsense." Since her hands were full, Kelsey kicked the door closed behind them, then toted the bundles to the kitchen and arranged the bags of supplies on the table. "Look at all this loot. You and Eric must have charmed the socks off those nurses."

Ruth laughed, a tickling, happy sound that warmed Kelsey to the bone. "They were awfully kind to us. I think they emptied the nursery's sample shelf, then chipped in to buy that wonderful diaper bag filled with baby things."

"One of the perks of being a mommy," Kelsey said. "The best part is that you both came through your physicals with flying colors."

"You sound surprised. I *am* a Sontag, after all, and so is my son."

"Of course," Kelsey murmured, unpacking one of the parcels. "There's only one package of diapers. You'll need a lot more, and I don't see any bottles. I know you're nursing, but you'll need bottles for water and—" A gentle touch on Kelsey's arm stopped her agitated speech.

Having quietly crossed the room, Ruth now stood beside Kelsey, her eyes soft with compassion. "I'm sorry. I didn't mean to be insensitive."

"Don't be silly." Kelsey offered a stiff smile and forced a reassuring tone. "There isn't an insensitive bone in your skinny little body."

Lifting her hand from Kelsey's arm, Ruth cupped the infant's fuzzy scalp, holding the tiny head against her shoulder. She started to speak, then appeared to reconsider her words. Instead she sighed and patted her abdomen. "At the moment, I don't feel particularly skinny. My face looks like a cantaloupe and my tummy pooches as though I swallowed a basketball."

Kelsey replied with an unconcerned flick of her wrist. "A temporary condition, my dear. In a few weeks, you'll be slipping into a size six with room to spare."

"Really? Gosh, that's terrific, because I used to wear an eight."

Kelsey grinned and shook her head, pleased to see that in spite of the ordeal, Ruth hadn't lost her sense of humor. "There are exercises that can hurry things along. If you're interested, I can show you."

"I'd like that." Ruth hesitated, then spoke solemnly. "You have helped me so much, Kel. Just knowing that you're willing to answer my questions and share what you've learned, in spite of how it must hurt you. I don't know how to thank you for being such a good friend."

Unwilling to dwell on past sadness, Kelsey squeezed Ruth's hand. "You just did. Besides, I love seeing that motherly glow."

"Speaking of glows, you seem rather illuminated yourself." Ruth playfully poked Kelsey's shoulder. "Does my brother have anything to do with that secret smile?"

With a haphazard shrug, Kelsey feigned interest in a container of baby lotion. "Maybe."

"I knew it!" Ruth looked as though she would burst with excitement. "What happened? Tell me!"

Kelsey set down the lotion and managed an aloof expression. "It's rather private, you know. Nice girls don't kiss and tell."

"Don't you tease me, Kelsey Manning...ah, Sontag? Oh, never mind. What went on between you and Luke? I'll just die if you don't spill every erotic detail."

Grinning smugly, Kelsey took Ruth's elbow. "Not in front of the B-A-B-Y. Besides, I have something to show you."

Ignoring Ruth's protest, Kelsey propelled her down the short corridor to the guest bedroom, then threw open the door with dramatic flair. "Ta-dum!"

Ruth gasped and clutched the baby even tighter. "Oh..." Stepping inside, Ruth stared at the beautiful, white-slated crib with eyes brightened with moisture. "I—I don't know what to say."

Kelsey clasped her hands together and anxiously scanned her friend's shining face. "If you'd rather have a different style—"

"No." Ruth sniffed, bent her head and awkwardly wiped the crook of her elbow across her damp face. "It's beautiful, perfect, the most perfect thing I've ever seen."

Kelsey relaxed, relieved that Ruth loved the crib as much as she did. "I'm so glad you like it."

"I adore it." Ruth walked slowly around the crib, taking in every nuance of its structure and design. One side rail had been lowered, and a darling baby-print sheet covered the waterproof mattress. A matching comforter had been neatly folded and laid inside. With a smile of sheer delight, Ruth lowered the sleeping infant into the crib and pulled the comforter over his little body. She straightened and used one knuckle to discreetly brush away another stray tear. "Thank you."

Kelsey cleared her throat and felt her own eyes stinging. "You're welcome."

The two women stood there for several minutes, watching the sleeping infant. Finally Ruth spoke in a husky whisper. "Was this your daughter's crib?"

"No. Pattie never had a crib." Kelsey crossed the room, then reached beyond the side rail and lightly touched the sleeping infant's back. "We were going to get her one, as soon as she'd outgrown the bassinet. This was the one I wanted, but I knew we couldn't afford it. Still, I used to go into the store just to touch it and marvel at how beautiful it was, and how sweet Pattie would look sleeping inside."

Suddenly Kelsey looked up, shocked at having revealed intimate feelings that she'd suppressed for so long. "I don't know why I said that. I never even told Luke."

"You told me because it was important to you." Ruth slipped a comforting arm around Kelsey's shoulders. "When my mother died, I cried for days, but Luke never did. Every time I mentioned Momma, he'd get that funny tight-jawed look and walk away. He would never talk about her, and he wouldn't let me talk about her, either, although I desperately needed to. I resented that at the time. Now I realize that he wasn't trying to pretend that our mother had never existed. Luke grieved for her as deeply as I did, but in his own silent way.'' Ruth paused, as though judging Kelsey's reaction. ''I suspect that you already know that about him.''

Momentarily unable to speak, Kelsey affirmed Ruth's statement with a jerky nod.

Squeezing Kelsey's shoulder, Ruth continued. ''It's not good to hold things inside. I needed to remember my mother, to talk about the wonderful times we had, and to express my pain and anger that she'd left me. If you need that too, I'm here for you.''

Kelsey turned and hugged her. ''You are the dearest friend anyone ever had. I'm going to be fine now, honestly I am. For a while, I questioned whether I would ever feel love again, or look forward to the next sunrise, but I can, and I do. Luke and I...well, I think things are going to work out.''

''I knew it,'' Ruth whispered, then started to giggle.

Unable to suppress the joyous swell of her own heart, Kelsey chuckled, too, and both women broke into tearful laughter.

A buzzer announced that someone was at the front door.

Kelsey wiped her eyes and grinned. ''That must be Luke. I left a message with Ernie that you'd be home today.''

Excited, Kelsey nearly skipped through the living room and whipped open the front door.

''Mrs. Sontag?'' A uniformed delivery man regarded her cooly.

Disappointed, Kelsey forced a polite smile. ''Yes.''

''This is for you. Sign here, please.''

Baffled, she scrawled her name on the indicated line and was presented with a legal-size manila envelope. The delivery man left, and Kelsey closed the door, eyeing the packing with confusion.

Ruth entered the living room. ''What is it?''

Kelsey replied with a shrug, then worked her finger beneath the sealed flap. She extracted a fat document that had been stapled and bound with blue paper. A row of numbers designated each typewritten line on the first sheet and Kelsey's gaze was riveted to one specific segment of the heading: *Sontag* v. *Sontag*.

An ominous prickling skittered down her spine and she hurriedly flipped through the pages. When she reached the last page, she saw the familiar signature and emitted a weak cry.

Alarmed, Ruth quickly crossed the room. "What's wrong, Kel?"

A peculiar numbness spread through Kelsey's chest as she laid the divorce documents on the entry table. Then, without a backward glance, she silently went into her bedroom and closed the door.

Chapter 15

Below the bedroom window, an awakening boulevard was clogged with predawn commuters. Kelsey idly watched the line of headlights winding down from the foothills, experiencing no joy in the new day. There was a hole in her spirit. She wondered if she'd ever be happy again.

A muffled wail filtered through the closed door, and Kelsey felt a surge of sympathy for Ruth. The baby had been fussing almost continuously for the past hour and although little Eric's crying hadn't awakened Kelsey—she hadn't been able to sleep anyway—poor Ruth needed some rest.

Kelsey slipped on a robe and went to the guest room. The door was slightly ajar, so she tapped lightly, then peeked inside. "Is everything all right?"

Ruth was pacing the floor, holding the infant against her shoulder, fatigue and frustration etched on her pale face. When she saw Kelsey, she jerked to a halt and seemed on the verge of tears. "I don't know. I've fed him and changed him, but he just keeps crying. Do you think he's sick?"

"I doubt it, but let's have a look." Entering the room, Kelsey gently lifted the baby from Ruth's shoulder, then cradled the crying infant in her arms. Eric responded to the shift in position with a quivering wail of displeasure.

"Goodness, we've got a hefty pair of lungs, don't we?" Kelsey tucked the baby in the crook of her elbow and used her free hand to tickle his teeny knuckles. Eric instantly took hold of her finger and quieted enough to blink unfocused little eyes in the general direction of Kelsey's face.

Wringing her hands, Ruth stared down at her son. "He's hardly slept all night. I don't know what else to do. There must be something wrong, Kel. Look, his face is all red and crinkly."

Kelsey smiled. "If you'd been screaming for an hour, you'd be flushed, too." When Ruth's lips quivered, Kelsey quickly reassured her. "He's fine, Ruthie, just fine. Your son has simply discovered that he can make noise all by himself and he's practicing, that's all."

As though to prove Kelsey's point, Eric's face crumpled like wadded paper and he emitted a pitiful cry.

Ruth winced as though the sound had driven a stake through her chest. "Do you think he has colic or something?"

"He doesn't seem to be in real distress." Kelsey sat on the edge of the bed and arranged the baby so his tummy rested on her thighs. His little head bobbled up, then fell back to her lap and his arms flailed with a series of jerky movements. Laying one palm on the baby's back, Kelsey used her free hand to stroke the fuzzy little head while her knees swayed in a gentle sideways motion. She hummed softly, and after a moment, the infant relaxed.

Ruth slumped into the bedside chair and shoved a mass of dark curls out of her face.

"You're exhausted," Kelsey said. "Why don't you go into my room and see if you can get some sleep?"

Rubbing her face, Ruth sighed, then dropped her hands into her lap. "This isn't fair to you, Kel. We've kept you up all night and you have to go to work."

"I was awake anyway. Besides, I'm going to take the day off. I have vacation time coming." Kelsey regarded Ruth for a moment, then broached the subject that she knew her friend would resist. "I've probably stepped beyond bounds here, but I made an appointment for you to see Howard Parlow."

Ruth's head snapped up. "Why?"

"I think you know why." When Ruth looked away, Kelsey used her most persuasive tone. "Sweetie, you need someone to look out for your rights. You can bet that Joseph is going to have a lawyer. You need one, too."

"I—I don't have any money."

"Nonsense. When we were in Santa Barbara, I found bank statements for three separate accounts. Granted, the balances have declined considerably over the past year, but there's still some money left and half of it is yours."

Ruth was silent for a moment, then spoke in a voice that quivered slightly. "I don't want to rush into anything. I mean, I'm sure Joseph realizes now that he has a problem. He might finally agree to seek help, and he'll need my support."

Every muscle in Kelsey's body went on the alert. "You aren't serious."

"People can change, can't they?" The question held an edge of desperation. "He's my husband, Kelsey. I can't just turn my back on him because things have gone a little sour."

Kelsey licked her lips and chose her words carefully. "The man tried to kill you. If you can forgive that, you're either a saint or a fool. Think of this baby, Ruth. Your first responsibility now is to protect your child."

"I know," she whispered. "I'm not going back to him."

"Then I don't understand why you're balking about seeing a lawyer?"

"Joseph is already in so much trouble, I just don't want to hurt him any more."

Kelsey was baffled and angered by Ruth's reluctance to prosecute a man who was guilty of such abuse, and she said so, then added, "Personally, I have every intention of pressing charges against Joseph, and as far as I'm concerned, he should rot in prison until Eric has grandkids. Look, Ruthie, you're an intelligent woman. You knew that your husband was sick. Why did you put up with him for so long?"

Ruth stared at her lap. "I thought he loved me."

"After everything he did to you? How could you believe that?"

"Because he told me that he did." Raising her gaze, she met Kelsey's stare with an agonized plea for understanding. "You don't know how much that meant to me."

Actually, Kelsey had a fairly good idea because she personally would have given the moon and six stars to have heard those three little words from Luke.

Ruth continued quietly. "When I was growing up, I don't remember my mother actually saying that she loved me. She did, of course, and so did Luke, but they both showed that love through their actions. When I was younger, I couldn't see that. I just wanted to hear the words."

Kelsey was beginning to understand. "And Joseph said those words."

Ruth nodded. "Repeatedly. Joseph could be cruel, yes, but he could also be gentle and charming. Now I realize that although he said exactly what I wanted to hear, he was only mouthing the words while his actions contradicted them."

A tingle of recognition tickled Kelsey's nape. All these months, she had been pining to hear Luke speak of love, yet in all the ways that mattered, he had been screaming of it. Every day he had expressed love through silent sacrifice, and she'd been too blind to recognize the priceless message.

After their daughter's tragic death, Kelsey's destructive myopia had continued. Unable to cope with her own guilt, she'd been too enmeshed in her own sorrow to recognize the depth of Luke's grief. For the past year, Kelsey had denied responsibility for the disintegration of their marriage. Now she realized that although Luke had actually walked out, she had been the one who opened the door, then figuratively forced him to walk through it.

Unfortunately, the signed divorce papers she'd received a few hours earlier proved that her sobering revelation had come too late.

Ruth broke the strained silence. "Look, Eric has fallen asleep. You have the magic touch."

Kelsey smiled ruefully. "I think he was just bored by tales of our woeful love lives."

Standing, Ruth bent and carefully lifted the dozing infant from Kelsey's lap. "My marriage is over, Kel. Yours doesn't have to be."

That statement surprised Kelsey, but she waited until Ruth had laid Eric in the crib before responding. "It takes two people to make a marriage work, Ruth. You, of all people, know that."

"Yes, I do." Ruth stood beside the crib and gazed thoughtfully out the window. "You still love Luke, don't you?"

Kelsey looked away. "Yes."

"He loves you, too."

"Agreeing to a divorce is a bizarre way to show that, even for Luke."

"Not really." Ruth sat on the mattress and took Kelsey's hand. "Think about it, Kelsey. What is the one complaint you and I have always had about my brother?"

Kelsey didn't have to think. "He's too protective."

"That's right, so from his perspective, what would be the most cherished gift he could offer, and the most difficult for him to give?" When Kelsey continued to stare blankly, Ruth sighed and answered her own question. "Freedom. Luke has offered you freedom."

"Well, I don't want it."

"Sure you do. You want to be your own person, and because Luke loves you he has finally accepted that."

This radical concept was a bit much for Kelsey's emotionally drained mind. Agitated, she stood and tried to grasp what Ruth was saying. "Do you mean that because Luke has agreed to a divorce, he's trying to say that he doesn't want one at all? That makes no sense."

"If my brother had wanted a divorce, he would have signed those papers the first day that he had them. Why do you suppose that he didn't?"

"I . . . hadn't really thought about it." That wasn't totally true, and Kelsey winced at the fib. Actually, she'd thought about little else over the past few months as the secret voice of her heart had hoped—no, prayed—that Luke would someday appear on her doorstep with a bag full of shredded documents and a declaration of undying love.

Ruth's knowing expression confirmed, however, that she was attuned to Kelsey's unspoken truth. "Luke didn't want to lose you. Now he's willing to give you up."

"Is that supposed to make me feel better?"

"Of course."

"Maybe I'm a bit thick, Ruthie, but I don't understand why I should be elated that the man I'm crazy in love with has decided, out of the goodness of his heart, that he doesn't want me anymore."

Frustrated, Ruth threw her hands in the air, then folded them reproachfully across her chest. "Honestly, Kel, you can be so stubborn. Go ahead, then—file the silly papers and regret it for the rest of your unhappy life, but I'm telling you that in his own muddling way my brother has given you something more precious than gold. If you don't recognize that, then maybe you don't deserve him."

Struck speechless, Kelsey could do little more than close her gaping mouth and allow the bizarre notion to spin around in her befuddled brain. Comprehension dawned slowly, like a sweet blossom opening its petals to the warmth of the rising sun. Ruth was right. Luke *had* offered her a precious gift.

It was a shame that she couldn't accept it.

"Go on, Ernie. I'll lock up." Luke didn't look up from the digital display on the emission analysis computer.

Seeming reluctant to leave, Ernie shifted his denim jacket from one arm to the other. "Sure you don't need help?"

"Thanks, I can handle it. Besides, your wife's probably got dinner on the table."

"My old lady never puts on the chow until I walk in the door. Says she's sick of ruining good food 'cause she never knows when I'm gonna show."

As the electronic printer chucked out a report, Luke straightened and rubbed his taut neck. "You'd better shape up, man. You've got yourself a choice lady there. Don't blow it."

Ernie cocked his head. "Like you did?"

Luke's eyes narrowed dangerously but he didn't dispute the remark. Denying the obvious was an exercise in futility; still, he wasn't in the mood to discuss the sad finale of his own marriage.

Apparently Ernie recognized the retreat signal, because he slung the jacket over one shoulder and backed toward the open auto bay. "Later, man."

"Right." Luke turned away, faking an interest in the computerized smog report until he heard the partitioned steel barrier slide down the track and slam into place. Once he was alone, he could put aside the swaggering, don't-give-a-damn facade that had fooled everyone except Ernie.

Closing his eyes, Luke leaned against the idling vehicle beside him. He was miserable. By signing those divorce papers, he'd relinquished his last chance of happiness, but he had given Kelsey what she so desperately wanted. He should take some solace in that, but it was difficult to feel noble with a belly full of regret.

Nothing seemed worthwhile anymore. Even this afternoon's visit from the city representative had done little to buoy Luke's sinking spirits. He'd listened to the offer with half an ear, then taken the guy's card and made a lukewarm promise to think about it.

Without Kelsey, moving uptown seemed a pointless gesture. Of course, he had a responsibility to his employees, and improved business would mean higher salaries and job security, so he should probably make the phone call and at least hear the guy out. Maybe things would look brighter tomorrow. Luke doubted that, but there was nothing he could do now but wait for sunrise and hope for the best.

Reaching inside the idling vehicle, Luke flipped off the engine, then clipped both the key and the smog report to the work order. He tossed the clipboard on his desk, turned off the garage light and trudged across the dreary parking lot to the shabby tin can that he would never call home.

The cold trailer seemed even emptier, more lonely than usual. Luke shivered and absently opened a cupboard. There were a couple of cans of soup, a box of crackers and one large bottle of whiskey. He took the bottle.

Unscrewing the top, he turned away from the acrid fumes and hesitated, knowing that if he just held his nose and swallowed, the blessed numbness would follow. Eventually, the pain would return but for those brief moments he could ignore the agony of his shattered heart.

It was a cowardly escape. He'd just fired a guy for using dope. Was an alcohol-indued stupor any better than that caused by a snout full of narcotic powder?

Disgusted with himself, Luke recapped the whiskey.

The tinny trailer door suddenly vibrated under the force of merciless pounding.

Startled, Luke called out, "Damn it, Ernie, I told you to go home."

The trailer latch rattled, then the pounding resumed with increased force.

Luke swore, then reached out and unlocked the door without stepping from his position in the cramped kitchenette. To his shock, Kelsey muscled her way inside carrying a brown grocery bag.

"What in the hell—" Luke flattened against the counter as she pushed by him.

Without favoring Luke with a glance, she upended the brown bag on the tiny table. A pile of shredded paper drifted out, followed by the discarded bag itself.

Whirling, she crossed her arms and faced Luke defiantly. "There's your divorce, Luke. Enjoy it."

Perplexed, he noted torn strips of blue paper amid the tangled mess. "Are you crazy?"

"Probably, but that's not the point."

"What *is* the point?" Luke encompassed the trash heap with a sweeping gesture. "You were the one who wanted a divorce."

"I have wanted many things in my life, Luke, but a divorce has never been one of them."

"Then why did you file in the first place?"

"Because you left me and I was hurt." Kelsey's courage cracked a bit, and her eyes darted nervously. "Two days ago, I took out my heart and handed it to you. I told you that I loved you now and that I had always loved you. Is that what frightened you away?"

"No." He raked his hair.

"Then I need to know why you signed those papers, Luke. The truth, this time, not just a bunch of asinine platitudes."

Luke's pulse was revving and his gaze was locked on that funny round mouth of hers, remembering how he'd spent the entire night dreaming about how sweet she tasted. Suddenly he couldn't even think for wanting her. Crammed into a three-foot kitchen with a woman who smelled good enough to eat had short-circuited his neurons and all he wanted to do was grab her.

The look on Kelsey's face suggested that that might not be such a good idea, so he jammed his hands in his pockets and sidestepped to the relative safety of the sofa, five feet away.

She folded her arms. "I'm waiting."

Pursing his lips, he thought back to the cabin, when he'd seen the madness in Joseph's eyes and recognized the murky reflection of his own soul. By admitting his own secret motives, he would reveal himself to be no better than the sick man his sister had married. "Can't you just let it go?"

"No, I can't."

Luke closed his eyes and spoke with great difficulty. "It was Ridenour."

"Excuse me?"

Sinking onto the lumpy sofa, Luke managed to meet her astonished gaze. "When we were up at the cabin, Ridenour started yammering about how Ruth belonged to him and how he had a right to protect his wife—" He broke off, and looked away for a moment. "I actually understood what the cowardly maggot was talking about. That scared me."

Kelsey touched her chest, as though reminding herself to breathe. "You can't compare yourself to Joseph."

"Yeah, well, I did and I wasn't too happy about it." Luke propped his elbow against the plywood paneled wall. "I felt the same way about you, Kel. I didn't want you to do anything or go anywhere without me, because I was afraid you'd get hurt. Fact was, I didn't want you out of my sight. So, you tell me what the difference is between me and my sister's screwball husband?"

"The difference?" Kelsey nearly choked on the question and steadied herself on the tiny counter. "Dear God, where do I start? For one thing, there isn't a cruel bone in your body, Luke Sontag. I'll admit that I don't like being con-

rolled and treated like an incompetent child, but that part
of our relationship was as much my fault as yours because
I allowed it. I just felt so guilty...." Her words evaporated
and she studied the peeling linoleum floor.

Luke frowned. Guilt? That was a new wrinkle. After all,
he was the one who'd failed as a provider. "What in hell did
you have to feel guilty about?"

She didn't raise her gaze. "For forcing you to marry me."

Now it was Luke's turn to be astonished. "Forcing?"

After taking a deep breath, Kelsey looked him straight in
the eye. "You never would have married me if I hadn't been
pregnant."

Leaning forward, Luke draped his forearms across his
thighs. "That's my line, Kel."

Her perplexed expression was endearing. "What are you
talking about?"

"Look, let's be honest. No way would you have married
a grease-jock like me unless you had to, right?" Luke
squirmed under her disbelieving stare. "I knew you'd married me because of the baby, but I figured that if I worked
hard enough I could give you a good life and maybe even
make you happy."

Kelsey simply stared at him as though he'd committed
heresy. Unnerved, Luke was sorely tempted to end the entire conversation by picking a fight and letting her stomp
away in a fit of pique. Something forced him to continue,
to expose every dark corner of his flawed soul. "After Pattie died, I knew it was all over. I figured that sooner or later,
you'd leave. My ego made it sooner, so I moved out. But I
couldn't sign those damned papers, because in my heart we
were still married."

In the strained silence that followed, Kelsey sagged against
the counter as though her bones had melted. "I never knew
you felt that way."

"Yeah, well..." Luke cleared his throat, unable to continue.

Kelsey moistened her lips. "So you don't feel that way
anymore? I mean, why did you finally decide to go through
with the divorce?"

"Ridenour kept referring to Ruth like she was his per sonal property, and he wasn't going to let her go because she'd been bought and paid for." Luke shrugged with nonchalance he didn't feel. "I got to thinking about how you were *my* wife, and I wasn't going to let you go, either Like I said, it was pretty scary stuff."

Shaking, Kelsey slid onto the small dinette bench, folded her arms on the table and bowed her head. "But you knew that I loved you."

Hearing those words just about undid Luke, but he man aged to stay put by digging his fingers into the seat cushion "My sister was in love with a lunatic. Weren't you the one who said that love isn't always logical? I finally figured ou that you were right. It isn't logical, and it isn't enough."

Kelsey cupped her hands to conceal her face. "Hoist wit my own petard."

Her obvious misery affected Luke deeply and confuse him totally. A discussion meant to clear the air had appar ently done just the opposite, and he was even more bewi dered than he had been.

During the past week, they'd come to terms with th tragedy that had torn them apart. Each of them had be lieved their child's death to be a personal punishment fo their own failures but now recognized that no blame coul be laid for a senseless tragedy. Still, he sensed Kelsey still hi some guilty secret, and something she'd said earlier sti gnawed at him. "Kel?"

She peeked over her fingertips. "Hmm?"

"Why do you think I married you?"

After taking a deep breath, she clasped her hands to gether and laid them on the table. "That's fairly obvious You are an honorable man, and marriage is what honor able men do when they unwittingly impregnate their par ners."

The hollow expression in her dark eyes damned nea sliced Luke's heart out. "I would have supported the bab and tried to be a good father, but I didn't have to marry yo to do that."

"I suppose not." Kelsey exhaled listlessly, then pressed her palms on the table and stood. "I'll have a new set of papers drawn up in the morning."

Luke stopped her at the door. "Where are you going?"

"Home. I've made a big enough fool of myself for one night." Shaking off his restraining hand, Kelsey stared at the floor and raised her arms as though to ward off his touch. "Don't. Please."

"Kelsey, for crissake, what have I said now?"

"Nothing, Luke. You haven't said a thing." A blast of cool night air entered the trailer as she pushed the door open. She paused. "That's not true. You've said a lot of things tonight, things that were difficult for you to express, and I appreciate your honesty."

"So what was this all about then?"

She shrugged helplessly. "Understanding, I suppose. There were things that I needed to know."

"Do you know them now?"

"I think so."

"Then why are you so damned unhappy?" Frustration sharpened his voice, because he wanted to drag her into his arms but had been rebuffed.

Reacting to Luke's tone, Kelsey raised her head and faced him with fire in her eye. "I'm unhappy because you didn't say what I wanted to hear."

"Now I'm supposed to be a damned mind reader?" Luke raked his hair and turned away, sucking in a quick breath before confronting her again. "What in hell do you want from me?"

"Your love," Kelsey snapped angrily. "That's all I've ever wanted from you, Luke Sontag, and it's the one thing in the world you've never offered."

"Are you nuts or something?" Luke rubbed his eyes as though trying to awaken himself from a bad dream. "Of course I love you. I've always loved you. What in hell do you think I've been trying to tell you?"

Her expression instantly softened. "Do you mean that?"

Luke swore under his breath and sulked.

Kelsey laid a soft palm on his taut arm. "Say it again, please."

With a discreet sniff, Luke stared over her head. "I love you."

Reaching up, she caressed his jaw with her fingertip, then urged him to meet her eyes. "Again," she whispered, standing on tiptoe until her lips were inches from his.

Luke's heart revved into the red zone. "I...love you, Kel. I love—"

Her sweet mouth cut off the words and he pulled her into his arms. The kiss increased, growing more fervent with each moment, until they finally stepped apart, shaken and gasping.

Keeping a firm arm around her waist, Luke laid his free hand against her cheek and was thrilled as she nuzzled his palm like an affectionate kitten. "I thought you knew, honey. I honest-to-God thought you knew."

"I should have," she whispered. "You showed me your love. I just wasn't looking."

Closing his eyes, Luke touched his forehead to hers. "So, what do we do now?"

Kelsey straightened and appeared to give the matter serious thought. "You know, my apartment is awfully crowded now, with Ruth and the baby staying there."

The point escaped him. "Yeah, so?"

"So, this is kind of cozy." She encompassed the tiny trailer with a sweep of her hand.

"You can't be serious." When she smiled sweetly, Luke stumbled back a step. "You *are* serious."

"Oh, yes."

Luke swallowed hard. "Listen, honey, nothing has really changed with me. I still work long hours and I don't make much money."

"I don't care."

"I do."

She patted his chest. "We'll work it out."

Luke captured her hand, pressing it against his collarbone. "I, well, I did send a few of my designs to a marketing firm."

Kelsey's face lit up like neon. "That's wonderful."

"I don't know if anything is going to come of it, but there's a chance they might find a manufacturing facility willing to do a couple of prototypes."

"Of course they will. Self-taught or otherwise, you're still a brilliant mechanical engineer."

Luke shrugged off the praise, although it pleased him immensely. "Maybe, if that happens, I'll have something to offer you. Then we can talk—"

Kelsey hand covered his mouth like duct tape. "If that happens, fine. If it doesn't, fine. You're not getting off the hook that easily."

Stepping back, she lowered her hand and faced him somberly. "Love may not be logical, Luke, but it is always beautiful. You can't compare what we have to Ruth and Joseph. Ruth loved him, yes, but Joseph never returned that love. When love is mutual, when two people commit to work hard to keep that love alive, then nothing else matters."

Luke absorbed that for a moment. "I didn't realize that you were such a dyed-in-the-wool romantic."

"Well, now you know." Nonchalantly brushing the lapel of her tailored jacket, Kelsey glanced around the cramped interior. "Let's see now, about closet space. That could be a problem, because I have a lot of business clothes...by the way, I have no intention of quitting my job. Is that a problem for you?"

Luke frowned. "No, but—"

"Good. Maybe I can put some kind of waterproof armoire outside. Yes, that might do it."

Good Lord, the woman was serious. For a moment, Luke was too stunned to speak, then sheer joy burst out of his chest in the form of rolling laughter. Startled into silence, Kelsey stared up at him. "No way am I going to let you live in this crappy trailer."

She hiked one brow. "*Let* me?"

Luke instantly reworded the statement. "*I* don't want to live here, honey. I hate it."

"Oh. Then what do you have in mind?"

Rubbing his chin, he gave the matter some thought. "Actually, I've been thinking about moving uptown and relocating the shop."

Her eyes widened in surprise. "Really? But you grew up in this neighborhood. I didn't think you'd ever leave."

"Things have changed. It's always been a tough place, but now it's rotting out with drugs and crime. This isn't what I want for my life . . . for our life.'"

A telling brightness shimmered in Kelsey's eyes and she managed a damp smile. "'Our life'—I like the sound of that."

He brushed his thumb below her wet lashes. "The thing is, I haven't been able to afford the move. Now, if I had a partner with a good financial mind and a regular paycheck, things might be different. Do you know anyone who might be interested?"

"Actually, I *do* have someone in mind. The problem is that she's terribly stubborn."

"I hate stubborn women."

Kelsey nodded soberly. "And she has an awful habit of speaking her mind."

"Wow. That's tough."

"But she can cook."

"There's a plus."

"And she has one other redeeming feature."

"What's that?"

"Allow me to demonstrate." Taking Luke's hand, Kelsey stepped down the steps and urged him to follow. When they stood in the darkened parking area, she gazed wistfully toward the garage, then slid him a shy glance. "I don't suppose that lovely old DeSoto is still in there." She shamelessly batted her eyes. "It's all quite proper this time. After all, we're still married."

Still married. Luke flat liked the sound of that.

He scooped up his wife and headed toward the garage. It was going to be one hell of a night.

*   *   *   *   *

Take 4 bestselling love stories FREE

Plus get a FREE surprise gift!

BELLE HAVEN

BY MAURA SEGER

Don't miss Maura Seger's BELLE HAVEN SAGA! Her four-book series features continuing generations of characters set in the fictitious town of Belle Haven, Connecticut.

Amelia Daniels discovers many things in the New World—first and foremost Garrick Marlowe—in THE TAMING OF AMELIA (Harlequin Historical #159, February 1993).

In August 1993, meet Deanna Marlowe as she struggles with two revolutions—in Belle Haven and in her heart—In THE SEDUCTION OF DEANNA (Harlequin Historical #183).

The feisty Julia Nash turns New York society upside-down in THE TEMPTING OF JULIA, a Harlequin Historical coming in 1994.

The saga culminates in late 1994 when Belle Haven comes of age in a contemporary romance from Silhouette Intimate Moments.

IMBELLE

INTIMATE MOMENTS®
10TH Anniversary

Celebrate our anniversary with a fabulous collection of firsts....

The first Intimate Moments titles written by three of your favorite authors:

NIGHT MOVES — Heather Graham Pozzessere
LADY OF THE NIGHT — Emilie Richards
A STRANGER'S SMILE — Kathleen Korbel

Silhouette Intimate Moments is proud to present a FREE hardbound collection of our authors' firsts—titles that you will treasure in the years to come from some of the line's founding members.

This collection will not be sold in retail stores and is available only through this exclusive offer. Look for details in Silhouette Intimate Moments titles available in retail stores in May, June and July.

SIMANN

continues...

Come back to Conard County, Wyoming, where you'll meet men whose very lives personify the spirit of the American West—and the women who share their love. Join author Rachel Lee for her fourth exciting book in the series, IRONHEART (IM #495). Gideon Ironheart didn't expect his visit to Conard County to embroil him in a mystery...or entangle his heart. But the magnetic half-breed with a secret hadn't counted on wrangling with Deputy Sheriff Sara Yates. Look for their story in May, only from Silhouette Intimate Moments.

To order your copy of of *Ironheart*, or the first three Conard County titles, *Exile's End* (IM #449), *Cherokee Thunder* (IM #463) and *Miss Emmaline and the Archangel* (IM #482), please send your name, address, zip or postal code, along with a check or money order (do not send cash) for $3.39 for each book ordered, plus 75¢ postage and handling ($1.00 in Canada), payable to Silhouette Books, to:

In the U.S.	In Canada
Silhouette Books	Silhouette Books
3010 Walden Avenue	P.O. Box 609
P.O. Box 1396	Fort Erie, Ontario
Buffalo, NY 14269-1396	L2A 5X3

Please specify book title(s) with your order.
Canadian residents add applicable federal and provincial taxes.

CON4